THE CHEFFE

Also by Marie NDiaye in English translation

Among Family (1997)
Rosie Carpe (2004)
All My Friends (2013)
Three Strong Women (2013)
Self-Portrait in Green (2014)
Ladivine (2016)
My Heart Hemmed In (2017)

Marie NDiaye

◉

THE CHEFFE

A Cook's Novel

Translated from the French by
Jordan Stump

MACLEHOSE PRESS
QUERCUS · LONDON

First published as *La Cheffe: roman d'une cuisinière*
by Editions Gallimard, in 2016

First published in Great Britain in 2019 by

MacLehose Press
An imprint of Quercus Publishing Ltd
Carmelite House
50 Victoria Embankment
London EC4Y 0DZ

An Hachette UK company

ISBN (TPB) 978 0 85705 890 4
ISBN (Ebook) 978 0 85705 891 1

2 4 6 8 10 9 7 5 3 1

Designed and typeset in Roos by Patty Rennie
Printed and bound in Denmark by Nørhaven

Papers used by MacLehose Press are from well-managed
forests and other responsible sources.

THE CHEFFE

OH YES, OF COURSE, SHE GOT THAT QUESTION OFTEN. Endlessly, I'd even say, after all, the Cheffe* was famous, and maybe she had a secret she'd give away, out of weakness or weariness or indifference, or by mistake, or moved by a sudden fit of generosity to counsel anyone interested in her trade and in some sort of stardom, or guaranteed acclaim, at least.

Yes, that fascinated a great many people, that glorious reputation she'd gained without really trying, and maybe they thought, maybe they imagined she was keeping the key to that mystery to herself, they saw a mystery there, she wasn't very bright.

They were wrong on two counts.

For one thing she was terribly intelligent, and for another you don't have to be as clever as she was to succeed in the business.

She liked being misunderstood.

---

* "Cheffe" is a recently-minted word in French; its meaning, of course, is "female chef". Because no good English equivalent exists, this translation will use the French word.

She hated people accosting her, prodding her, she hated the threat of being unmasked.

No, no, she had never had a confidant before me, she was too reticent for that.

Very often people asked her that question you're thinking of, and inevitably she shrugged, smiled with the look she liked to put on, faintly mystified, distant, a look of sincere or feigned modesty, it wasn't clear which, and answered, "It's not hard, you just have to be organised."

And when they kept pushing, she told them, "It just takes a little taste, it's not hard," and turned her high, narrow forehead very slightly away, pinching her thin lips as if to say not only that she'd tell them no more but also that she'd put up a fight if anyone tried to forcibly unclench her teeth.

The look on her face, and even on her body – hard, closed, removed – turned dull and dim and ridiculously adamant, and that put a stop to the questions, not because people were sorry they'd troubled her but because they thought she was thick in the head.

The Cheffe was fantastically intelligent.

How I loved to see her delight in being taken for a simple-minded woman!

Our sly, shared awareness of her vast intelligence felt like a bond between us, a bond that I cherished and that she didn't mind, a bond I wasn't the only one to feel, since there were others, longstanding acquaintances, who knew just how sharp she was, how perceptive, and who also sensed she wanted to keep that a secret from strangers and meddlers, but I was the youngest, I didn't know her before, back when she cared less about secrecy, I was the youngest, and the most in love with her, of that I'm sure.

But also, she thought there was something excessive in the praise people had begun to heap on her cooking.

She found the phrasing of those panegyrics ridiculous and affected, it was a question of style.

She had no taste for preciousness or grandiloquence, and no respect.

She knew all about the force of the senses, after all it was her work to awaken them, and she was always enchanted to see that force show on the diners' faces, she strove for nothing else, day in and day out, for so many years, virtually without rest.

But the words people used to describe it struck her as indecent.

"It's very good," was all she wanted, all she could possibly ask.

To analyse in graphic detail all the causes and effects of the pleasures offered by her green-robed leg of lamb, say, since today that's her most famous dish and the emblem of her style (what people don't realise is that towards the end she didn't want to make it anymore, she was tired of it, just as a singer tires of the same beloved song she's continually asked to repeat, it sickened her a little, she resented that magnificent leg of lamb for being more famous than she was, and for having let so many other dishes languish in undeserved obscurity, dishes that took far more work and skill, dishes she was far prouder of), to subject that rapture's many and varied forms to minute analysis was in her mind to expose something intensely private to the full light of day, something in the eater and by extension in the Cheffe, it embarrassed her, at times like that she wished she'd never done anything, offered anything, sacrificed anything.

She never said so, but I knew.

She never would have said so, that too would have been revealing too much.

But I knew it, from the cold, stubborn silence she closed herself up in when she was dragged from her kitchen to hear out a customer who insisted on offering his compliments, who, whether intrigued, troubled or spurred on by the Cheffe's silence, refused to give up until he'd got some sort of answer, and to be done with it she slowly shook her head from right to left, as if, modest as she was, that gushing praise was a torment, she didn't say a word, she was ashamed to be exhibiting herself, stripped bare, and the customer too, even if he didn't know it.

And afterwards her mood was dark, as if she'd been not praised but criticised or insulted.

If I was there looking on, or if at least she thought I was (often wrongly, since I always tried to slip away when the Cheffe was forced out into the dining room), I sensed that she held it against me, her dignity had been wounded in front of me.

And yet for my part – and mine alone, I wish I could say, but how to be sure? – nothing could ever diminish my reverence and tenderness for the Cheffe, not even the spectacle of a scene in the dining room when, as did sometimes happen, she met the complaints of the very occasional dissatisfied customer with her usual lofty silence, offending the customer, who thought she was scorning him when she was only ignoring him, in her reserved way, just as she did her admirers.

Yes, that's right, no happier with applause than with attacks. At least those attacks never aspired to eloquence, and their words didn't aim to penetrate the Cheffe's heart and soul.

Yes, that's right, the complaints concerned only the food, the Cheffe's decision to combine this ingredient with that (even the celebrated green-robed leg of lamb, for instance, before its renown grew so great that today it can't be questioned, there were those who found fault with its sheath of sorrel and spinach, they would have preferred one or the other, or even chard), whereas the applause soon turned to glorification of the Cheffe herself, and then ventured into the secret world of her presumed intentions, a longing to know her truest being, the only possible source for those sublime dishes.

"Idiots," the Cheffe once said to me, of all that to-do.

She also claimed she couldn't understand a third of what people wrote about her cooking – confirmation for those who thought her dim-witted, who were convinced her gift had come to her purely by chance.

Yes, they thought the severe, intransigent god of cuisine had chosen to become flesh in the form of that difficult, slightly dense little woman.

As I've told you, she was perfectly happy to be thought simple-minded, it was a way to be free.

She wasn't one of those people who play stupid for so long

that they become stupid, forgetting it started out as an act, no, playing that part only made her wilier, shrewder, maybe a touch cynical, I don't know.

She was sharp, she was prickly, but for all that I've always thought the girl she once was – eager to please, keen to enchant everyone even as she stayed behind the kitchen door, finding pleasure enough in the contented murmurs filtering through as they savoured what she'd conceived and created – that lonely girl, ever searching for friendship and compassion, was still nestled deep in the Cheffe's breast, and sometimes she rose up, suddenly remaking the Cheffe's face, tempering her words, surprising even her.

She often showed me a softer face, she had faith in herself, and I'd get no more out of her than that.

Still, she was ambitious, yes, why not?

She wanted to be someone, but in her own way, without fuss, without having to talk about it, someone people don't forget even if they never actually knew her.

She wanted to leave only a vague, marvelling recollection in the eaters' minds, so when they tried to remember where that delectable image had sprung from, and that melancholy image too, like a happiness that will never come again, they'd remember only a dish, or just its name, or its scent, or three bold, forthright colours on the milky white plate.

The Cheffe would have rather they not even remember her name, rather they never saw her face, rather they had no idea if she was plump or slender, short or tall, if her body was pleasingly put together.

Which turned out not to be possible, it wasn't the Cheffe's habit or style to work at shaping her legend.

She never hid, even if she didn't like showing herself.

She did this and that, she posed for a regional newspaper, standing with her employees at her restaurant's front door, and that photo, amateurishly shot by the food critic, with the Cheffe grinning broadly at some off-the-cuff joke from the sous-chef behind her, with the Cheffe looking more, in her strange, self-satisfied cheeriness, squinting a little in the bright noontime sun, like a mother just awarded a medal for her flourishing fecundity than the inflexible, austere boss we all knew, resolutely close-mouthed, discreet, sometimes unknowable, that photo of the Cheffe is the best-known today, and every article on the Cheffe is now illustrated with a close-up of that laughing, frivolous face, as if that were the Cheffe's real face.

It wasn't, I assure you.

At the same time, because she had no sense of strategy, the Cheffe always said no to being photographed in the dining room with important customers, politicians, actresses, CEOs, and people resented it, they thought her cheaply manipulative or arrogant when in fact she was only skittish, timid, and tired too, of course.

Had she said yes, I have no doubt that those snapshots, showing her distant, uneasy face, adamantly closed over her inner complexity, would have portrayed a far greater truth than her impish picture in *Sud-Ouest*.

And in any case she wasn't fond of that photo, not because she didn't recognise herself in the look on her face, that's one thing she might have liked, since the Cheffe always tried to throw people off where she was concerned, but rather because she was afraid that deeply incongruous picture might make people think the photographer had captured her genuine nature, and might make some of them hope they too could one day flush it out, could maybe even convince the Cheffe that that was her true self, that at heart she was that jovial, serene, earth-motherly woman she herself didn't recognise.

She didn't particularly care if people misunderstood what she was, if they were convinced she was friendly and open and so on.

It's just that she didn't want anyone talking to her with that absurd misrepresentation in their heads, she didn't want anyone trying to summon up her beaming, beatific face by pushing her into places she'd never been, places that weren't hers at all.

She didn't want anyone wondering if that was a true or a false image of her real self, and she didn't want them to have any reason, like that photo, to care or even think about that question.

That's how she was. At least I think that's how she was.

The Cheffe kept the deepest part of her nature hidden even from me.

Understandable, yes, since I was her employee, and we were separated at least as much by age as by rank, by experience, even by gender, if you like, though I never thought it mattered, in my quest to understand the Cheffe's soul, that I was a man, I never saw it as a handicap.

Quite the reverse? Yes, possibly.

I try even harder, I question everything I think I know, sense or interpret.

Yes, if I were talking to you about another man I would possibly or even probably analyse his behaviour by my own in some similar circumstance, and that would of course be a terrible mistake, because I've learned that I'm not like most men in the way I feel certain emotions, in the very nature of those emotions, whereas my innermost heart could always read the Cheffe's, even though she was a woman, even though she was twice my age.

Forgive me this little boast, but I think I'm fairly perceptive.

Which was exactly what the Cheffe feared most, she tried to push me away and she couldn't.

There's nothing you can do faced with the loyalty of a loving, impassioned person.

Did she accept that? Resign herself to it? Yes, of course, she loved me too, in her way.

You give me a cold smile and ask, "What about the childhood of a Cheffe?" assuming I don't get the reference, you're convinced I don't have much of an education.*

You're right, I didn't learn much in school.

As soon as I walked into the classroom I felt a groundless terror contracting my bladder, and also, and worse, draining my memory of everything I'd crammed into it the night before, at home, in many diligent hours of anxiety and desperation to please, to be perfect, and so the precious fruits of my attempts

---

* The allusion is to Jean-Paul Sartre's short story "L'enfance d'un chef," usually translated into English as "The Childhood of a Leader".

to learn and remember vanished into thin air, the mere smell of the classroom – sweat, leather, dust, chalk – instantly turned my brain into a helium balloon, ready to fly out of my skull if I made just one move, and I knew what that move was, and I struggled in vain not to make it: it was my trembling, breathless little body hunching down as the teacher looked for someone to call on, making me look guilty, like some laggard who doesn't even have the nerve to assert his boredom and laziness, when in fact I was yearning to cry out "I know all this backwards and forwards, there's not one question I can't answer!" and then the balloon started to rise, drifted out through the open window, climbed into the autumn sky to join all the others that broke free before it, the balloon of my memory, my work, my intelligence, leaving only the shell of my true being on the chair, limp, tiny, stupid, pathetic.

I've mostly lived alone.

And even more alone now, now that the Cheffe is gone, even if my apartment in Lloret de Mar has more visitors in a week than my Mériadeck studio saw in several years, I still feel profoundly alone, and just as profoundly glad of it.

I've made what people are quick to call friends here, odd sorts of friends I'd never dream of confiding in, whose lives I know next to nothing about, at least not the lives they led before they came to live out their old age in Lloret de Mar, who see me as one of them even though I'm far younger, they're fond of me because I'm like them and I like being with them, downing endless aperitifs together on their terraces or mine, which is exactly like theirs, overlooking the shimmering, luxurious, bottom-lit pool, I like that because they expect nothing from me but pleasant companionship, and neither they nor I want to burden our memories with stories we might feel obliged to tell if we were in France, our luxurious exile drapes us in a very cosy mystery.

I read a great deal, I believe I'd even call myself lettered, as people used to say.

I don't cook anymore, in fact I never have cooked for myself.

Yes, of course, the Cheffe told me about her childhood, at least what she was willing to have me know of it, but isn't that what we all do?

I knew her daughter well, and she described certain places, explained certain happenings, and although that woman only spoke of her and the Cheffe's past to show me how terribly she'd been wronged at every moment and in every place, I picked up enough overlapping details from their stories to reconstruct that time I never knew in the Cheffe's life.

Let me say first of all that the Cheffe did not have an unhappy childhood, no matter what may be said by those who place their faith in facts and dates, they mean nothing, virtually nothing.

You thought so too, that her life was pure misery from her earliest childhood on?

So what do you do with the Cheffe's own experience, facts and dates aside, of ways that many young people today, raised with all the comforts of a respectable upbringing by parents who want them to know everything about life but never run into anything unpleasant, must find terrible and unjust and incomprehensible and archaic?

I don't mean to say that they aren't all that and worse.

They may well be.

But if the Cheffe felt differently about those facts, wouldn't it be condescending not to try to judge them from exactly the same angle as she did?

She's the one who actually lived them.

And so, since all through her certainly poor and even destitute childhood the Cheffe found many opportunities for fun, and could later even say she was as happy as a little animal bursting with health, perfectly attuned to its environment, unwilling to change it for anything, then we've got to believe her, in all simplicity, and not do her the disservice of presuming she dressed up those early years in a joy they never held.

You're thinking, and I once thought the same, that no-one could genuinely remember himself or herself as a happy, fulfilled child in that kind of environment, I certainly wouldn't have been happy, I would remember that time with sorrow, the sorrow I would most certainly have felt at the time.

So that child can't possibly exist, and the Cheffe was misremembering or deluding herself, it makes no difference which.

But no, not at all. I'm certain everything she said was the truth.

It's our job to work at reaching her there, in her early happiness we find so hard to imagine.

Yes, it's almost too much to ask.

"Such a wonderful childhood I had," the Cheffe used to say when she talked about Sainte-Bazeille, where she'd spent her first fourteen years, where her parents hired themselves out here and there as farm labourers, dragging her along with them, putting her to work once they were reasonably sure the boss wouldn't notice, that was already forbidden back then, hiring children.

And like them she pulled beetroot or gleaned corn, ever ready, on a prearranged sign from her mother, to drop whatever she had in her hands and mime some sort of play, should someone who might report them come near.

Yes, the Cheffe was born after the war, in '50 or '51, I never knew exactly, for all my digging.

I went to see that little house in Sainte-Bazeille where the Cheffe claimed she lived the best years of her life even though she never went back to it, even though she refused to make the briefest detour to see it again, like that time we were driving from Bordeaux to Grignols to buy fattened ducks from a promising new farmer and I suggested we make a quick side-trip through Sainte-Bazeille.

She was silent for so long that I said it again, thinking she hadn't heard me, I imagine my voice was filled with the repressed but tremulous, proud, happy excitement of someone who's sure he's had a wonderful idea, and I turned my head to glance at the Cheffe, very pleased with myself, I so wanted to make her happy, to satisfy her every wish, I so longed to give her the tiniest pleasure, even at the expense of my own, I mean my immediate pleasure, which meant nothing to me because at the time I found my happiness only in the Cheffe's.

And although her face had been unusually serene ever since we had taken the main road out of Bordeaux, I saw a shadow come over it then, and even two angry little creases fencing off the corners of her mouth.

The clear, silvery, majestic light of that November morning so precisely set off the Cheffe's head, her hair pulled back and imprisoned in a pitiless chignon on her nape, her long, straight neck, smooth and solid as a young beech trunk, that for a moment I thought it wasn't the Cheffe there beside me on the passenger seat but only her image, two-dimensional, without flesh or life, but nonetheless captivating, grand and aloof, as she often appeared in my dreams, or as I saw her, felt her beside me when I found myself in my room after work, alone but because of that never truly alone.

A very tight chignon, yes, almost torture for her poor hair, grown fine and lank from having been too long pulled tight.

She never wore her hair any other way, and it's only another effect of the cursed *Sud-Ouest* photo that you find that surprising, because it's true that in the picture you see her with a cloud of soft, brown hair that seems less to surround or encase her skull than to float delicately around it, and since as I told you that photo misleadingly accompanied every article ever published about the Cheffe, all sorts of people who'd never met her, who could never have hoped to meet her, were convinced she let her hair spread out like that, like a weightless nimbus, all around her temples, her brow, a freedom that in truth she never granted it, and I can't imagine why, on that day of days when that deceptive picture was taken, she had.

No, I'm not in the photo, I wasn't yet working for the Cheffe.

But I know she always bound her hair behind her head, and not only for the obvious reasons of kitchen hygiene, I know she would have been happier with no hair at all, and if such a thing were conceivable back then she would have shaved it all off rather than torture and blight it by strangling it in a rubber band twisted over and over.

She would have liked to be only that face I saw against the cold, bright November light coming through the car windows, she would have liked her art to be incarnated, since it had to be, in only the plainest way, the strictest way, the most neutral: by nothing more than a face.

Oh no, I'll come back to that, being a woman mattered to her. I'll tell you about that later.

But it had nothing to do with her face.

It wasn't a feminine face, there in that pallid, distant light, and even less, if this makes any sense, a masculine face.

It was the idea of a face, the emblem of a face, proclaiming, in that exact, impartial morning light: "Since my cooking must be represented by a human face, here's the face that best expresses its deep simplicity, even its poverty, because this face isn't seductive or pretty or adorned, it's a face beyond all consideration of beauty or ugliness."

Which is why, even though I never knew the obviously random and anomalous reason why the man who took her picture found her that one day with her hair set free, yes, it's true, almost proudly shown off, even though I never knew that reason because no-one would tell me the precise circumstances of the photo shoot, in the very middle of the day, in front of a restaurant that must have been packed at that hour, I'm sure the Cheffe was later sorry that on top of everything else she'd displayed that mane which in a way didn't belong to her, that mane she tolerated only for the sake of convention, in every way incompatible with the essence of the face she wanted to show the world.

And then I saw how deeply she was annoyed by my suggestion of a pilgrimage to Sainte-Bazeille, the place of her childhood.

Without even a fleeting look to soften her words, she murmured, "That's none of your business."

And of course she was right, I couldn't deny it, but it was still a cruel blow to my sensitivity, which was always particularly tender where the Cheffe was concerned.

Stupidly, not out of pride, with her I had none, but because, reeling, I must have thought a kindly insistence on my part would bring a less brutal answer, one that would partially wipe out the first, I added: "You were so happy there, it might be interesting to . . ."

"Will you be quiet, be quiet, you don't know anything about it!" she shot back, her voice muffled, contained with great difficulty, and the effort I could see her making not to let her irritation explode in a furious shout crushed me just as much as the words she was saying.

I mumbled my shamefaced apologies and she shrugged, tense, irked, suddenly all the sunniness this outing had brought her was gone, and it was my fault.

It came back when we drove home to Bordeaux with three

little crates of beautiful fattened ducks that she would come up with the idea of glazing with white-fig jelly and slow roasting for hours in a pastry-sealed pot.

But I never forgot her sharpness that morning.

When, much later, I went to Sainte-Bazeille on my own, telling no-one, and after asking all over the village finally located the house she grew up in, I wondered if she was afraid of coming face to face with what I then discovered in all its sadness: not so much a house as a hovel shabbily built by the side of the road, on a plot of land ringed with sagging barbed wire, and to be sure everything about the place suggested no-one had lived there for years, the windows were all broken, maybe by the same people who'd covered the cladding with tags and graffiti, but even at so long a remove it was all too clear that a family of eight (yes, the Cheffe had five brothers and sisters) who lived in such a place had to be among the poorest in the village, and even very likely the poorest of all, especially, as the Cheffe once let slip, because her parents were only renters on that tiny patch of land, an embankment where nothing much grew, despite all her mother's efforts to make a vegetable garden.

Maybe the Cheffe would have been embarrassed to show me that house, maybe she was ashamed?

No, the Cheffe was never ashamed of anything that wasn't her doing, and besides, at the age I was then I meant far too little to her, she couldn't have cared how I might judge her or feel about her.

No, I think she feared her own pity at the sight of so vivid an image of her parents' misfortunes, the whole family's public disgrace.

Because, the Cheffe used to say, her parents always managed – were always trying – not to make their troubles seem fewer and slighter to their children but to teach them to find those troubles far less interesting and therefore less serious than what common sense told them, common sense being embodied in Sainte-Bazeille by their neighbours and teachers.

So the Cheffe could always counter pitying words and veiled looks of disdain or reproachful contempt with her parents' healthy optimism, the expression of their indomitable spirit, and in this case their heroism.

They always assumed things would get better, and they thought they'd been proved right when things simply didn't get any worse.

Which is why, since the Cheffe so loved her parents, so protectively watched over their memory, and since all their lives her parents had worked at not being pitied (or pitied only in a global way that wasn't aimed specifically at them, didn't touch them), she would have thought she was betraying their memory if she'd felt, if she couldn't help feeling, a stinging sympathy at the sight of that Sainte-Bazeille hovel, even if hers would have been slighter than mine on seeing that jumble of boards where by some miracle her parents gave her a luminous childhood, or, yes, the illusion of a luminous childhood, but aren't they the same thing, since it's all about memory?

As far as I know, her brothers and sisters never talked about those days.

They were reserved people, uncomfortable opening up, and in any case they wouldn't have dared take a position different from the Cheffe's, she was the only one who'd succeeded, the only one who'd made money.

They were all younger, but they all died before her (Ingrid excepted), two of them apparently by suicide, the Cheffe never spoke their names, what could she have done?

What could she do, with the hard-working life she'd chosen, the almost total lack of time off, the worries that don't punctuate a cook's life, don't accompany it, but are the very stuff of it once you've climbed as high as she had, what could she do for them but get in touch once or twice a year and, when they came asking, lend or give them various sums of money, always keeping her geographical and emotional distance, since for all those reasons and no doubt still others she couldn't possibly look into the exact nature of the problems pushing them to ask for her help, problems the two youngest chose to escape, one by throwing himself under a train, the other, I believe, by hanging?

She never turned them away. She never abandoned them or anyone else.

But what more could she do for them?

Wasn't that already a lot, signing those generous cheques?

Never demanding they justify it, never asking any questions at all, and even if her tact was inspired by a determination to keep clear of endless, depressing, unsolvable problems, her brothers and sisters didn't know it, they could only be glad she was at once so discreet and so generous.

They at least never complained. Certainly not, that would have been very foolish.

You've heard the Cheffe's daughter's claims, she who knows next to nothing about it, and as is so often the case you'd rather believe the slanderer than try to hear, in her very silence, the one being wronged.

I'll tell you about that in due course.

The Cheffe would never have boasted of the money she gave, or hold it up as evidence in her defence, in the end she thought it better or less painful for no-one to know, for people to think her an unfeeling person, devoid of sisterly sentiment.

She didn't mind being misjudged, never being asked her side of the story, that was fine with her.

That it was her own daughter misleading everyone, in vengeance for who knows what wrong, that must have hurt her, yes, terribly, I think.

But what truly tormented the daughter was life itself, she was nothing but a victim, always and forever, of having been forced to be born.

She had no will. She was too absorbed in herself. I'll tell you about all that later.

In any case, just as the Cheffe vehemently refused to revisit her house in Sainte-Bazeille, so she wouldn't run the risk of betraying her brave, worthy, carefree parents in her heart, I'm looking for a way to tell you about her childhood and not feel I'm betraying her in *my* heart, she who was so grateful to her parents for her happy upbringing.

She went to school on and off, when she had time.

To hear her tell it, school was a chore to get through, whereas the work she did for her parents, however monotonous and exhausting, always gave her the pleasure of feeling useful, and so of feeling alive.

Yes, very likely, sitting in a classroom, thinking of her parents having to do without her, having to work even harder and longer just so she could warm a chair in a school for a purpose she couldn't imagine, since she was absent too often to see any coherence in the things she was taught, very likely, yes, being kept away from her parents under those conditions she might well have felt only impatience and repulsion for school, most of all because she was painfully aware of everything that made it impossible for the teachers to like her, despite laudable efforts from some of them: her hostile, bored, closed manner, her hardworking but absurdly cavalier parents, always satisfied with everything, neither arrogant nor humble but, shall we say, inexplicably carefree.

She wanted them to like her, and more than anything she wanted them to like her parents.

If they did, she would have thrown everything she had into her schoolwork, and more besides, both her and someone inside her who hadn't come out yet, whose secret, larval existence she would learn of only when she discovered cooking.

No, that's true, she could have taken not being liked, it wouldn't have saddened her in the least.

I agree with you there.

But I still say she couldn't bear the lack of friendship or admiration for her parents, she couldn't accept that the few times they'd consented to come to the school for a meeting their exceptional, flamboyant personalities didn't immediately snuff out all the harsh words the teacher was planning to say to them, that he did say to them, as if they were bad parents, neglectful, crude, greedy, blind to their child's capacities, or maybe simply indifferent.

And to make matters worse they never answered, they left in the same cheerful mood as when they came, having done their duty, docile but impenetrable, bucking the school as they bucked all institutions, yes, submissive on the surface because they were fundamentally easy-going people but deep down immovable and obdurate and not even aware of it, like two little donkeys wrapped up in their own mysterious world.

And had just one teacher realised all the wonderful things those parents were hiding beneath their destitution, thought the Cheffe, then she would have approached her schoolwork with the same tenacity, the same tireless intelligence, the same ingenuity she devoted to helping her parents in the fields, where, even as a tiny girl, she'd come up with many perfectly respectable tactics to fight off the pain or fatigue that came from too much time in a stressful position.

But since no representative of the school ever congratulated her on her parents, or held back the unpleasant things he thought it only right that they hear (having to do with the Cheffe's many absences and the outlandish parental excuses she wrote out and signed herself, not wanting to trouble them), she came to see herself as the enemy of the teachers, of the headmistress, of anyone, her classmates included, who took the world of the school for the world of truth and goodness, and who recognised neither the truth nor the goodness of her parents' strange world.

It's true: if the Cheffe were attending that school nowadays, her teachers would have received those mystifying parents with an open mind, without judgment or indignation, they would have seen the stoical coherence and decency in which, for all their many failings, the Cheffe's parents were raising their children, they would have tried to relate to those parents' stubborn, feral but perfectly peaceable approach to getting along in society, they would have tried to understand all that and they would have been the better for it, they would have been edified, perhaps even inspired, and the Cheffe wouldn't have thought she was being disloyal to her parents if she felt a fondness for school, if she simply consented to participate in it.

That's right. She didn't.

At fourteen she left school forever, having learned to read but just barely to write, though she was good at arithmetic, she had a natural talent for numbers.

On the suggestion of a farmer they sometimes did jobs for, the parents sent the Cheffe off to a family in Marmande, relatives of his, since it was winter and the parents were having trouble finding work, and as it happened those people in Marmande were looking for a maid, and so the Cheffe discovered city life, the oddly self-conscious authoritarianism of the newly met mistress of the house, the very unfamiliar and for her bewildering relationship she had with the two other employees, a woman who cooked and a man who tended the grounds.

Of those two, the Cheffe couldn't help but say, decades later, with a wry little smile, "Life with them was no bed of roses."

And then she'd say it again, she always repeated that sentence, but the second time the wry smile was gone and her lips turned down gravely: "Oh no, life was no bed of roses."

It was a long time before I learned just what sort of mistreatment the Clapeau couple's cook and gardener inflicted on the Cheffe, and I must confess that, not knowing, my suspicious, melodramatic imagination showed me images of the Cheffe, a tiny creature not fifteen years old, in a setting where the outright rape of a child would have been told or remembered by the protagonists and the victim herself fatalistically, like a necessary step in the initiation into adulthood.

Yes, I used to think, it would be just like her to have been raped at fourteen and a half and say her life was no bed of roses, and I was so furious with the Clapeaus' gardener and cook that I would have gladly set out to hunt them down, to grasp them by their grey hair and pull their faces up to the height of their crime.

Yes, that's how I was, perhaps a little excessive but above all tormented that I couldn't protect the Cheffe from the start, from the moment the bus brought her and her poor cardboard suitcase from Sainte-Bazeille to Marmande and the Clapeaus', where she found herself offered up to greed, to depravity, to lies respected as a way of getting along, she whom her parents had enveloped in an oblivious innocence that was theirs alone, which they weren't even aware of, which was as natural to them as the air they breathed.

No, I never did try to find out what had become of them.

It was only because of my endless questions, gentle but obstinate, that the Cheffe finally told me the details of the life she led in Marmande.

Not that there was anything to hide, it's just that she took years to realise how much it all interested me, and it was good that she did but not only good, because, realising it but not understanding it, she was cautious, as she was of anything she didn't entirely grasp, she carefully weighed everything she told me, and sometimes she chose to say nothing.

But she didn't hesitate to tell me that the Clapeaus' cook and gardener treated her like a thing of no interest, pretended they didn't even notice she was there, even though the cook had to share her room with the Cheffe.

By mutual agreement or not, they let their gazes vaguely glide over her without ever landing on her, not running through her either, and so she felt like she'd become a mass of dead, formless flesh, as repellent to the eye as to the mind.

They never said a word to her, and since apart from reprimands and instructions the Clapeaus weren't in the habit of speaking to the staff, the Cheffe had to get used to keeping quiet, she whose parents never minded her chatter, as she said, she who even took a certain childish pride in her ability to rattle on and on, and in so doing entertain and amuse her family, whose words came out sparsely and laboriously.

You ask me, you're wondering, why the Clapeaus' cook and gardener pretended to see the household's new maid as a colourless obstacle for their gazes, how they could have failed to see she was only a sad, lonely child, ripped away from the warm, nurturing environment that was all she'd ever known, you're wondering and asking me why they should have been so unkind when there was no conceivable question of competition between them and the Cheffe.

As it would turn out, the Clapeaus' cook wasn't wrong to be hostile to the little creature she'd been forced to make space for in her already cramped room.

But she had no way of knowing that when the Cheffe started at the Clapeaus', no way of knowing she wasn't wrong.

Did she sense it?

I don't know. The Cheffe didn't know.

"What did they have against me, right at the beginning?" she used to ask me. "Later on, I understand, but right at the beginning . . ."

Was there something about the Cheffe that made her off-putting or intimidating?

Did she bring into the Clapeaus' banally corrupt, unexceptionally venal household the intransigent purity that reigned at her parents', that showed on their very faces, the Cheffe asked me more than once, still wondering after all those years, even as her memory was perhaps exaggerating her parents' miraculous innocence (I don't know if it was, I don't know anything about them, we never met), wondering in ever greater perplexity, and almost despair and delight, what could have made such guilelessness and joie de vivre possible in a couple so bereft of everything that constitutes other people's happiness?

Had the Cheffe, not knowing it and not wanting to know

it, brought a little of that insufferable integrity into the Clapeaus' house?

Did the goodness that quietly, permanently illuminated her parents' faces show on her face as well?

I don't know. The Cheffe didn't know.

It must be said that the Clapeaus themselves felt none too at ease with the Cheffe, although, and this is important, the face she'd inherited from her parents was a face that never judged, so any discomfort they felt in her presence came not from some stern disapproval they thought was directed their way (to which they would have been entirely indifferent) but from the questions the peculiar look on that childish face forced them to ask about their own decency, by which I mean their lack or failure of decency.

I'm not talking about money or even behaviour, I'm talking about goodness of soul, I'm talking about the very basic fact of having a good soul and feeling it.

Feeling it, not knowing it, because there's no room for pride in these things.

In later times, the Cheffe would always believe her talents and intuition and the exceptional career that grew out of them had robbed her of the face that was hers in those days, she'd always think her success and ambition had dragged her far, far away from the pure shores her parents lived on, and at that she felt a loss and a deep sadness.

Life with the Clapeaus, in that atmosphere of icy hostility on one side and timid imperiousness on the other, soon grew so wearing that after six or seven weeks she decided to run away, to go back to Sainte-Bazeille and her parents, never doubting for a moment that they'd give her complaints and unhappiness a loving, sympathetic welcome.

She imagined herself simply resuming the happy, arduous life her time at the Clapeaus' had interrupted for no good reason.

But as she walked along the main road out of Marmande, on the grassy strip between the pavement and the ditch, in the fading afternoon light, she pictured ever more clearly what would be going on in her parents' house at that hour and at that hard time of year, she saw them both coming and going in the three little underheated rooms, her father restless and bored in such a small, crowded house, knocking into things everywhere he went, too tall, too massive, her mother hunched over the youngest child she was still breastfeeding even though, thought the Cheffe, she was so scrawny, so ill-equipped just to provide for herself, she could see everything that was happening at that moment, unchanged by her absence, she could see it all, and little by little, her pace slowing, she began to think there was no room for her in that picture anymore.

The space she'd vacated when she left, which her brothers and sisters must have immediately filled with their confined, hungry young bodies, was a space she couldn't let herself take up again, even if she could find a way back into it, she couldn't let herself do that, she thought, standing still by the roadside, separated from Sainte-Bazeille, from the wonderful life she remembered in Sainte-Bazeille, not so much by the kilometres she had still to walk in the dark as by the sudden thought that her parents wouldn't be able to fight off an ambivalence on seeing her come home.

And that was the first time the Cheffe ever dared think her parents capable of ambivalence.

Oh, I think she was wrong.

As I imagine them, they would have accepted their daughter's return with no show of emotion, would have asked no questions, wouldn't have taken her to task, would have been able to forget, immediately and to their deepest depths, all about Marmande and the Clapeaus.

But very likely she wanted more than that, she wanted to surprise them and see them visibly happy and proud of her for fleeing the Clapeaus.

And how could they be? she suddenly thought, standing by the road, unable to go on.

Although she'd always found the official reason why she was sent to Marmande petty and in a way unworthy of the fanatical veneration she felt for her parents, she now suddenly realised it was probably the modest salary the Clapeaus would pay her that had convinced her parents it would be useful for her to leave Sainte-Bazeille, not, as she'd preferred to think – though no-one had ever told her any such thing, and so hadn't lied to her, hadn't "put one over on her" – the many advantages of living in a city, gaining solid professional experience, etc.

Yes, she understood, shivering by the side of that deserted, dark road, no longer sure which way to go but sensing she would be turning back, not knowing it yet, only sensing it, re-luctant, disgusted, but resigned, she understood that anything she earned and ate elsewhere meant that much less her adored parents had to provide.

How, then, could they be entirely happy to see her back with them?

The Cheffe was ashamed to assume her parents would be torn between joy and disappointment, it felt like her heart had suddenly turned cynical, it felt like life with the Clapeaus had corrupted her, complicated her, but she didn't think she was wrong, she was sure her parents would feel an ambivalence when they opened the door to her – but it was as if her own faintly sordid intelligence were creating that reaction in her parents, from a distance.

Instead of telling herself "Now I realise they can feel two conflicting emotions," she told herself, strangely, "If I hadn't had that thought, their love for me would still be as whole and untroubled as ever."

And for that she rebuked herself, and thought she'd suddenly turned wicked.

She did what her intuition had already told her she would, she retraced her steps, quickly this time, almost running, for fear the Clapeaus might have noticed she was missing.

Our smart apartment building in Lloret de Mar was designed almost exclusively for retirees like my friends, well-to-do French people whom a new life, strangely anonymous between fresh, neutral walls, seems to cast, with no sacrifice, no diabolical repercussion, into a kind of youth they never knew, alcoholic, vaguely communitarian, shallow and coolly hedonistic, we laugh and joke, we gather on Santa Cristina beach in tiny swimsuits and minuscule bikinis and drink lots of white

wine, we fear no judgment in our uninhibited, incurious, insistently
frivolous little circle, we've never been so free, so deliberately juvenile.
I'm not their age, nowhere near, but our similar lifestyles and inter-
changeable apartments make us equal on that score as well, I forget that
I'm not old yet and they indisputably are, our health is good, we look
after ourselves, we're immortal, we look after ourselves and no-one else.

She went back to life as a maid, doing housekeeping and
errands, laundry and dishes, and in her mind the change in
the cook and gardener's attitude, easing from silent, deliberately hurtful animosity into ordinary indifference punctuated by
the occasional curt and impersonal remark, was forever bound
up with what happened to her on the road to Sainte-Bazeille:
she'd had a thought that faintly dishonoured her parents, and
that flash of insight meant not that they no longer deserved her
unwavering devotion but that she'd done something wrong,
she'd defiled a purity of spirit.

She'd lowered herself to the ignoble level of the cook and
the gardener, she thought, and that's why they'd laid off her.

They must have seen what was gone from her eyes when
she came back after her brief flight.

They saw the absence of what once had incensed them.

They were always calculating, designing, anticipating, unlike her parents, who were as improvident as could be but so
perfectly thoughtful.

Her parents, the Cheffe had always thought, were happy to
be poor.

They believed, the Cheffe had always thought, or rather
they sensed, that they would lose something vital if ever they

found their way out of the poverty that clung to their bones.

Such as? Oh, the best part of them.

I used to be disgusted by that attitude towards their poverty, there was something about those parents, or at least the Cheffe's vision of those two paragons, that vaguely annoyed me when I was young, and vaguely sickened me too.

But now I understand the Cheffe, and I'm sad and sorry I can't tell her so.

Even if they didn't know it, the Clapeaus too showed her that something about her had changed after her encounter with doubt on the road to Sainte-Bazeille, because now they were more open with her, more sympathetic.

And so, all things considered, the Cheffe wasn't far from feeling at home in Marmande – not happy, because she thought she could never be happy again, now that she'd drifted so far from the spirit of her parents, but reasonably content, she was curious, she was eager to learn.

And besides, even if the Clapeaus' new friendliness constantly reminded her of what she saw as the ruination of her soul, as time went by she came to appreciate its warmth.

Yes, she was very young. No-one judged her more severely than she did, you know.

She never cast stones at anyone but herself, maybe the child she once was, but after all that was still her.

The Clapeaus were in their sixties, with four grown-up children who brought their families to lunch every Sunday, and many acquaintances they often asked to dinner, which justified their having a live-in cook.

Maybe they didn't dare admit that they themselves needed fine dishes cooked for them every day, because they loved eating with a fervent, unrelenting love, stronger than they were, that forced them to keep food in the foreground of their thoughts at all times.

It disturbed them a little.

Maybe they only had so many guests to give themselves an excuse for that obsession.

Because it frightened them, loving to eat as much as they did.

"You have to give your guests a decent welcome, decent food," they often said, since they couldn't say: "We really invite people over as an excuse to stuff our faces."

Did the Cheffe, at her age, realise the Clapeaus didn't entirely like being what they were, that they wished they could take a tamer, more ordinary interest in cuisine, that they felt in a sense possessed by eating and the pleasure it brought them?

I don't know. I only know that she always found a way to let the people she cooked for never feel ashamed that they passionately loved having her cook for them.

Oh yes, she hated people feeling guilty because of her, because of the pleasure she could bring them, which happens, she hated that.

But at the Clapeaus' she was probably too young to understand how deeply those otherwise reasonably friendly and uncomplicated people hated that weakness, that ardour for fabulous, varied, new, memorable meals.

Had she understood the remorse that faithfully visited them

after every feast, then she would have seen more sense in their strange behaviour with the cook, the way they fawned over her and harassed her at the same time, praised her with unfeigned enthusiasm in front of the guests and lashed her with baseless, strange, disjointed rebukes when they were alone with her, which the cook, viscerally aware of her power and standing, perfectly grasping what she would have found hard to put into words, answered with serene, impudent, weary effrontery, not fooled for a minute: "Yeah, yeah, you loved it and you know it," she told them, unless she didn't actually say those words but simply conveyed their meaning – it's the same thing, I know the gist of what happened and not the details, I know the spirit more than the letter, of course, but isn't it the spirit that matters?

In any case, after some time the Cheffe realised the cook had a powerful hold over the Clapeaus.

Whenever they'd berated her too violently on some empty pretext they themselves didn't believe in even as they were making so much of it (blushing, stammering, looking away), they always came hurrying back to beg her forgiveness, one or the other of them, and everything about them was a plea: "Don't leave us, forget all those stupid things we said, not under the effect of alcohol, alas, we never drink enough to break free of our foolish guilt, we stay mired in that guilt instead of springing away with a joyous, intoxicated kick, no, it wasn't our usual *cru bourgeois* that made us deluge you with vague, incoherent complaints, it was only our irremediable sense of shame and dishonour after an exquisite dinner, as yours was yet again this evening, thank you, thank you, please don't leave us."

Busy cleaning the kitchen, whisking a broom over the floor tiles glistening with cooking fat, the Cheffe heard every word of what went on between the sneering cook and the remorse-drunk Clapeaus, but I'm sure she never glimpsed the erotic aspect of the exchange, and the cook's vengeful, arrogant sense of sexual triumph when she afterwards turned to the Cheffe and cried, joyless but with a thrill in her voice, "I sure showed them, I've got them eating out of my hand, you see that?" was something the Cheffe simply couldn't perceive.

Later she could, of course, and she hated it, she would hate it for as long as she lived.

What exactly? Oh, you know what I'm talking about.

That way some dinner guests, men or women, have of treating the man or woman who cooks for them like a lover or mistress, since they lack the imagination to dream up any other image of the person who has so lavishly catered to their pleasure and happiness.

And with that there come poses, gazes, even words, that – spoken with no ulterior motive or hidden meaning, almost innocently shall we say – so overtly evoke sexual pleasure that the Cheffe, who had a real loathing for invasiveness, came to dread any expression of gratitude or admiration, as I told you before, she didn't like coming out into the dining room, didn't like meeting the customers.

She didn't like feeling her body close to theirs, didn't like seeing their tongues, their lips, their post-meal glow.

You're right, I called it a lack of imagination and I shouldn't have.

Not because it's wrong or not what I really think, but because you're going to ask how in that case the Cheffe would have liked to be thanked, in what register of ideas or feelings she wanted to be praised.

That's what you're about to ask me, right?

Because even for a woman as exceptional as the Cheffe, working and slaving and often suffering, and sacrificing any chance of rest or more or less anything like a private life, a family life, on the altar of extraordinary cooking, all that would have been hard to endure without thanks.

As I told you, she wanted no part of worship with erotic overtones, real or perceived.

She wanted it to be spiritual, she wanted the eater to fall into a state of quiet, modest contemplation, she wanted him to speak to her, if he so wished (but she would have rather he didn't), as he would to the officiant of a ceremony at once simple in its presentation and elaborate in its conception, and then she, the Cheffe, the celebrant, could be complimented for having so skilfully organised the phases of that ritual, she could be thanked, she could be praised for her thoughtful and sensitive observance.

That, she could tolerate, it could sometimes be a pleasure, she could put up with it, yes.

It was in that spirit that she practised her art.

Otherwise, she would have said, why bother?

She didn't want money or responsibilities, she wasn't greedy, had no taste for luxury, wasn't interested in her legacy.

Cooking was sacred.

Otherwise, why go to so much effort?

No, of course, that's not how she saw things in the days of Marmande and the Clapeaus, she didn't see anything, she wasn't really looking.

But she was feeling, concentrating the rays with her tireless little magnifying glass, secretly absorbing and transforming everything offered by the part of her working day that she spent helping the cook, that woman who would never be her friend. Very simple tasks, yes, peeling, washing, slicing.

One of the Clapeaus' grandsons was kind enough to send me a copy of Madame Clapeau's cash book from those days, and the entries for meat, vegetables, groceries and wine fit perfectly with the dishes the Cheffe remembered seeing the cook make, which she tried to describe in detail when I asked her about her informal education at the Clapeaus', she loved remembering that sort of thing, how she later mocked the heaviness of those menus!

For the Clapeaus, you couldn't give your guests a decent or even, in a sense, a friendly reception without a first course of charcuterie and then another of fish in sauce, a main dish of roasted or braised meat with multiple vegetable sides, a generously crouton-topped salad, a huge cheese board, a tart or a cake, all of that followed by fruits, chocolates, petits fours.

They loved a platter of pork charcuterie, they loved pâté en croûte, meat pies, galantines, ham croissants, which they didn't trust their cook to make but had delivered from a shop in Paris, I've forgotten the name, they claimed it was the place to find the best of all things pork.

The Clapeaus had a serious passion for meat, and since, strangely, they seemed to find that passion as acceptable as their fondness for fine cuisine was shameful, they sometimes exclaimed, in a tone of exaggerated, faintly absurd pride, "Meat galore, that's what we like!" – hoping to hide the fact that in truth they loved everything, creams and flans, roasted vegetables, warm goat's cheese on toast, and that deep down what they really loved was eating, even if organising their dinner parties, planning the menus, choosing the products, endless deliberations with the cook on the choice of a dish supposedly favoured by some guest, all those falsely anxious, ostensibly fraught preliminaries (everyone was supposed to believe those many invitations were a duty and a chore the Clapeaus were shouldering) brought them enormous pleasure, a pleasure so ill-concealed that the Cheffe saw it almost immediately.

Yes, it was the Clapeaus who first gave her an example of the pleasure the vocabulary of cooking can inspire, they pronounced the words carefully, repeated them needlessly, kept each one in their mouths as long as they could before going on to the next.

They also gave her an example of what it is to be helpless and lost, not because good food was the only thing they ever thought about but because their own nature shocked and alarmed them, and they looked at themselves with the same stern, censorious gaze they would have given anyone whose life was ruled by an obsession.

They hated that about themselves, they couldn't even understand it, that was why they were lost, unworthy of respect, people mocked them behind their backs, sometimes hardly behind their backs at all.

That was what taught the Cheffe you should only let your obsessions show if you're proud of them.

What did they look like?

I couldn't tell you. I never saw a photo.

The Cheffe never described them, except to say they weren't in any way unusual.

I'm not sure she would have told me even if they were enormously fat, I can imagine her conscientiously keeping that to herself, out of politeness, compassion, esteem for those people who, in the end, treated her well.

So it means nothing either way that she didn't say if they were or were not grossly overweight.

The Cheffe was the most loyal person I ever knew, and that's what lay behind so many of her mysteries.

She kept quiet or concealed the truth out of faithfulness to loyalty, if I can put it that way.

I myself have to take care to be both loyal and accurate, to be faithful to both loyalty and accuracy, and it tortures me terribly, talking with you I've often found myself deeply discouraged, yes.

I'd like to tell the Life of the Cheffe the way people write the Life of a Saint, but that's impossible, and the Cheffe herself would have thought it ridiculous.

So I try to make plain honesty my watchword, but sometimes I hear the clear, calm voice, slightly tinged with a terrifying threat, the threat of a withdrawal of her trust and affection, sometimes I hear the voice of the Cheffe saying, "Do you really think you have any right to talk about all this? If I never did, why should you?"

Yes, it's very hard for me to accept that one day, as I'm talking away, I may commit an infidelity to loyalty and not realise it or realise it too late, and I know that vanity, in this case the temptation to impress by revealing some secret, lies in wait for me with every sentence I speak, I know it well, it's very hard.

I'm feeling my way, I'm not sure of anything, I want the Cheffe to be thought an admirable woman.

Horrified by that idea?

Yes, she certainly would have been, but she would have been wrong, that's the conviction I've come to.

I can go on talking to you about the Cheffe as long as I feel certain that she would have been wrong to fight it with her old resistance to anyone taking an interest in her.

Because I realised that had become a reflex for her, and I also realised she didn't dare ask herself if it was really so impossible to feel happy or curious about the many requests she got, at the end, from journalists eager to meet her.

She'd long since convinced herself that she couldn't.

It was like a sin to her, that idea of meeting, of telling, but it was a sin she'd made up, and she didn't know it.

The Cheffe would have found that misstep far less grave if she'd realised no-one else saw it, I'm almost sure.

She was proud, but there was no vanity in her pride.

She admitted her lapses in judgment, the illusions her untamed heart sometimes dreamt up, she knew she was strong-headed, too quick to accuse herself, punish herself, too quick to feel guilty.

I myself make plain honesty my watchword, and I put my love for her after that, because I know the Cheffe valued honesty over love, she thought people could do terrible things in the name of love, but never in the name of honesty.

The love between a man and a woman never interested her much.

Long before I met her, cooking had commandeered all her capacity for loving, for giving of herself, for suffering, for hoping, both the act of cooking and especially the thinking behind it, and the little capacity for love that managed to slip free of cooking went to her daughter, the Cheffe's daughter, you may already have met her, if you ask me she didn't deserve that love.

But it was a love heavy with despair, so maybe it wasn't really love at all.

I've often thought my feelings for the Cheffe kept me from becoming a great cook, but I don't regret it.

Every day I get something from what my love made of me, and if I can live my life on good terms with myself it's only because my exclusive, absolute, imperishable love transformed the boy I was, conventionally eager to succeed, ordinary, pragmatic, into a young man capable of marvelling and sacrificing.

How could I regret becoming a far better man, morally and spiritually, than the man I would have been had that love not caught hold of me?

I can't regret that.

Forget my dreams of becoming a chef, for me it will be

enough to have practised my trade decently, and made from it only what I need, which is very little.

I can't regret the swelling of my courage, the blossoming of my cramped heart, no-one would regret that, man or woman, no-one.

Once you've seen that elevation of your consciousness, even at the expense of more concrete ambitions, then you can only be grateful, and you'll set aside disappointment and frustration for all time.

That's why I can't regret devoting my talents to loving and serving the Cheffe instead of myself, I can't regret that.

In Lloret de Mar, readying my terrace for this evening's aperitif hour, thinking of other things, unfolding the metal chairs and wiping the table and sweeping up the blue petals gently falling from the old jacaranda that protects me from the sun, it occurs to me that the days go by so uneventfully and identically that my friends and I might almost have discovered some ingenious tactic for shielding ourselves from the withering passage of the years, sheltered from time in our harbour we see others growing old and we look at ourselves and we find that we never change, not even alcohol reddens our eternally tanned faces, we think ourselves lucky and attractive, we never give doubt or anguish or existential chagrin a chance to sneak into our happy hearts, our carefree hearts, our hearts gone cold, and we all see ourselves in the flattering mirror of the others' unchanged faces.

As I was saying, the Clapeaus had come up with the odd idea that by parading their unbridled taste for meat they could hide their mania for food in general, which is why meat was the daily fare at the Clapeaus', and why they even considered it a therapeutic necessity, they claimed meat protected them from various illnesses they never failed to catch when circumstances deprived them of pork or beef at every meal.

The Cheffe would remember the dishes she saw the cook make, in a large, sunny, modern kitchen looking onto a little urban garden enclosed by high walls and abundantly planted with espaliered pear and peach trees, a kitchen the Clapeaus were so proud of that they showed it to all their guests, proclaiming "The most important room in the house!" with feigned sarcasm, trying to sound caustic, exasperated by it wasn't quite clear whose laughable ambition to have the kitchen thought of like that, maybe the cook's, but all their friends and relatives knew that in truth they alone seriously and solemnly saw the kitchen as the most important room in the house, the cook certainly didn't care, it wasn't her house, and nothing belonged to her – the Cheffe would remember those dishes as made up of nothing but meat, day after day, vegetables being added only for visual effect, and in a sense as penitence.

There was brined pork and Lyonnais sausage accompanied by a few very thin leaves of white cabbage, there was breaded and pan-fried fillet of pork topped with anchovy butter, there were kidneys from all sorts of animals, inevitably sautéed in butter and glazed with Madeira sauce, there was rabbit with shallots and mushrooms, beef tongue au gratin, pigeons with peas, there were veal escalopes in peppery cream sauce, black pudding studded with chopped onions or offal and served on slices of baked apple, fried chicken croquettes, lamb cutlets à la Villeroy, that last one was a great favourite of Monsieur

Clapeau's, he called them his little darlings, he liked them thickly breaded, crisp on the outside and just barely cooked inside, he wanted a faint taste of blood.

The Clapeaus tired quickly even of dishes they loved, and their perpetual craving for new tastes grew stronger as they grew older, as if they were afraid they might die before they could explore every flavour, every combination of textures and appearances, every way of cooking and seasoning, every sensation the act of eating could offer their very imaginative minds.

They pressed the cook to produce something they couldn't name, and since they couldn't name it something they couldn't describe, they didn't mean to but they put her in a very difficult spot, called on to cook something they couldn't begin to imagine.

They brought her recipes they'd found in strange old books, written in a language she could scarcely understand, and told her to use them simply as inspiration, to reflect and meditate on them, and then, with those mysterious recipes in her mind, to open all the doors of her imagination, to open them as wide as she could.

The cook scarcely pretended to glance at them.

She never loathed the Clapeaus as much as when they came to her in that mood: astir, hopeful, but at the same time expecting to be disappointed, and so at once pleading and dissatisfied, frustrated, furious, hating themselves.

The Cheffe saw that, took note of it, shall we say, but she didn't judge, didn't think anything about it, because even then her powerful intuition was telling her, warning her, that she was too young and too ignorant of humanity's ways to allow herself an opinion of people who, however naive the Clapeaus sometimes seemed, had seen so much more of life than she had.

And when she became an adult, it would still be the Cheffe's way to withhold her judgment on the things people did.

She wanted to understand all their motivations before she opened her mouth, for the sake not so much of justice as of accuracy, she feared she might not always see things as they are.

Which is why people sometimes called her too cautious, afraid to offer a prompt, clear opinion, always holding back.

They couldn't have got her more wrong.

The Cheffe was almost incomprehensibly indifferent to what people thought of her ideas.

But the possibility that she might find herself in the dock of her little inner courtroom, where her rigorous integrity was always quick to summon her, facing charges of prejudice, incoherence, misinterpretation and vanity, that possibility she found hard to bear.

People must have been all the more surprised by that reticence, which in anyone else could easily have gone unnoticed, because the Cheffe had a quick, categorical opinion on anything connected with cooking, and was never shy about questioning a dish or an ingredient, even if it might earn her animosity or – almost worse, for her – excessive approval.

The Clapeaus never watched themselves around her, they forgot she was there when they were talking to the cook.

And when she saw them that way, intense and imploring, dubious but longing, she invariably wondered, puzzled: Why don't they cook for themselves? Why grant that cook, whose mediocrity the Cheffe was coming to recognise, the power to make them unhappy?

They knew so much more about cuisine than that cold, morose woman, they'd developed an interest in gastronomy so much broader and better informed than hers, that they might well have come close to the undiscovered foods they were dreaming of if they'd taken on the task themselves, they could have experimented and striven and not had to explain and describe, not had to fruitlessly search for the words that might make something they themselves didn't know understandable to a cook who was hostile and resistant before they even began. Why don't they do that, the Cheffe wondered, deeply troubled by their pathetic, forced devotion to the cook, its shameless- ness, its twistedness.

She thought there was no good way to disentangle yourself from such a perverse relationship, she thought that for all her ill will the cook wasn't wrong to balk at the Clapeaus' demands, as vague as they were desperate or imperious, and neither was she wrong to feel she didn't have to slavishly obey people so ashamed of their appetites.

But the Clapeaus weren't wrong either, she thought, to fault the lack of inventiveness of that bitter, sullen woman, who cooked with a truculent fervour and a scarcely concealed ambition never to give them quite what they wanted.

The Cheffe long delayed telling me what she knew about

the Clapeaus, how she understood their apparent conviction that they couldn't possibly cook for themselves.

She always stopped short of that, as if suddenly certain words eluded her.

She was waiting to know me better.

She already knew, when she told me of her education at the Clapeaus', that I wouldn't snigger at anything she might say, that I wasn't the sniggering sort, that I could in fact safely be judged capable of anything but sniggering.

She knew that, but maybe she wanted to be sure I wouldn't snigger even to myself, to make sure I'd take everything she said seriously and literally, sure I'd believe every word without hesitation.

If, she explained, the Clapeaus didn't think they were allowed to cook, it was because no communication can be had with the object of your worship except by way of an intermediary knowingly or unknowingly destined for that role, and that was the cook, who even with her many failings did indeed perform all the duties of that very special, undelegatable mission.

The Clapeaus would have thought they were committing an unpardonable offence against the sacred laws of cooking if they arrogantly set out to enter into contact with it, to lay their hands on it, shall we say.

No-one would have punished them, said the Cheffe, but they would have known they'd done something wrong, and more than wrong, criminal.

And the cook must have seen that, she understood the Clapeaus better than she understood herself, closed and aloof though she was with them, and sometimes, in a spirit of intentional cruelty, she spat out, "Here, why don't you try it for once!" and cackled as they recoiled in horror, sure of her unbounded power in the space of the altar, meaning that her limited abilities didn't matter, since she was sanctified and they weren't, and never would be, because they were afraid.

Sorry? Yes, I'm getting carried away, you're right, no, I know you're not saying it but you're right all the same, I'm becoming ridiculously grandiose. And for what?

But I find it hard to keep my demeanour serene and my tone moderate when I'm talking about things that meant so much to the Cheffe, my old fervour always comes back, entire and unchanged, and I can see myself, young, ignorant, alone with the Cheffe in the kitchen after the other employees had gone, raptly listening but taking care not to show any of that raptness, that hunger to know everything about her, as in her clear, crisp voice she told me what I'm telling you today, her eyes fixed on mine, as if to make sure she saw nothing in them to trouble her, no boredom, no fatigue, no restlessness.

And if she were to glimpse in my eyes the shadow of an interest greater than she considered plausible, or an emotion stronger than she thought permissible, I knew she would stop at once, and then I might never again spend those late-night hours with her in the just-cleaned, orderly, empty kitchen, my mind almost blank with weariness, sometimes trembling with cold or exhaustion, no, I would spend them alone in my Mériadeck studio, just as awake, seeing the Cheffe as if I were standing beside her, unable to bring herself to leave the kitchen even when there was nothing more to wash or put away, seeming to dread going up to bed in her apartment over the restaurant, her lips moving, facing the counter I leaned on to listen to her, and I wouldn't be there, and she'd scarcely notice.

But, from the solitude of my bed in Mériadeck, I would know I wasn't there, and I'd suffer terribly for her, even if she was not a woman to be pitied, and suffering for her was no better.

No, she didn't sleep much.

She would have liked to make herself sleep exactly as long as she needed to recover her strength for her work, but she couldn't.

Instead she drifted around the deserted kitchen, telling herself again and again she should go up to bed, then looked at the clock and discovered in dismay that she'd been telling herself that for an hour, two hours, and there she was still downstairs, wandering among the counters and ovens, not even knowing what she was thinking about.

I'm telling you all this, the business with the Clapeaus and the cook, to explain how the germ of a conviction that never left her might have been planted in the Cheffe's mind: cuisine is a thing to be touched by authorised hands only, respectful, delicate, mindful of what they're doing.

No matter, in a way, if they're not expert, so long as they've been ordained.

By whom? Oh, by yourself, it's nothing to do with a diploma or a master's blessing, no, you have to feel whether the breath of cooking has entered into you.

The Clapeaus were too given to fear and tangled feelings for that spirit ever to enter their mixed-up hearts.

They spent a few weeks every summer at their house in the Landes, bringing the cook along with them, but the summer the spirit of cooking took root in the Cheffe's heart, the summer she turned sixteen, the cook refused for the first time to make the trip, she wanted to go visit her family, to spend some time with her children, thereby informing everyone that she had children, in Champagne or I'm not sure where, a long way from Marmande.

The Clapeaus watched her pack her suitcase, not for a moment thinking they'd see her again, little doubting that the children in Champagne were a pretext to quit without saying so, and it gave the cook a sharp pleasure to see them so distraught, vainly trying to hide their panic at the thought of going a few weeks without her, she liked that because she hated their need for her, and she said nothing to suggest she'd be back, she knew she would, she didn't say a word about it, too bad for her.

There comes a time, the Cheffe always thought, and so do I, when so much contempt for others and so inflated an idea of one's own worth can no longer be rewarded, a time when it must in fact be punished, by decision or by accident.

So too bad for her, the Cheffe always thought, and so do I, and I assure you that the Cheffe, in all her love of fairness and decency, not to mention compassion, the Cheffe who readily and completely forgot other people's every little mistake, the Cheffe never shed a tear over the fate of the cook, never tried to find out what had become of her, if she was happy in her new position.

Because when they got to the Landes the Clapeaus realised they didn't feel up to the arduous task of finding a suitable cook, which is to say one who knew and understood them. The cook knew them perfectly and understood them perfectly, even if, hating them as she did, she often pretended she neither knew nor understood them.

Sitting in the armchairs still draped with dust covers in the house in the Landes where they only set foot in summer, the Clapeaus looked around and their eyes lit on the Cheffe, just turned sixteen, busy uncovering the many pieces of unnecessary, uninteresting furniture that cluttered that house, like the house in Marmande.

"You're going to take the cook's place for a while," they told her, as if it went without saying, and maybe it did, but it wasn't their tone that convinced the Cheffe she was capable of the work.

The Clapeaus' offer or order roused something in her that she must have felt for some time, ever since she first witnessed the Clapeaus' futile discussions with the cook and imagined herself in her place, musing on what she would have said, even deciding that if she were the cook there would never have been any such discussion.

Because, she'd told herself many times, she wouldn't have aimed her work just far enough from what the Clapeaus wanted to make them labour to explain what they were hoping for but not so far away that they could legitimately complain they hadn't been listened to.

She would, she thought, have striven not to fulfill their wishes, which were in any case vague, contradictory, unworkable, but to cook with such little regard for the contingencies of their respective situations, with a will so bent on creating a perfection far beyond the chance likes and dislikes of all concerned, them and her alike, that the Clapeaus would have to surrender to her, happily, gratefully.

She would, she thought, have cooked in a way that couldn't be argued with.

I asked her: "So no-one would have the right to criticise you?"

She answered: "Oh yes, of course they would, as you know I myself criticise everything set before me."

No, it was the sincerity of her quest for a culinary ideal that the Clapeaus wouldn't be able to question, they would understand and admire it, because they themselves were searching for a gastronomical experience that would raise them above mere gluttony, that would let them forgive themselves for being what they were.

Which is why, listening in on those scenes between the Clapeaus and the cook, the Cheffe always sensed, unable to find the words in her mind but feeling it with all her being, that the cook wasn't the person they needed, and that, as in an unhappy marriage, the one side's failings and follies only aggravated the other's.

She froze, her hands still hovering over a dust cover they were about to lift off, then stepped back and crossed them over her stomach, calmly answering, "Yes, of course, gladly," and already her mind was racing, almost bolting, coursing with images of dishes it had invented before she fell asleep at night, when, unlike the early days in Marmande when she saw only her parents' faces, she reviewed what she considered the cook's mistakes, the improvements that could be made to the pork-and-chicken-liver terrine the Clapeaus rightly found a little bland, the ingredients it would be best to use sparingly, like flour and bouillon for sauces, yes, even then the Cheffe wasn't fond of flour in cooking.

Did she eat or taste everything the cook made?

Yes, I believe she did, apart no doubt from grilled meats served in individual portions – rib or sirloin steak, veal, pork, lamb cutlets – and even that I can't guarantee, because to their great credit, or maybe it was simply their guilty conscience, I'm not quite sure, the Clapeaus wanted their servants to eat well and abundantly, even overeat, as long as drinking didn't come with it, they had no tolerance for drunkenness.

As a rule they took no heed of expenses where food was concerned, so I would imagine that what the Clapeaus couldn't decently consume would have been more than enough for the Cheffe, the cook, and the gardener to finish, but it wasn't even a matter of finishing it, I'm not talking about leftovers, I mean whole servings given to each.

The Clapeaus would never have dreamt of forcing the cook to make separate meals for herself, the Cheffe and the gardener, no, they were never petty like that.

That was how the Cheffe had gradually learned to judge the cook's skills, and above all her inspiration, and as she told it the skills were beyond reproach but the inspiration was essentially nil.

She used to tell me, "It was like you were eating the same thing every time, no matter what kind of meat or vegetable or grain she was using, everything turned into the same handful of tastes, it was tedious."

And every sauce was a béchamel, with different seasonings depending on the dish, or else a cream or butter liaison, and the sauces were inevitable and excessive, ladled over everything in exactly the same way, you couldn't tell fish from meat or potatoes, as the Cheffe told herself many times, at night, before she fell asleep.

Bold ideas came to her, which she didn't write down but mentally filed away by category, for example the idea of allspice, and this was how she fixed it in her memory: try adding it to vol-au-vents, to beef bouillon, to the rum that raisins and candied fruit are soaked in for fruitcake.

Or again, on the subject of crème fraîche: avoid it, except in blanquette de veau.

Those decrees were naive, and they expressed not so much some special precociousness in the Cheffe as her limited experience, since the only dishes she knew were the ones made by the Clapeaus' cook, and the only tastes she knew were the Clapeaus'.

But at that early age the Cheffe acquired the habit of never going to sleep without first thinking back over all the food that was eaten that day, evaluating, analysing, judging everything she'd put in her mouth and everything she'd studied with her sensitive eye, the arrangement of colours on a plate, the severe beauty of cast-iron casseroles, already sensing the interest, both for the eye and for the appetite, of bringing the casserole straight to the table rather than, as the cook did, as everyone did at the time, transferring whatever had been simmering inside it – soup, jugged hare, ragout of beef cheeks – to a tureen decorated with fussy, old-fashioned flowers, or a silver platter whose grey patina made browned meats seem dreary and off-putting, she always thought, which is why when she had her own restaurant she never served anything on silver, and also why she always took great care choosing the colour of her enamelled casseroles, thinking of the tinge the food took on in the last stages of the cooking.

The morning the Clapeaus told her she'd be filling in for the cook, that morning when the Cheffe's strong, square little hands realised they would finally be put to the use they sensed they were made for, the Cheffe was convinced she had to dazzle the Clapeaus with that first dinner, she had to crush them under the irrefutable weight of her talent, ingenuity and charm.

Yes, at that moment she wanted to cast a spell on them, nothing less.

And if her cooking would later show that she mistrusted beguilement more than anything else, that she avoided any technique suggesting an ambition to please, to pamper refined tastes, that day, in the living room of the house in the Landes, with the bright summer-morning sun struggling to shine through the pine trees, the old rust-branched pine trees that derived an ascetic, minimal existence from the sand, the thought of bewitching the Clapeaus excited the Cheffe's intelligence, her thoughts raced at such a clip that she feared she might not be able to keep them in line, she panicked.

She told the Clapeaus she'd have to go out and do some shopping immediately, and never before had the Cheffe told the Clapeaus what she had to do, only the Clapeaus had the implicit right to say such things, and yet here she was on that inaugural morning telling them just that, her gaze fixed not on the two Clapeaus slumped in the armchairs still draped with dusty covers but on the desiccated branches of the pine trees, so old that only the very tops were green, so that from the house's windows there was nothing to see but what looked like dead trees, bare, rust-red branches that sometimes pressed up against the glass.

It was summer, the season of the Clapeaus' perennial holiday, and the pines surrounded the house with a rusty, dry wreath that stretched all the way to the ocean, whose languid murmur the Cheffe had now heard for the first time in her life, it was summer, and the Clapeaus stoically endured that time and that house, the prison of the rust-red pines, the ceaseless murmur of the ocean, the damp smell of the house, its meagre comforts, they endured that obligation, imposed by a tradition they themselves had invented, to spend long weeks each summer far from their beloved house in Marmande, the only place where they felt at peace.

"The kitchen's not as well equipped as in Marmande, of course, and it's much smaller, too," they said to the Cheffe, suddenly almost humble, as if in such conditions the Cheffe might refuse to take over.

They stood up together to show her the kitchen and cooking things.

It was a small room in the back of the house, its tile floor gritty with sand, kept dark all day long by the thick, rugged trunk of a pine tree growing just outside the narrow barred window, and yet when she walked into that kitchen the Cheffe felt a happiness she'd never felt before.

For the first time in her life she felt she was in a place that would be hers and hers alone.

There was a newish gas stove and an old wood-burning oven, many pots, pans and casseroles of all sizes, and a hodge-podge of out-of-date spices and condiments, like jarred ashes, accumulated by the cook who'd taken care not to label or name them, guarding her secrets, the Cheffe immediately thought, not that she was unhappy with what she was finding, since with the cook's past appearances on this stage erased she wouldn't have to follow in her footsteps.

She said nothing of all that to the Clapeaus, nothing of what she was thinking, didn't confess her emotion on discerning, in that little room severely guarded by an old pine tree planted just outside, the brand-new elements of a happiness and a rapt-ness she was now feeling for the first time, though she'd had a glimpse of it when she lay in her bed at night mentally draw-ing up menus, lists of perfect dishes, corrections to the ones she'd eaten, but only a glimpse or an illusion, and now the reality of that happiness, that raptness, now the plenitude of that happiness and raptness was spreading all through her sixteen-year-old body, eager, as she said, to finally go to work.

And when the Clapeaus anxiously asked what she thought, when they announced they could always go to a restaurant this first evening, give her some time to get used to things, she answered with concern on her brow but joy in her heart that she would gladly make that first day's dinner if they didn't mind driving her around to buy the things she would need, and all the while she was peering into the cupboards, pulling out drawers to inspect the knives and spatulas, her steps quick and lively on the tiles dusted with grey wind-borne sand, and she made it so clear that she'd taken possession of both the room and the Clapeaus' hungering flesh that they took a step back, huddling in the doorway, no doubt convinced they'd done well to entrust this girl with that mission, but once again feeling left out, never called, never chosen, never worthy of the work.

And that girl, so young and so small, that girl who still had the cheeks and the long, delicate, flyaway hair of a child, that girl they hardly knew, whom they'd taken so little interest in, that girl was firmly pushing them back towards the hallway with her gaze, which had taken possession of them just as it had of the little kitchen, and at that moment the Clapeaus must have known she would still be their cook when they went back to Marmande, they had yet to eat a single dish made by her hands but they knew it, they saw what had settled over her, what never settled over them, and they knew it.

They didn't ask what she was planning to make.

With one hand she silently brushed the sand from the table,

a sand so fine that it worked its way in at the windowsills, under the doors, then tore a sheet from the notepad hanging by a string on a nail near the sink and sat down to write out a shopping list, her back turned to the Clapeaus so they wouldn't see she wrote slowly and clumsily, holding the pencil very straight over the paper like a tool meant for piercing or gouging.

She didn't really need that list, that was simply an image of her she thought she had to give the Clapeaus in those early days.

The Cheffe kept a record in her mind of everything she needed for her work, just as she did every thought that came to her about cooking, her memory was vast and remarkably organised, and in any case her difficulties with reading and writing made reliance on written words pointless, since in a very concrete sense those words said nothing to her, evoked some object in her mind only at the price of a strenuous, disheartening effort.

Yes, the Cheffe had a phenomenal memory.

People who knew of her illiteracy and thought her simpleminded and so went into ecstasies over her culinary gifts, which they saw as the revelation of some unexpected, titillating sort of primal intelligence, always overlooked or underestimated her prodigious memory, thanks to which the Cheffe never needed written recipes or notes, she kept all her recipes meticulously archived in her head, she had the most methodical mind I've ever known.

I can never remember which terrace I've been invited to for a party, I often have to work, as I sit on a metal chair or stand at the railing, forearms on the hot aluminium, hips thrust back, buttocks bulging

*under my eternal Bermuda shorts, to remember if this is my terrace or
André's or Florence's or Jacky's or Véro's or Dominique's or Manuel's
or Sylvie's, to remember if I have hosting duties or if it's one of them
who's supposed to be offering me yet another drink, a grilled sausage,
a bowl of tabbouleh, I settle the question by looking down at the pool,
measuring the distance, since from my apartment, the only one of the
bunch on the ground floor, you could easily straddle the balustrade and
dive without danger into the gilded glistening water, it's been known
to happen, all those scenes mingle in my memory and the overlit water
soon gives me a migraine, I should turn away but a stupor rivets my
forearms to the aluminium railing and my blurred, flickering gaze to
the water, clearly you wouldn't dare dive from this terrace into that pool
far below, so am I at Jacky's? Am I at Pascaline's?*

And as the Clapeaus' massive Citroën pulled away from the
house, turned onto the sandy road through the pines, so dense
and rust-red that they eclipsed the blazing noonday sun, allow-
ing only a dull-red halo of dusty light around their trunks, the
Cheffe wasn't thinking – too new to all this for such things to
occur to her – that she was sitting in that vast leather back seat
as if she were the boss and the Clapeaus had to drive her wherever she wanted, the two of them crammed into the front and
eager to hear her wishes, to learn what shop they'd be taking
her to once they emerged from the dense, rusty, innumerable
ranks of pine trees reducing the unclouded July sun to scattered, quivering patches on the grey sand.

"First of all, a good chicken," said the Cheffe, "and then
I'll need various kinds of fish, and leeks, carrots, potatoes and
other things I'll tell you as we go."

The Clapeaus conferred.

Their voices were almost sharp, atypically tense, as they discussed how best to go about finding all that.

Monsieur Clapeau had stopped the car at the end of the dirt road, just before the main road, as if reluctant to cast off into the vibrating blaze of the sunlight, which made liquid mirages undulate on the asphalt.

When, a half-hour later, they drove into the yard of the Joda family's farm, the same bleached, shimmering light made puddles as undeniable as they were chimerical on the packed dirt – which is why, I'm sure, the Cheffe could never separate the exaltation of cooking, the effervescence of mental energy focused solely on the invention of a meal, from the extreme, inhospitable heat, from the livid, liquid, scintillating light of a late summer morning in southwestern France, she closed her restaurant during the winter months, her imagination failed her at that time of year, she turned sad and hard.

Yes, she could be hard, but I like to think I was the only one who felt it, who knew it.

She never let it show.

"My heart is a brick," she would tell me when I went to see her in her apartment above the closed restaurant, when I sat down in my usual armchair and asked why she was keeping her thick, dark-blue velvet drapes half drawn instead of letting in the meagre January light, "My heart is a brick," she would say with a weary shake of her head, and that was supposed to explain everything, the half-open curtains, her silence as I laboured to entertain her with stories I'd read in the local paper, her slightly blank gaze, her refusal to make even the most cursory attempt at politeness, she who generally had such exquisite manners.

That's where it all came from, from that blinding white sunlight on the road outside the rust-red cover of the pines, it came from the heat and the sight of non-existent but undeniable rippling water on the packed earth of the Jodas' farmyard that summer when the spirit of cooking recognised the Cheffe and the Clapeaus saw it in her and on her, never in them, but they could still see it, that's where it all came from: the morose winter sun would never have brought her out, the Cheffe always told herself, she would have gone on being invisible, unknown even to herself, untouched by anything, had the summer light of her sixteenth year not been there to reveal the thing in her that could have stayed veiled forever.

Do you realise that all the Cheffe's best recipes, the most popular but also those dearest to her heart, like her little vol-au-vents with Camargue oysters, her clam and green asparagus soup, her calf sweetbreads flambéed with Armagnac, they were all inevitably conceived and developed at the height of the summer, when you couldn't stand in the restaurant's kitchen without gasping or feeling an oily sweat overflowing from the hollows of your flesh, the Cheffe was at the peak of her powers and ingenuity while we were all drooping around her, seeing to our everyday tasks by pure force of habit, with nothing like thought guiding our hands, and in those stifling weeks the Cheffe's instincts were at their apogee and her joy at its peak, no oily sweat ever trickled over her skin because her joy absorbed everything, exhaustion, the unbearable heat, the thick, stifling air, the joyful grace of creation absorbed it all, her skin shone with a gentle, fresh, quiet glow.

She never spoke of it, but I knew, having walked past the restaurant on those summer nights when the choking heat drove me out of my Mériadeck studio, when I decided I'd rather wander the dead, dark streets than toss and turn between my damp sheets, I knew the Cheffe spent a good part of those nights alone in the kitchen, experimenting with some idea her imagination had offered her.

I saw the harsh white glow of the lights shining onto the pavement from the three barred ground-floor windows, and I painfully envied the Cheffe who was working inside, in the inspiring solitude of the night, in the infinite, intoxicated hours of the night, chopping, cooking, testing, all alone and all-powerful in the thick silence of the night, how I envied her for not being weighed down by love, for doing what made her happier than anything on earth, with no-one and no sad thoughts of anyone (apart from her daughter, but was that love, wasn't it crushing despair?) troubling the pure, simple joy of her favourite thing, of creation fixed solely on itself and perfectly happy to have nothing exist around or outside it.

How I envied her, yes.

But I wouldn't be telling the whole truth if I didn't add that I was perfectly happy loving the Cheffe as I loved her.

Who knows which is better?

The Jodas offered to sell the Clapeaus a very fat chicken they'd slaughtered two days before.

The Cheffe inspected it closely before she agreed to the purchase, and when, decades later, she described how intently she'd pinched the deep yellow skin to gauge its thickness, tried to break a bone to check the bird's vigour, how she'd gravely inspected the gizzard and liver to be sure they looked healthy and fat, she couldn't hold back a little laugh of embarrassment and amused disbelief.

"When I think what I was planning to do with that magnificent chicken," she always said, "when I think I'd made up my mind to demolish that wonderful meat!"

And of course she made allowances for her youth and what she saw as her obligation to show the Clapeaus all the talents she was certain she had, which necessarily implied, she recognised, some degree of artifice or display (showing off, she called it), but she was still ashamed that she hadn't yet realised, that glorious summer, had felt no stirring of doubt, no need to silence her sensitivity, that she hadn't realised the one and only justification for putting an animal to death lies in the respect, care and thoughtfulness with which you treat its flesh and then take that flesh into you, bite by bite.

Forty years later, that still bothered her.

Because the spirit of her cooking was so fundamentally contrary to the spirit that whispered the idea for that first dinner in her ear that she found it hard to imagine she'd once been that girl.

The Cheffe would later devote all her care to respecting the products she used, she inwardly bowed down before them, paying them homage, grateful, honouring them as best she could, vegetables, herbs, plants, animals, she took nothing for granted, wasted nothing, damaged nothing, mistreated nothing, defiled no creation of nature, however modest, and the same went for human beings, even if her work didn't involve chopping them up, the same went for all of us, she never humiliated us. For the Cheffe, everything that lived was to be esteemed, everything that existed.

She never tore into anything or anyone, ever.

Except, perhaps, for that beautiful chicken from the Joda farm, yes indeed, and she never quite got over it, haha.

Had they been asked, the Clapeaus would surely have held a very different opinion, they would surely have cherished an enchanted memory of that first dinner in the Landes, a memory soon magnified by their obsessive habit of making something legendary of a meal they'd especially enjoyed, but the Clapeaus' judgment would have changed nothing for the Cheffe, she knew that to them there was no such thing as a morality of cooking.

That question would have been simply beyond their understanding, their minds weren't made for considering or even perceiving such things.

The Clapeaus' car pulled away from the Joda farm and drove on to Vieux-Boucau in the infernal noontime heat, all the windows rolled down, but to the dazed Cheffe that searing wind only made the leather car seat all the hotter, only blasted her face and bare, pink forearms all the harder, there was no-one else out on the steaming road at that hour.

For the first time in her life the Cheffe felt privileged, regal, even if at that moment she was physically suffering, even if she was starting to worry, seeing the time go by, wondering if it might have been a mistake to accept that decisive challenge, the challenge of making a meal in just a few hours that would forever leave the Clapeaus in her thrall.

Meanwhile, they were on their way to Vieux-Boucau because the Cheffe wanted fish and shellfish, even though she'd never seen the ocean and at the time couldn't have cared less about the ocean, scarcely turning her head when Madame Clapeau pointed out the shoreline on their left, too lost in her thoughts of the soup she'd planned as a first course.

The Cheffe didn't know the first thing about fish, not their names, not their uses in cooking.

But, having accompanied the cook to the market in Marmande and tasted the soup she made every Friday, she was convinced that if that weekly, inevitable, impoverished soup – obediently downed, without a word, by the Clapeaus – was so flat, if its aftertaste was almost soapy, it could only be because the cook made it from her very thin vegetable bouillon, into which she simply dumped a few fillets of whitefish that imparted no flavour, not even their own subtle, fresh, seaside taste, that only created a dull-white foam whose look and smell always sickened the Cheffe.

She didn't like seeing that soup brought to the table in Marmande, she didn't like fish soup being thought of that way, as something obligatory and dreary, inevitable and repellent, and in her nightly meditations, reflecting on the day's meals as she lay in her bed, she concluded it would take virtually nothing, just a little effort, to make fish soup delightful, and she felt entirely capable of that little effort.

And so, as a way of making the Clapeaus her captives, she'd thought it an obvious decision to try to conquer them with a soup whose mere mention had always made their faces fall. And here's what the Cheffe set out to make once they were back in the house shaded and guarded and intimidated by the rust-red pines, here's what she conceived, what she created by the grace of an admirable resolve, and not only for the sake of those two Clapeaus from Marmande, of course, but also quite simply to prove to herself she could cook.

And if she could cook, if she knew how to cook, then her aim was within reach, she'd have only to marshal the troops of her vigour, her tenacity, her quickness, her daring, and marshalling those troops was nothing to her, even then her will was enormous, almost obsessive, no effort daunted her, her work could have killed her and she wouldn't have noticed and wouldn't have cared.

Here's how she worked in that house in the Landes, the summer she was sixteen.

She began with the Jodas' magnificent chicken, whose tender, plump, yellow flesh would have to be sacrificed to her goal, which as I told you she would later condemn, but in that dark, sandy little kitchen she wasn't yet thinking that way, and it was with an untroubled sense of doing exactly the right thing that she carefully stripped the meat from the carcass and chopped it very fine, then put that dense, tender flesh through the meat grinder, even though its very essence demanded that it be taken into the mouth just as it was, simply cooked, and above all perfectly intact.

She mixed that chopped meat with five eggs, herbs, trimmed bread soaked in milk, a little cumin and clove, and then, in a wondrous feat of dexterity, she flawlessly reconstructed the shape of that sumptuous chicken, moulding the meat around the bones, sculpting it over the carcass so it would seem that the chicken had never been touched, and then she draped it in the delicate, corn-coloured skin to make the illusion complete, to lead the Clapeaus to believe that that monstrously reconstituted chicken, remade with an aggregate that could never rival the original, had come to them just as it was from the farmyard, a dizzying *trompe-l'œil*, something the Cheffe would later reject, almost unreasonably, but which that afternoon seemed to her the very summit of her art, the magisterial affirmation of her superiority over the Marmande cook, who could never have managed to pass one thing off as another.

How the Cheffe would later hate all shams.

She stuffed the carcass with the leftover meat, and now the chicken looked even plumper, seemed about to burst with the excess of its own excellence.

It was a miracle of legerdemain, the Cheffe would grant, there was no way to tell that the animal had been brutalised, taken apart and then put back together in a sort of sick joke.

She put it in the oven, generously basted it with melted butter, and then an hour later surrounded it with new potatoes, coarsely chopped carrots, turnips, red onions, whole heads of garlic.

Her solitude, in that little kitchen dimmed and grimly defended by the rough, aged trunk of the pine blocking the view from the window, filled her with a kind of calm, quiet jubilation whose matchless pleasure she would later never stop seeking – that was the first time she'd ever been left alone to work, left alone to come up with ideas, and therefore alone with the prospect of potential disappointment or possible praise, and it was precisely that intoxicating creative aloneness I glimpsed in her and envied her on those stifling nights in Bordeaux when, as I told you, I went to seek out the lights of our kitchen, it was precisely that ardent, intense solitude, at once reflective and rapt, whose acidic tang the Cheffe never tired of describing for me, something I myself have never really known, not with that fullness and purity, since I never had the kind of impregnable detachment from everything not immediately involved with cooking, the kind of ungiving withdrawal into yourself without which you can't seriously think or invent, and which, I long ago realised, is a paradox of that trade, since in those moments the very people you want to delight, to fascinate and to subjugate, the diners, have been completely eliminated from your mind and your memory, even if your every thought is devoted to their future pleasure.

I could never put the people I was cooking for out of my mind, I always feared they might not be happy, I always tried to tailor my work to what I assumed were their tastes and desires, that's why I've always been average, virtuous but anxious, that's why I've never reigned over anything, not that it ever brought me serenity, I've never been free of mundane cares, I've never known peace, never known the calm, cold exultation of perfect aloneness in the act of creation.

In that rudimentary little kitchen amid the pines, the Cheffe felt, perhaps, not happier than she'd ever been (she was happy with her parents, happy in her strange, rough childhood), but happy in a way she'd never known, finer and more expansive than any other pleasure she could imagine, happy for reasons that came only from herself, her endurance, her boldness, her faith in her abilities, and not because someone else, not even her beloved parents, was trying to make her happy, which she never trusted, and very likely that destroyed any possibility of her prizing or accepting the love of a man: she wanted to owe the emotion and sensation of happiness to herself alone, and having so long wanted that, she made herself incapable of finding pleasure or profit in a man's aspiration to bring her joy, that bored her, everyone bored her but her daughter, who did all she could to bring her the opposite of anything like joy, but did she really love her, was that love at all or was it guilt-racked despair, I have my own opinion, you've met her, you've seen that unpleasant, sterile woman, arrogant and vain and now trying to peddle specious anecdotes about the Cheffe to the whole wide world.

I hate her, I have no qualms about saying so, I hate her and I have contempt for her, she never deserved to be the Cheffe's daughter.

Enough of that, hatred and contempt don't make you any bigger when you're nothing much.

What I was trying to make you understand is that in that

rudimentary, pine-smothered kitchen the Cheffe tasted the exquisite fruit of a calling recognised and understood by every part of her body.

Her feet went back and forth over the cement tiles, quick and lively as two perfectly trained little animals that delight in their task, instinctively and miraculously avoiding every danger, any wasted step, all the treacherous obstacles of the space they've been ordered to move through, and it's a fact that I never saw the Cheffe make a motion or gesture that wasn't marked by a magical precision, even in the most cramped or cluttered quarters, every tiny part of her diligently obeyed her order to make every move precise, and did so gracefully, what's more, with a radiant eagerness that suggested everything she did in the ritual space of the kitchen was done in accordance with the precepts of beauty and necessity.

It might have happened, I don't claim to know everything, but I never saw the Cheffe hurt herself when she was working, never a stumble, never a bump.

What I did see was the incredible virtuosity of her strong, square little hands, and the inconceivability of those hands not forever obeying their orders with the utmost exactitude, and I also saw that the Cheffe's expert hands discreetly led their own life, and could stay busy on the chopping board while, for example, the Cheffe, with the telephone wedged between her ear and her shoulder, talked of things utterly unrelated to what her hands were doing, and her hands never went astray, her short fingers could think and decide and never misjudged, her hands never slipped up.

And that was something the Cheffe discovered in that little kitchen in the Landes, she discovered her own body, which until then she'd used only as a single thing, like a reliable machine she controlled from her heart: now, moved and joyous, she realised her body was made up of many little animals who'd learned to work flawlessly all on their own, and who, that afternoon, happy, modest, at once obedient and quietly enterprising, showed her all their *savoir-faire*, working as a tight-knit team that in a sense excluded the Cheffe for her own good, working for an efficiency the Cheffe could never have achieved had she gone on trying to control the machine that until then she'd thought her body was.

That's how she used to talk to me of her limbs and her organs: like independent beings, clever and devoted, which it was vital she not command, since she didn't understand them as well as they understood themselves and each other.

Sometimes, openly marvelling, giving herself little slaps on her thighs, she'd say, "These legs never get tired, there's nothing I can't ask them to do."

And, squeezing her stomach, she would say, "It can take anything, it never gets sick, and it's never full, the poor thing."

And since she didn't think she was in charge of the little animals working together in her body, didn't think she had any hold over them beyond the friendship they felt for her, she took no pride in her vigorous constitution or her body's exceptional capacity for work, she felt nothing but gratitude, it was a gift from nature, and the only thanks could be modesty.

Once she'd finished that chicken masquerading in its own

generous, innocent flesh, she started a fish stock: into a pot half-filled with water she dropped the two kilos of fry she'd bought from a Vieux-Boucau fish shop – smelt, loaches, sprats, little sardines – then added carrots and celery, rounds of leeks and onions, cloves, and, just to see, what little wizened, pale saffron was left in the one labelled jar she found in the spice cabinet.

Alone, hard at work, silent in that little kitchen transformed into a steamroom by the damp heat of the cooking (and – not because it tortured her, it didn't, but only to prevent an excess of steam from affecting her perception of tastes and smells – she opened the narrow window almost entirely obscured by the massive, rugged trunk of the old pine, and the air that drifted in was heavy with the odour of turpentine and dark, hot sand, so thoroughly disconcerting the Cheffe, unused to those oily exudations, that she immediately pushed the window shut again, and for a moment she felt like she was a prisoner of the pines, of their austere, unsettling benevolence), the Cheffe could hear only the fleeting little noises made by the trusty companions collaborating inside her, and the instructions she gave herself under her breath.

But although she heard no sign of life from the other rooms of the house, she thought she could make out the Clapeaus' panting breath just behind the kitchen walls, she could see them, multiplied and impatient, teeming, anxious, too excited to feel their usual shame at their gluttony, listening intently as she progressed in the creation of their ecstasy, the two of them perhaps thinking, with a shiver, "Our happiness is in the hands of that child," yes, she suddenly saw them in great numbers, watching over her, seconded by their spies the pines, dozens of Clapeaus not so much doubting or mistrusting her talent as trembling in terror at the thought that she might turn out to be utterly unequal to the task, and that lacerating fear wasn't exactly about her in a way, in fact it protected the Cheffe as a person because the Clapeaus wouldn't hold it against her if she disappointed them, they would blame only themselves, would accuse only their folly.

She thought she could hear them coming and going along the kitchen wall, both outside among the coolly complicit pines and in the hallway between the kitchen and the dining room.

That didn't disturb her.

She didn't tell herself so, she almost didn't realise it, but she profoundly understood the Clapeaus, she accepted them as they were, folly and all.

She accepted, finding it neither good nor bad, that the prospect of a meagre or mediocre dinner would plunge them into a sadness that she thought in no way trivial or ridiculous, or worthy of reverence either.

Although . . . you're right. I'm probably wrong about that.

She understood the Clapeaus' distress at a lacklustre meal far better than she would have understood indifference, and she found the Clapeaus' petrified apprehension entirely worthy of respect, even if she didn't envy them their folly in any way.

But the fact that they'd expanded the shrunken dimensions of their lives with a passion for food, that they'd allowed that mania to structure every moment of their days, she could understand that, respect it, already feeling in herself the stirrings of a very similar mania, more enviable only because she would make it her way to fame, because she would let it carry her but never overpower her, until her last years, at least, when that mania might indeed have finally submerged her.

But in truth the thought of a multitude of prying Clapeaus trying to learn what she was making in that little kitchen, the thought that they'd managed to trick the lofty, puritanical pines into adopting their own inquisitive gaze (she couldn't forget the old trunk at the window behind her, she sensed its rough breath as it vainly tried to insinuate itself into the kitchen), none of that bothered her, she held nothing against anyone, she worked quickly, her mind clear, happy, always a step ahead.

Yes, that's something I always noticed about her, she never accused anyone but herself.

She didn't complain, she didn't criticise.

Interested in people, as you put it?

Oh yes, she silently watched people, not seeming to, with that slightly distant face of hers, that still face, sometimes almost frozen in a neutral mask that could be unsettling for people who came to her in friendship and fraternity, and since her eye turned judgmental only when it lit on a slab of meat, a crate of vegetables, or any other object or ingredient required for cooking, since it seemed to dim when it moved from a nimbly filleted piece of fish to the face of the apprentice handling the knife, you might have thought it was only the fish that interested her, not the apprentice, you might have thought she found more to study and judge in the filleted fish, perfectly complete in its simplicity, than she ever would in the complicated, changeable face of the person before her, but if you did you were wrong, as you realised from some remark she discreetly slipped in about one or the other – because then the words she chose struck you by their unerring rightness, like so many arrows in the centre of the target.

You could never have come up with such words yourself, you would never have thought words could so precisely tell the truth of a face, its expression, the sense of a way of standing or moving, and the moment you heard them those words seemed not just implacably true but also the only ones possible, and the Cheffe could come up with them because, appearances to the contrary, for all her withdrawn air and opaque gaze, she studied and interpreted faces more deeply than the rest of us, we who confronted the mystery of a face with our big, amiable grins, our faces ripped in two by sociability, all mystery banished.

A sharp tack, some called the Cheffe, but if you ask me those ill-chosen words expressed only our difficulty in defining her, she was clever but not calculating, curious but aloof, firmly turned towards her own inner world, which no-one knew the first thing about, I would claim, except perhaps her daughter, whose unstable, ungrateful, selfish, cruel ways forced the Cheffe to reveal her one weakness, no, it wasn't love that brought her out of her secret refuge, it was sadness, it was despair, it was bitter incomprehension at seeing what her adorable, cherished little girl had turned into, it wasn't love that brought her out of that refuge, and certainly I never managed to bring her out, since the things I know about the Cheffe, the things I'm telling you now, aren't things she revealed to me, they're things I think I've realised on my own.

Neither my love for her nor her deep affection for me would have been enough for that.

She could be naive, so strangely naive!

Now and then, in the lull at the end of the shift, she would express her surprise at something a customer or employee had done, and we'd laugh and tell her we were surprised at her surprise, we all thought it blindingly obvious that such a person could only do such things, and she would gently shake her head, murmuring, "That's not how it seemed to me at all."

Then, in a joking tone that was only camouflage for her dismay at finding us young folk so jaded, she would say something like, "How could you possibly have seen that? You'd have to be just as debased as he is!"

And we all laughed, and she laughed along with us, we were so happy we'd amused her (we thought we were amusing her), and even happier that we'd taught her something about life, that for a moment we'd had that small superiority over her who knew nothing of the world outside her kitchen, we thought, just as we thought knowing the world meant never letting yourself be taken in, doubting plain kindness, mistrusting an honest face.

So yes, she could be wrong, but always in the same way, when her study of a face led her to believe in a goodness that wasn't really there.

I don't believe she ever mistrusted someone who turned out to have a generous heart.

Why do I think it's important to tell you about that side of the Cheffe, and why am I trembling?

You tell me I'm trembling, it's possible.

Too many people who didn't really know her, too many who in some cases scarcely got near her, have called her insensitive to other people's existence, walled up in the narrow, fervid universe of her passion, venturing out now and then only to give voice to a severity and a hardness that, to hear those ignoramuses tell it, were the only thing that could draw her out of herself, yes, I know, it was particularly her daughter who said that, the daughter the Cheffe never said no to, the daughter she always forgave, until at last she discreetly distanced herself from that dangerous woman, although she never stopped loving her with the tormented love she'd come to inspire in her, I sometimes saw her read – devastated, whispering words of despair and incomprehension – one of those furious e-mails her daughter was forever sending her at the end and then turn a contrite face to me, as if she were the one who'd done wrong, and the words she mumbled were always words that excused her inexcusable daughter or recalled the sweet child she'd been, as if the memory of the child could lessen the idiocy and cruelty of the adult, or make them seem insignificant, or even not entirely real.

So I who can boast of only one thing in my life, which is that I knew the Cheffe better than anyone, I can say she was loving and compassionate and understanding, sometimes more than was good for her, and the proof is that not one of her employees ever bad-mouthed the Cheffe, not that they weren't encouraged to by the many people who found it boring to have nothing negative to say or write about her, the Cheffe as she really was bored them, with her generous heart, her compassionate heart, more understanding than was good for her.

And so the Cheffe worked in that little kitchen in the Landes, at once confident and tense, just as she always liked to be, with the kind of controlled, dynamic, galvanising intentness that attracted miraculous ideas and received them without triumph, as if they were owed it, as if it went without saying, an intentness whose disappearance, once the work was done and the scale of the accomplishment measured, gave rise to a faint dizziness, an exhaustion, and a wonderment less marvelling than incredulous: How could I have been capable of such a thing?

Only that intentness, the Cheffe always said, could make the merciless toil of cooking bearable.

When you didn't feel it, or when you felt it but found no pleasure in it, and looked on the dismembered animals, the dirt-crusted vegetables, everything hiding the secret of its taste and waiting, gravely, unhelpfully, for you to figure out what to do with it, then an enormous weariness and nausea might make you wish you could just run away, the Cheffe said, and never again feel yourself bound up with that dead, stinking flesh, the entrails, the fat, the tedious labours, the inevitable filth, and the pain of all those, human and animal, by way of whom an ineloquent, mindless food made its way from kitchen to table, the animals' shrieks, the humans' exhaustion, you wanted to run away as far as you could when that monotonous misery hit you full force, when the cool ecstasy of creation wasn't protecting you, said the Cheffe with her little oblique smile, "and sometimes I did, and I thought I was freeing myself, but of course I always came back," said the Cheffe, "because I was even unhappier freed from the trials of cooking than enduring them, and I didn't often have to endure them, whereas when I was far away from them I suffered all the time, no two ways about that."

"I could never be happy for long outside my kitchen," the Cheffe used to say, and then add, quickly and dutifully, "except with my daughter," and we both knew it wasn't true, or at least I did, just as I knew the Cheffe felt obliged to invent and to trumpet a joyful motherhood, not for herself, not out of pride, but in the hope of convincing her daughter, wherever she was, she was never with her, as if such words, repeated year after year, might in the end impregnate the air her daughter was breathing someplace in this world and disarm her forgetful but rancorous heart, her heart that preserved no memory of the love she'd been given but kept rigorous track of every perceived slight.

You're going to meet her?

You'll see it straight off, she's a deeply deceitful person, inhumanly self-centred, but at the same time not very bright and so not as harmful as she'd like.

I'm not worried, you'll see it straight off, I don't think I'm being too harsh, oh no, I'm not worried.

Hate me? Oh, yes.

Feel contempt for me? Naturally.

Put yourself in her place: how could she not hate the one person who never doubted her lifelong ambition, the only one she ever had: to undermine her mother's mental and physical forces so that, once she'd worn her down, once she'd brought her low, she would see her swallowed up by the mediocrity, the laziness, the self-indulgent, self-pitying inertia she herself deliberately made the stuff of her life?

I can understand her hating me.

I never played the Cheffe's game, which meant nodding and beaming when she spoke of her glorious, talented, lovable daughter, showing perhaps a tinge of envy or regret if your own child was less remarkable, and other people generally did cooperate in that little charade, never suspecting it was one, they weren't so interested in the Cheffe's life and her daughter that they'd think to distrust those claims, and they agreed for the sake of politeness, noncommittally.

I alone held back, didn't nod, didn't smile.

And the Cheffe understood that I knew what she strove in vain not to know, which is that her daughter was in no way the clever, confident person she claimed, that she never would be, that in fact she used all the meagre resources of her very limited intelligence to try to make her mother guilty of her failures, to make her feel guilty and become guilty, since the daughter was always dragging her into situations she had to pull away from if she didn't want to drown with her – and she would have drowned for good, but the daughter would soon have surfaced, I'm sure of it, she's very attached to life and her little comforts, in spite of her perpetual threats to end it all.

No, the Cheffe was never angry that I refused to be duped when she launched into her stories of a daughter who existed only in her imagination.

It was a flutter of wings just by her ear.

Yes.

A quiet rustle that came from my devoutly sincere mind, and our eyes met, and then, possibly grateful or relieved, she saw my scepticism, I might even say my honesty, so she kept her hold on reason and when she went back to describing her miraculous daughter she knew full well she was telling tales.

"If it weren't for you I would have gone over the edge," she once told me, almost casually, and I never felt the need to ask what she meant, or make some lame attempt at denying it, I understood her at once: had she gone on too long exalting her daughter as an admirable young lady who loved her and gave her every motherly satisfaction, had she kept that up too long with no-one ever contradicting her, not even with a fluttering aerial caress on her forehead, she would have succumbed to the temptation of believing what she was saying and so lost a piece of her sanity, no-one would have thought she'd gone mad, no-one would have noticed or cared, but, she thought, that loss would have sapped the very foundation of her engagement with cooking, which for her seemed to depend on a constantly clear and confident mind, and so she would indeed have gone mad as she understood it, since she would have lost her vigilant concern for truth and precision.

Hence her gratitude that I refused to feel sorry for her, or uncomfortable or afraid, that I refused to feel obliged to greet her tales of her daughter with polite acquiescence.

I held fast to my doubts and my horror of that woman, I crossed my arms, took a step back, and looked at the Cheffe, sending her my loyal, gentle, truthful thoughts, and the Cheffe never resented it, on the contrary, and she realised I'd saved her from a peril even more terrible than believing in the virtues of that despicable daughter.

Once her bouillon of little fish was thoroughly cooked, once she'd made sure you could no longer tell the bits of vegetable from the pieces of fry, the Cheffe dredged out the biggest bones, then emptied the pot into the blender and found herself pleased with the resulting soup: thick and coarse, bright yellow from the saffron.

She put in a cod loin and a fillet of pollack, let them cook for a few minutes, then turned off the heat.

She'd never made or seen someone else make a fish soup that way, nor read any recipe, in fact she never would read very much, deciphering words wasn't her strength.

And yet, as she told me, everything the Marmande cook's lifeless, inexpressive dishes were missing had indirectly tutored her, pushing her, at night in her bed, to come up with ways to make what she'd tasted far better, and so, she liked to say, in a perhaps slightly mischievous paradox, she thought she'd learned far more, and got much more exercise for her inventiveness, from the dreary, unwitting teachings of Marmande than she would have got training under some brilliant chef, in any case even decades later she still felt a quiet, surprised pride at the fine work she did in that little kitchen in the Landes, spied on by the pines enlisted by the Clapeaus, by the Clapeaus themselves, by the swarm of feverish Clapeaus frantic with desire and uncertainty and by the less trusted but no less respected pines, by the oppressive old pine at the window.

The surprise, at herself or at that strange sixteen-year-old girl who so oddly happened to have been her, would come only much later.

Nothing surprised that girl in the serene bustle of her work, in the deep concentration of her thought, nothing came as a surprise, inventiveness least of all.

Everything seemed to happen by itself, her quick progress, her precise movements, the laconic dance of her sturdy, neat little body, of which she was calmly, happily aware as she strode back and forth, never wasting a step, now and then remembering, with a sharp aesthetic disapproval, the halting, uncertain, irritable way the Marmande cook moved through that big room whose proportions she seemed out of loathing to have resolved not to note, no more than she saw all the tiny details that made it the kitchen it was and not some other kitchen.

To the Cheffe, the Marmande cook always seemed as if she'd been abandoned just that morning in some brutal, back-stabbing environment she had to steer clear of for the sake of her safety or dignity, whereas even then the more resourceful Cheffe could draw on her own inner harmony, unruffled and adaptable, happy and beautiful wherever she was cooking, at peace, focused, delighted, a friend to the meddlesome pines, aware of and at one with her surroundings, and at the same time magnificently somewhere else.

When I close my eyes and picture her in that little kitchen in the Landes, I'm convinced she already had that moving, enviable ability to be perfectly happy in herself, in an easy, friendly rapport with her open and obliging body, with her enormous but controlled ambition, with her temperate desires and well-regulated heart, that's how we thought of her, that's how we saw her, at first, when she was our boss, vaguely and respectfully believing she didn't need anything because she found everything she needed in herself, even cooking was an extra, a challenge to take on, a suitable pastime for a queen with no love of idleness, we thought she could easily do without everything – cooking, her daughter, love, all of us – which of course I now know wasn't true, and outside the kitchen she found her own company hard to endure, she was less at home with her rich, expansive personality than we were with our stunted little souls.

Who do I mean by we?

Oh, my co-workers back then, back when I first went to work for the Cheffe, when she took me on as an apprentice and I joined a team of young men who'd been with her for some time, whose feelings and opinions I made my own, in my ignorance, before I realised I saw the Cheffe very differently from them, I was in love with her, and I strove to understand her with all the subtlety I could muster, I wasn't sophisticated, I was very young, sometimes my attempts to see into her failed and I was totally blind, but I kept at it, with love's help I conquered my weaknesses, I came to know the Cheffe better than anyone, I don't doubt that for a moment, who ever loved her like I did?

Her daughter? I take it you're joking.

It troubles me to think she might already have hoodwinked you, it makes me feel less free to talk to you candidly.

I need to believe you're good people.

How good can anyone be if they're so easily taken in by a woman that crude, that predictable, that transparent in her pettiness?

And how can I talk to you candidly, with an unguarded sincerity that's not like me at all, that shakes me to my depths, the memory of which sometimes wrenches me awake in the night, terrified that I dared fill in the Cheffe's silences, revealing a few of my own secrets at the same time, and I lie there sweating and depressed, hating myself and you too in a way, I can't get back to sleep, my eyes open in the dark and the blood pounding in my neck – how can I talk to you candidly if I think my words are falling into the deep hole of scepticism that even the briefest conversation with the Cheffe's daughter will have dug in you?

Because then you'll question everything I say, you'll compare it to her daughter's radically different telling and try to give equal weight to both sides, and you won't realise you're insulting me so cruelly that I find it simply grotesque to suffer so for the sake of the truth if it only means I'll be compared to that wastrel, that liar, placed alongside her, given the same credence.

The whole thing becomes ridiculous, you understand?

*It would be easy to smirk at my Lloret de Mar friends, they have
no idea they belong to a type that seems to exist only to be smirked at,
with their bright, practical clothes, their overblown good humour, their
lack of inhibition and the resulting ingenuous display of flesh, but the
way they've rigorously winnowed down their lives to end up happily
reduced to whatever will fit into their sixty square metres in Lloret de
Mar fills me with fond respect.*

The Cheffe was never much interested in desserts, though
she did see their usefulness, even their necessity, which is to
say that, having gone over and over that question in her mind,
having tried out various final courses that were nothing like
treats but rather made a very slightly rugged epilogue to a perfectly cadenced journey (sorbet of green olives, for example,
or diced cucumber cooked in honey, to follow a dish of oxtail
with leeks), she accepted that it might seem ungenerous or
high-handed to cancel the traditional conclusion, sweet, melo-
dious and uncomplicated, the dulcet, consensual last word of a
statement that was always delicious but sometimes a bit rough,
the Cheffe's cooking could be brusque, especially later on, in
its almost fanatical plainness, yes, her cooking could be hard
when you first encountered it, could be uncongenial, but once
you'd learned to love it you felt only repugnance for any man-
nered, pandering cuisine, anything soft and creamy, you felt
like that food didn't think much of you, as if you were someone not much could be expected of, who's never asked to show
what he's capable of, his fearlessness, his curiosity, who knows
what, you don't feel respected as a customer and an eater, you
feel ashamed for the cook.

But the Cheffe never found the way, and in the end she stopped trying to defy the age-old, deep-seated desire for a sweet ending, a moral to the story, if I may, a moment of universal agreement, all the tablemates united in happy, distracted concord with the cook's intentions, whereas the Cheffe was still working – up to the last moment, the final mouthful – to spur on not the eater's capacity for surprise, not his resistance to provocation, she never liked to provoke people, even if, it must be said, she often did, but rather his quest for a seriousness and cool reserve that she herself strove to make the masters of everything she did.

And those virtues she was so intent on attaining, and on imparting to those who liked her food, seemed to her impossible to find in the everyday, easy sweetness of a dessert.

But she preferred to step away from the field of battle, she chose to say no more about it, to think no more about it, as if the very notion of dessert had never existed, and to serve at the end of a meal something that just happened to be more sweet than savoury, more sugared than sharp, that could only with difficulty be remembered as a confection pure and simple.

When you first tasted the Cheffe's cooking and, if you knew nothing about it, assumed that some luscious reward would crown the private efforts you'd put into appreciating each dish at its full, very demanding measure, you might have seen what played the part of the dessert as a discreet test of your merit, and almost of your soul, because then, in order to find the delight you were looking for, you'd have to stifle your childish desire for the gratification of something sweet, but you did most certainly delight, if you could find it in yourself to be bold and curious, and as you delighted you felt you'd been elevated, taken seriously, and as you pushed back your chair you sent the Cheffe this thought that would long make of you, in your happiness, her debtor: "You brought out the best in me."

Yes, you delighted, and strangely that delight demanded an investment of seriousness and resolve, in return for which you would never forget a moment of the experience.

And if you then went back to more obliging desserts, I believe you had to feel something crumbling inside you, a backsliding not into some weakness or eccentricity but into everything that's most trivial about you, and in time, to be sure, that would fade, with your busy life and its everyday ways, but I like to think a regret would still smoulder inside you, flaming up whenever you realised you'd shown a lack of boldness or style, the regret was there and you couldn't remember where it came from or what it was trying to tell you, no more than you can remember the distant cause of certain sadnesses that sometimes come over you, on seeing a golden light against a little patch of wall or the glistening chrome of a radiator grille on a dull summer day, the regret was there, the regret that you'd lacked the ability or desire to stay on the exceptional plane that, for the duration of a meal, the Cheffe had raised you to by the spirit of her cooking.

Tears? No, it's my eyes watering, that's all, it doesn't mean anything.

I'm not the type to shed tears in public, you know, that's

not in my upbringing, my mother would have mocked me heartlessly.

Yes, that's right, I never met my father, but let's not talk about my life before the Cheffe, it's completely without interest, because I truly came into this world the day I opened the door to her restaurant, hoping for work.

I didn't see much of my mother after that. I didn't have the time.

Completely without interest, I'm telling you.

The Cheffe's unwillingness to make a dessert that would satisfy only the pursuit of pleasure was something she discovered that very afternoon in the little kitchen in the Landes, it's the oldest, most unchanging facet of her character as a cook, it almost dizzied her, and she stood still for a few minutes at the table, her hands flat against the wood, wondering if she was right to be like that, and although she didn't know it already fearing the excessiveness of her instincts, but perhaps understanding that she had to obey them if she wanted to keep the flame of her mission burning high and bright.

Yes, the Cheffe was a quiet visionary, a sober fanatic, her incandescence was hidden and deep, only the pine tree saw it as it watched her through the glass, its own ascetic ardour sealed away beneath its bark, deep in the trunk.

What she knew for sure was that she wanted at all costs not to imitate the Marmande cook, who made the Clapeaus the desserts most likely to tickle their bottomless gluttony as well as their wretched, contorted shame at that gluttony.

She found that unspeakably repugnant, but she was disgusted by her repugnance, and she wanted no part of any of it.

Lying in bed at night, analysing the vague impression of a mistake set off in her by a coffee parfait, an egg custard, a sponge cake, or a plate of soufflé fritters, she realised that what united all those desserts in her dislike, her sense of an endlessly repeated misstep, was that they were all very sweet, very fatty, very insipid, and that they appended themselves to the meal in a crass, intrusive way, they were never, the Cheffe felt in the meditative solitude of her bed, the restrained, concise, discreet conclusion to the necessarily more important, more serious, more scintillating meal, they were always out of place, they were an unwelcome protuberance on an interesting, precisely calibrated form.

She was sometimes astonished at the Marmande cook's enthusiasm as she made the desserts the Clapeaus so loved, her ardent concern for their tastes in that one area, she who was perpetually disgruntled and dyspeptic and could go on working for the Clapeaus only so long as she knew she wasn't giving them everything they wanted, she who always carefully kept her work just short of completeness, in which way a little of her bitterness was drained off and the Marmande cook could preserve untouched what she gloomily loved to contemplate, thought the Cheffe, because she would never offer it up to anyone, her illusory treasure: her power of creation.

But the cook went out of her way to charm the Clapeaus with her desserts, which were nothing but monstrous inanities of sugar and butter, as if, the Cheffe imagined, she permitted herself to mine her virtuous resources of invention only insofar as she saw it as a chance to corrupt the Clapeaus, who not only knew that vast quantities of sugar and butter were bad for them – though I can't think that they cared, a good dinner meant more to them than the prospect of old age – but who most importantly had chosen to identify sugar and butter as the primary culprits in their weakness, reserving a very particular and visible hatred for those ingredients, even as they knew, or maybe they didn't, I'm not sure of anything, that with a little effort they could have given up sugar and butter, whereas well-marbled meats, rich, fatty terrines, dry-cured ham, those they could not do without, they couldn't hate things that brought them so much pleasure, and so they despised sugar and butter, which they needed less.

They could have given them up, they couldn't bring themselves to do it, their loudly proclaimed hatred assailed something that wasn't their real problem at all.

And the cook sensed that, she knew the Clapeaus better than she knew herself, she knew them the way you know your children, your pets, all your house's little creaks and cracks, she sensed that sugar and butter mattered less to them than the rest, she threw her colossal, boundless rage, a rage that had no reason to relent, that couldn't relent, into making sugar and butter indispensable to the Clapeaus, and so to make the Clapeaus, who could still vaguely see the path, lose their way forever.

As I say, the Cheffe wanted nothing to do with all that.

She wanted to illuminate the Clapeaus with the cold, intense, irresistible brilliance of her mastery without having to enter their clammy hearts, without having to brush against their warm, sticky skin, neither provoking nor flattering, neither condemning nor excusing their tortuous emotions.

And so she put together a dessert without thinking of them, not trying, as she had with the denatured chicken or the fish soup, to dazzle them.

Her dessert would be intransigent, uningratiating, but irreproachable within the severe boundaries of its intention, only that intention could be criticised or mocked or indignantly rejected, not the drily perfect dessert it produced.

Quickly, with all the assurance she'd seen in the Marmande cook, she made pastry for a tart without butter, just flour, two eggs and water.

On that pastry she laid quartered peaches in serried ranks, then sprinkled them with a pinch of sugar, a little salt, and, distantly, pretending almost not to notice she was doing it, some finely chopped verbena picked at the foot of the back stairs.

She wasn't sure that the tart would be delicious, nor that the Clapeaus could even finish a helping, so strongly did the recipe go against their habits, and neither was she sure she herself would find any pleasure in that tart, or rather that any pleasure she did find in it would derive from something other than the knowledge that she'd created a dish of absolute rightness, harmonious and balanced in its austerity, a dish that, to use the expression the Cheffe would later often borrow from the vocabulary of couture, "draped" to perfection.

She didn't know how much pleasure that dish might give, but she was sure, almost, that it would be a success in a larger sense, and she liked that, she thought she had to be right, not because she wanted to sway others but only so she could privately know she hadn't gone wrong, that her intuition had guided her well, and that the thing she'd had in her mind, floating at the very edge of her thoughts, like an image you see in a dream – precise, more real than reality, obvious and implacable, ugly perhaps, but with an ugliness full of dignity and presence – she'd managed to re-create as surely and finely as could be.

And so, having called up in her mind a simple, idealised image of a peach tart, its amber colour underscored by something she thought might be verbena, with the faintest gilding, subdued and matte, of caramelised sugar (the Marmande cook always plastered her tarts with a thick syrup of sugar and apricot jam, they glistened as they were set down on the table, as polished and glazed as gravestone ornaments,[*] and the Clapeaus would exclaim, "Isn't it beautiful! It's too pretty to eat!", remembering which the Cheffe wondered unconcerned if the Clapeaus might find her tart too homely, too unenticing to touch, she imagined that unconcerned, with a touch of anticipatory disappointment, she hated waste, and she knew that she herself would only go near her dessert for a sample), she was pleased, when the tart came out of the oven, to see no disparity between the thing and her premonition of it, and so she forgot the idea and conferred on the real tart the status of a model for all her desserts to come.

And that way she could like making and serving desserts, she could do it without feeling she was demeaning herself

---

[*] The large slabs of stone covering graves in French cemeteries often bear tributes or remembrances in the form of thickly laminated plaques.

and pandering to the customer, she would bring integrity and self-respect to dessert.

The dish that "draped" perfectly, yes?

Other fashion expressions the Cheffe liked to use?

None that I can think of. No, clothes didn't really interest her, she thought fashion was trivial and pointless.

What is it exactly you're wondering?

I imagine she was wearing one of her two cotton skirts in that house in the Landes, that summer when she was sixteen and the spirit of cooking danced before her brown eyes and then was suddenly inside her, one of them was pale grey and the other navy blue, high-waisted, gathered, calf-length, and a beige short-sleeved blouse buttoned up to the neck, it was a neighbour in Sainte-Bazeille who'd made her those very simple, very unadorned clothes, the Cheffe was fiercely attached to them, they reminded her of Sainte-Bazeille and her cherished parents, and they also had something of the uniform in their impersonal rigour, which the Cheffe liked because they revealed nothing, no vanity, no desire to please, and no grim determination not to please either, both the cut and the fabric were plain and forthright, innocent, they weren't trying to say anything, they were trying to say nothing, and that's just what they said.

Those clothes were only what they were, good fabric well tailored, perfectly suited to what was asked of them: nothing more than the protection of a body that was equally innocent and mute and devoid of intention, the Cheffe's little body in that house in the Landes, her compact sixteen-year-old body, sturdy and discreet, which the Cheffe treated with reasonable, modest care, like a tool needed for a task, something you wouldn't want to damage but for which you feel neither fondness nor scorn, that body she never looked at, wasn't jealous of, was never surprised by, couldn't have said if it was breathtaking or badly flawed, that stolid body that would go on virtually unchanged as the years went by, as if preserved by the Cheffe's very disinterest, held fast in an eternal, detached youthfulness.

For cold days the Cheffe had two other skirts cut on that same pattern, one made of plaid wool, the other brown wool jersey, and two beige flannel blouses, her growth slowed when she was thirteen, the same clothes still fit her three years later and would for a long time to come, she vaguely imagined keeping them forever, since she wasn't too hard on them, as she said, she liked to imagine herself wearing those Sainte-Bazeille clothes forever, cladding herself each morning and for all time in the memory of Sainte-Bazeille, covering herself with the purity of Sainte-Bazeille.

Much later, when the Cheffe opened her restaurant, she bought several identical work outfits to wear under her big white apron, they were a little like those Sainte-Bazeille clothes except that the skirts were replaced by straight trousers, black or dark grey, also buttoned high on the waist, clasping the hem of a sand-coloured blouse with a short, pointed collar, always buttoned up to the very top.

The Cheffe seemed so perfectly made for those clothes, so uniquely made for that sobriety without pretention or ostentatious modesty, for that plainness deliberately stripped of meaning, that when I ran into her one Saturday afternoon on Place de la Victoire, it took me a moment to realise that it was her, this woman with the Cheffe's face and dark, thoughtful, calm gaze, but who was dressed as I'd never seen the Cheffe, as I would never have dreamt I might see her, dressed in a way that would, I thought, have horrified her had someone suggested it, like pulling some stranger's skin over your own, with all its secretions and humours.

The Cheffe recognised me, she stopped walking, not happy.

She said a few words in a sullen, distant voice, then her gaze turned away from mine and hovered somewhere beyond my shoulder, I realised she was embarrassed and irked to be seen this way, in the skin of a stranger she didn't at all care for, a stranger who even disgusted her.

She was on her way to the wedding of one of her nieces, and she'd thought it best, so as not to seem superior and disdainful to the family she loved loyally, unconditionally and sadly, who wouldn't have appreciated seeing her appear at the big event in a dark trouser suit and an ecru cotton blouse, they would have assumed she didn't want to spend the money, thought too little of them for that (and I believe her family's judgment was the only one she feared, even if she kept them at arm's length, she feared it with a sad, desperate fatalism), she'd thought it best to dress as the other women at the wedding would be dressed, with a conspicuous, tragic attempt at elegance, and so she was wearing a fuchsia satin dress, somewhat short, slightly clinging, with a thin black leather band for a belt, a little black fitted jacket, black lace tights and low-sided stilettos, the whole thing striving for sexiness in a graceless, laboured way it deeply saddened me to see.

The Cheffe was trying to please Sainte-Bazeille, but where was the clarity of Sainte-Bazeille?

The timeless freshness of Sainte-Bazeille?

She knew nothing was left of all that, now she was only trying to appease Sainte-Bazeille, to earn Sainte-Bazeille's shallow approval, I was disheartened and overjoyed as her gaze shifted from one side of my shoulder to the other and she fingered the tassels on the fine leather belt wrapped around her ill-defined waist, ashamed and irritated at me for crossing Place de la Victoire at the same time as her, she couldn't look at me, and she offered herself up to my judgment and my shock with a gloomy stoicism, with a grim acceptance of the stunned or mocking thoughts that must, she was telling herself, be vying for space in my mind at that moment.

And as the sun shone on her disarmed face, undefended by her gaze, now occupied elsewhere, I saw the odd orange tint of her foundation, the pale pink of a lip gloss applied with a clumsiness I thought laden with rage, as if the Cheffe had done all she could to display absolutely no skill in a domain she had no patience for.

Why overjoyed?

Oh, I can explain, I was fighting back the urge, the burning desire to kneel before the Cheffe and throw my arms around her black-lace-clad legs, yes, that's just what I ached to do, right there on Place de la Victoire with the cars rushing by, fall at the Cheffe's feet and embrace her, thank her for letting me see her like this, I was shocked and absurdly grateful, because the Cheffe hadn't wanted me to see her and because she thought it a stroke of bad luck that I had run into her that afternoon on her way to the church, her niece wanted a church wedding, the Cheffe couldn't understand that affectation of religion, and maybe she secretly disapproved of it, her parents always acted as if they had no idea there were such things as religions even as everything they did demonstrated the most rigorous sort of morality, but the niece was getting married in the church and to the church the Cheffe was obediently going, just as she obeyed the tacit injunction to show up "nicely dressed" according to the code that governed her siblings, she obeyed that order to show that she loved and respected them even in what was least respectable about them, she submitted to them and them alone, out of impotence, out of nostalgia.

They were Sainte-Bazeille, she thought, but where in them was Sainte-Bazeille's innocence?

That satin dress, its hard, sharp sheen, the way that dress displayed the charms of a conventional femininity, crying out in a shrill fuchsia voice: "Get a load of what's under here!"

And what was under there was the Cheffe's neat, solid body, her competent, powerful, well-maintained little body, which a man could imagine himself desiring and passionately loving, as I sometimes did in my Mériadeck studio, if the Cheffe meant more to him than anything in the world.

Because that proud, skilled body had no reason to be exhibited in a crassly shimmering dress, it was beautiful and dignified in its vitality, its endurance, its animal perfection, and that tight satin showed none of those things, no, the clinging satin cruelly, stupidly showed that her body wasn't pretty enough for it, that her stocky, hard-working body couldn't live up to it, to that horrible glistening satin, flattering only to young, willowy figures unused to labour.

I knew the Cheffe's sisters and sisters-in-law would be wrapped in a similar satin or a fierce jersey, my own mother dressed like that on special occasions, her flesh was as dense and muscular as the Cheffe's, and any light, flowing, shimmering fabric mocked her, any frivolous fabric, they mocked the hard-working musculature bulging mannishly under the silly glimmer, it mortified me and filled me with venomous pity to see my mother dressed up in those incongruous, heartrending clothes.

So, you understand, where was the special splendour of Sainte-Bazeille in all that?

The Cheffe's parents were long dead the day I ran into her on Place de la Victoire.

Their children had carried on none of their parents' untamed grandeur, which, I told myself, would have shielded the Cheffe's mother from the merest idea of appearing at a wedding in a short pink satin dress, I told myself she would have gone in a dress tailored in her image by the seamstress of Sainte-Bazeille, perfect and unshowy, gravely majestic.

Evidently the Cheffe's brothers and sisters had inherited none of that spirit.

It made me angry at her parents, they hadn't managed to make themselves imitable, edifying.

I often wondered why it was that the Cheffe alone seemed to be aware of her parents' admirable oddity, a tearful and guilty awareness, because she was convinced that cooking had dragged her into compromises and calculations her parents never resorted to (perfectly happy in their poverty, remember), and because unlike her none of her five brothers and sisters had ever shown any desire more consuming than the desperate, sad, unproductive desire to escape Sainte-Bazeille forever, to escape Sainte-Bazeille's tranquil, serene destitution.

How could it be that those parents the Cheffe so adored appeared to the other children in the form of repellent, disturbing, pathetic examples to be avoided?

And that they couldn't prevent the church and the fuchsia dresses, any more than the suicide of their two youngest children?

And I was angry at the Cheffe's parents for, I assumed, dying before they could grasp their failure to transmit the clarity of Sainte-Bazeille, for, I believed, dying in the false certainty that they'd raised their children well, whereas the Cheffe's body shockingly encased in satin and the others' relentless insistence on living and behaving like the harshest critics of their parents' ways offered sad proof, I thought, that they'd made enemies of their children, even if some trace of love lingered on in them, some fondness, an imperishable attachment, in the same distraught, hopeless form that those emotions took in the Cheffe's relationship with her daughter.

Because the Cheffe's brothers and sisters must have both fondly remembered their parents and hated everything those parents were in their humble Sainte-Bazeille isolation, I told myself as I watched the Cheffe walk away on her unsteady heels, that afternoon when we met by chance and I saw myself, as clearly as if I'd actually done it, kneeling before the Cheffe, pressing my face to her thighs, telling her both that I was irrevocably in love with her and that I was happy to see her so vulnerable and so flustered in her satin disguise, almost as happy and moved as if I were taking in my arms her naked, trusting, hungry body, as I imagined doing every night in my Mériadeck studio (meaning that I wasn't thinking about the restaurant or potential improvements to such and such a dish, I was thinking only about the Cheffe who by some miracle loved me and desired me and would come and join me in that studio to which in reality she never came, and never would have thought of coming, that's why I couldn't be a great cook, I was perpetually bedevilled by love, by desire and illusions).

The Cheffe said a few words that I've forgotten and hurried off across the square, awkward in those pumps and that dress, hobbled, no doubt humiliated by my stare, and without quite meaning to she glanced back over her shoulder to see if I was still watching.

And since I hadn't fallen at her feet, since I hadn't clasped her legs, I tried to fill my gaze with all the tenderness I felt for her, all the understanding and gratitude, which I desperately wanted her to see and be sure of before the flood of traffic separated us and before, in the kitchen that evening, discretion forbade us to speak of that moment when I'd seen her so unlike herself, so helpless and so docile.

Her glance was troubled, possibly startled.

Had she ever seen my love for her before that?

No, it would never have entered her mind, it couldn't have interested her, I meant far too little in her eyes.

She liked me, yes, and she was happy with my work, but I was only a very diffident young employee whose private life and burdensome emotions had never attracted her attention, and that's what shook her just then, realising that I adored her just when she was feeling diminished and preposterous in her satin and lace, that was what shook her, even if I was no-one who mattered, no-one she would have been glad to be admired by, I was also too young, unremarkable in every way.

But now she'd have to look at me with that knowledge in her eyes, I told myself as I watched her wavering back disappear into the crowd on Place de la Victoire.

My one hope, fervent and fearful, was that her astonished discovery of my love wouldn't change the way she treated me in the kitchen, which shows very clearly how little I knew her at the time, since I later thought it self-evident that no such revelation could affect the Cheffe's ways in the kitchen, her behaviour was always attuned to the demands of the work, and she would never have let any emotion come between the exacting attention demanded by the work and the work itself, she would never have let any awkwardness, any pleasure or displeasure, alter the impeccable professional relationship we'd built up, not even if no-one could see it, not even if it did no harm to the work. Only her daughter, as you may already know, had the power to undermine her career, I'll tell you about that soon.

We also love Lloret de Mar's short winters, even if we pretend to long for the summer, the sunbaked terraces, the gold-tinged sunlit pool, and our constant high-spirited inebriation, we're more sober in the winter at Lloret de Mar, we go for drives in the unremarkable house-strewn countryside, we take Spanish lessons, we reconvene the book club we'd abandoned in the sunny season. It's just us French folk, and we're spared the tiresome task of meeting strangers in a language we haven't quite mastered, not that that bothers us, nothing bothers us, and we don't bother anyone, we go for drives on the roads lined with ugly houses, we sing in Michèle's or Christine's or Martin's car, forgotten by time, time that ravages everyone else's faces and bodies, the grey rainy winter is so short in Lloret de Mar.

You're wondering how her parents died?

I hadn't yet met the Cheffe, I only heard about it.

At the restaurant, from co-workers, discreetly.

I don't like telling that story, it makes it seem there's some necessary connection between the Cheffe and those terrible deaths when in fact it was nothing but chance, that's how vicious rumours are born, the Cheffe must have been tortured enough by that horrible accident without people piling on, rooting around in a wound I imagine must still be raw today, wherever the Cheffe may be.

Her parents died together in a car the father was driving, a car the Cheffe had bought them the week before.

Inexplicably, the father went through a stop sign. A car on the main road hit them from the side at full speed.

The father got a driving licence during his military service, but he'd never owned a car before that brand-new Fiat the Cheffe gave them, she'd tried to give them so many things, most particularly a house so they wouldn't have to live in that Sainte-Bazeille shack, but the parents turned it all down, the house, the furniture, the appliances, they turned it all down with, I imagine, the same affable, courtly, steady, uninterested look that once came over their faces when a teacher asked to meet with them, and like that long-ago teacher the Cheffe understood she couldn't fight that very gentle, unspoken, limpid refusal, couldn't insult that incorruptible resistance with cheap trickery: she would never have dreamt of backing them into a corner with a gift brought or delivered in the guise of an impulse buy.

I know their hard-headedness tortured the Cheffe, even if that almost irrational side of them was one reason why she adored them.

But she found that side of them frightening and unjust when it made no distinction between her – their daughter, with her immense, respectful love – and everyone else who'd ever tried to bend them to their will.

Because she didn't want anything from them, she only wanted them to accept the idea of a comfortable old age, an undramatic poverty, and maybe she also wanted, but very modestly and fleetingly, to feel loved back, and that would have been a way for them to show their love, she thought, skipping, just once, the sovereign dismissiveness that was their quiet, inevitable answer to adversity – and wasn't she their friend, very likely their best and truest friend?

How could they imagine she wouldn't feel sad, even hurt,

that she was rich and still had to go on visiting her parents in that Sainte-Bazeille hovel?

Was that the beatific spirit of Sainte-Bazeille, that inability to say yes? To recognise the offering when it's given with love, to graciously welcome it into the house?

That's me saying all that.

The Cheffe saw nothing to be hurt about, she saw only her parents, whose health was declining between the damp, rotting walls of the house they wouldn't leave, and they didn't say but might well have thought: We're perfectly happy as we are, we want nothing from anyone, why must she pester us with her worries and her wishing we had a better house than we do, we who never yearned for anything better, who in fact always ran from anything better, dimly sensing it wouldn't be good for us?

But I took offence for the Cheffe when she told me of that fruitless battle, in a light-hearted voice so I'd think none of it mattered, and once again I was outraged at her parents, those two fine people with their tightly closed hearts, incapable of sacrificing their freedom to accept a gesture of pure affection and devoted attachment that asked for so little.

The Cheffe never went any further than that in the story.

What came next, which I both imagined on my own and gleaned from my talks with one of the Cheffe's sisters, has always struck me as just the kind of bad decision mulish people are prone to, an incomprehensible fit of boldness, the last card disastrously slammed down on the wrong table, plunging everyone into confusion, into a sort of daze that for a time wipes out any possibility of reasoned reflection, and so it was that the parents, having once again declined the Cheffe's offer to buy them a nice house in Sainte-Bazeille, told her out of the blue that there was one thing they did want and that was a car, and I don't know if they meant that or if it was simply what they'd come up with to placate the Cheffe, to quell her need to heap kindnesses on her parents, I don't know, but maybe they saw it as a way out, a way to be left alone and not have to give up living their own life as they pleased, since a car would be a considerable gift, extravagant, and from their point of view insignificant.

The joy of hearing them finally ask her for something blinded the Cheffe.

She who usually thought of everything, how could she have dreamt of letting her father drive, when he'd essentially never driven in his life?

Her sister had no answer when I asked her that, she shrugged, then surmised that neither the parents nor the Cheffe seriously thought the car would be driven, that it might have been enough for all three of them to implicitly understand that the vehicle taking up much of the front garden was an expression of the Cheffe's love, and her polite, closed-hearted parents' recognition of that love, I added to myself, and it could be, the sister went on, that the parents were vaguely planning to give that car to one of their children once what the Cheffe would see as a suitable period of time had gone by. "It could be," said the sister, "but alas, that's not how it was, and against all expectations and all reason our father sat down behind the wheel, and you know how it ended, you can't explain a thing like that."

The sister also told me the Cheffe let out a sort of hoarse, chilling wail at the funeral in Sainte-Bazeille, and then fainted.

The Cheffe never told me about that, and when she spoke of her parents in our sometime late-night talks in the empty kitchen, her wording and persistent present tense gave me every reason to think they were still living, and so I would have thought had my co-workers not told me that story in my first days on the job, probably more or less incidentally, and then, I found myself thinking, not incidentally at all but with a bright-eyed intensity and an eagerness to show me they knew a few of the Cheffe's secrets, to tell me they had the power to strip her bare, possibly to hurt her terribly, she who let no-one approach her – "Don't touch me," seemed to say her inward-looking gaze, her body wholly given over to the injunctions of the work, her brief, unjoking, cordial smile, which nonetheless protected another smile, a smile I think few but me ever saw: broad and gentle, tender, confident.

What's that? Oh yes, the Cheffe's daughter must have seen that precious smile hovering over her when she was a child, but I have no doubt that suspicion, sadness and disappointment wore it out by the time she was a teenager, and from then on the best the Cheffe could do was joylessly pull back her suddenly tight lips, whether she was face to face with her daughter or forced to think of her by a ridiculous, belligerent e-mail, she tried to stop thinking about her, you know, but she couldn't ignore her daughter's e-mails, and when I was at her side, as I always was towards the end, I could see her mouth distend into a horrible smile, misshapen and dejected, as she stared at the screen, and then I knew she'd just heard from her daughter, and I put my hands on her shoulders, very gently.

"It's my daughter again," she murmured, and I whispered back, "Don't worry, I'm here."

My hands lay lightly on her shoulders, I could feel the warmth of her skin, I was sure I could feel her relaxing, sure she loved me, needed me, loved me.

No, I don't know if the Clapeaus ever saw the Cheffe's real smile.

I don't think so.

When they came to set the dining-room table, drained by apprehension and doubt, and so wearing faces fit for a disaster, sagging, grave and oddly pious, they seemed to be training their ears no longer on the kitchen, where their young employee had been hard at work for hours, their sixteen-year-old maid whose promotion to cook suddenly seemed an insane idea, it frightened them a little, such recklessness wasn't like them, maybe they were angry at themselves for so rashly entrusting that girl with such a responsibility, and at her for so impetuously accepting it – they seemed to be training their ears no longer on the kitchen but on the pines that guarded and surrounded the house, that saw everything, knew everything, and the pines kept their silence.

The Clapeaus sat down facing each other at the table laid for two. They waited wordlessly, solemn and hopeless.

Then the kitchen door opened, the Cheffe's determined little form appeared, and the mysterious, deep-rooted faith they'd suddenly felt just that morning came flooding back, they saw the profound joy in her dark gaze, without quite knowing it they felt the vehemence of her tension, hermetically contained in that calm face, in that slight, not-visibly-pounding chest, a tension perfectly sealed away, perhaps seeping out just a little in the form of tiny drops of sweat at her hairline.

They sensed the girl's joy, but also the fear creeping its way into her carefully stilled heart, she hadn't yet fully mastered her miraculous, single-minded focus on cooking and so couldn't drape herself in practised detachment as she imagined the Clapeaus' formidable anticipation and then their reaction to what she would put before them, it wasn't yet time to be trembling, she was doing her best to fight it off, it was hard, a fear was creeping in.

She let the Clapeaus see her and went back into the kitchen, leaving the door open.

She hadn't spoken a word, and neither had they.

The only tureen she could find was decorated with painted roses, which she thought utterly wrong for fish, so she brought the soup out in the austere, pitted cast-iron casserole, set it on the table, snatched away the heavy lid.

She knew she was going against the Clapeaus' conventional tastes by forcing them to look upon what they must have thought of as that hideous old pot, she knew it might even offend them, like some obscene move on her part, but she was hoping the rough, violent majesty exuded by that ugly, irreproachable, proud casserole juxtaposed with the embroidered linen tablecloth and silver cutlery brought from Marmande would serenely silence any objection from the Clapeaus, would snuff out their sense of an inelegance, not that their notion of what deserved a place on the table would be changed just like that, but because the power of the casserole (regally decreed by the casserole itself) would intimidate them, having caught them off guard.

The Cheffe gently sank the ladle into the soup, stepped back, and turned towards the kitchen, she was planning to let the Clapeaus serve themselves, she thought it essential that they see the untouched ochre soup between the black walls of the pot and take palpable measure of its full, rich consistency, so different from the cheap bouillon of mortification the Marmande cook used to inflict on them, she was determined to astound them and win them over, she reminded me, as if seeking forgiveness and wanting to justify what she would much later come to see as pure vanity, that insistence on making everyone at the table wonder at your handiwork before they get down to eating.

She would later take care to serve nothing whose form had to be marvelled at, nothing meant to arouse oohs and aahs, on the contrary, she strove to give each course and each plate a presentation so delicate, so rigorous, so pure that it would only strike the eye if the eye was open to that pleasure, only if it was ready for it, only if it wanted it.

And if it didn't, if it never noticed that cool beauty, the Cheffe didn't think it mattered, she thought people could still appreciate a dish even if something about it eluded their eye, just as she had nothing against people who wolfed down their dinner like they were shovelling in some lunchroom slop, she didn't think they were savouring it any the less.

She thought any dish that made a show of itself was hiding something, and she didn't like what that thing was – a pointless or unfounded pride, a childish plea for attention, maybe an attempt to distract from the rudimentary work done by a cook who hadn't thought it necessary to treat the primary ingredient with the kind of brio he lavished on a puff-pastry swan or a stunning nougatine gondola.

The Cheffe hated even the idea of showiness, that was the source of her refinement.

And I've always thought the splendour she humbly created on a plate lingered on in the minds even of people who didn't realise they'd noticed it, awakening their souls to harmonies of another order, it made them more perceptive and sensitive and the Cheffe knew nothing about it, couldn't know anything about it, must not think of it for even a moment, something wondrous happened by way of her and she didn't know it, must not know it, must not understand it.

But at that first dinner in the Landes she chose not to ladle out the fish soup so the Clapeaus would have to look into the pot and see the rough, pleasing balance of the colours and substances, the pink-tinged cod loin, still whole in the glossy soup, the rugged sides of the proletarian casserole, which, in its stern dignity, was not honoured to be containing and presenting that refined soup, not gratified, no, rather it consented, with a slightly crotchety grace, to grant that soup the favour of its own indisputable elegance.

The Cheffe was hoping the casserole's self-assurance would make the Clapeaus forget the tureen with the little painted roses, would even make them forget that such things as tureens with little painted roses existed.

And the Cheffe was also hoping to tell the Clapeaus she meant no offence, quite the contrary, she dared to confront them with that casserole, with its almost alarming power, only because she had deep faith in their discernment, which wasn't entirely true, the Cheffe believed in the Clapeaus' power of perception only to the extent that they'd already been subjugated by the pines when they sat down at the table, mindful of the need to replace their usual cook by any means necessary, and ground down, flattened by the pines, which knew them and didn't speak to them, which knew their failings and weaknesses and didn't mix with them.

"Don't let the pot frighten you," the Cheffe would have liked to say, realising the pot might not be quite forceful enough to rattle or overturn the Clapeaus' little world, she almost wished she could caress their troubled brows with her confident hand and reassure them, soothe them, she liked seeing them happy.

She withdrew to the kitchen and saw to taking the chicken out of the oven, keeping one ear on the little sounds coming from the dining room.

She heard only the clink of spoons on porcelain, she knew the Clapeaus weren't fond of chitchat at the table, they focused all their attention on the sensations afforded them by the food, even when they had guests they scrupulously avoided all small talk, little caring what the others might think.

Before long they had finished with the soup, from what the Cheffe could make out, and still she didn't hear a word. That worried her a little.

But she came out of the kitchen shielded by a protective, hard-won calm that made her every move seem to take place outside herself, as if she were controlling and commanding her mind from a slight distance, and she took care not to look too directly at the Clapeaus as she carried off the dishes and then the pot, but her gaze once fleetingly met Madame Clapeau's, she'd glanced up at the Cheffe almost timidly and then immediately looked down at the table again, a flash of fright lingering in her eyes' wake, and the Cheffe could see that the bowls had been emptied, with only a thin sheen of soup left in the pot, and she was relieved but all the more troubled by the flare that had shot from Madame Clapeau's eyes, which she thought she could still see faintly gleaming between herself and her employer, didn't that fear mean that she, the Cheffe, was a witch?

In its blood-red enamelled cast iron oven dish she brought out the huge chicken she'd massacred and then resuscitated, like a savage joke, surrounded by little vegetables still sizzling in the modest pool of golden, perfumed fat conscientiously and honourably exuded by the Jodas' admirable chicken.

She held out the dish and briefly displayed the glistening, tanned skin, stretched to splitting point over the stuffing-swollen breast, the abnormally inflated legs, she wanted the Clapeaus to think they knew it was just a plain oven-roasted bird so the deception would stand out in the fullest relief – and her virtuosity as a magician in the brightest light, the Cheffe would reluctantly admit to me, with a shame I rarely saw when she told me a story.

Because afterwards she took the chicken back to the kitchen to be sliced and arranged on a green earthenware platter, then came back and set it down on the table, Monsieur Clapeau, at the mere sight of that strange overflowing flesh, cried, "She's turned the whole chicken into one big cromesquis!"* and from Madame Clapeau's throat issued a sound that did little to soothe the Cheffe's nerves, that even nearly tore a hole in her composure and struck her as the sonic equivalent of the thin flame of terror she thought she could see still burning, bright and quivering, between Madame Clapeau's face and her own, denouncing her as an amoral little sorceress, not because she'd humiliated the Jodas' beautiful chicken but because, the Cheffe vaguely sensed, she was letting herself flaunt the hold she thought she had over the Clapeaus, the hold she now incontestably did have, which Madame Clapeau no more contested than she rebelled against the pines' cool authority, which she, Madame Clapeau, would nonetheless rather have felt enfolding them intangibly, unspoken, not nakedly exposed on a green earthenware dish, in an impudent casserole, and then a prison closed over them, and Madame Clapeau shivered, broken.

---

* A cromesquis is a croquette made of chopped meat in cream sauce, breaded and fried.

I went too far, the Cheffe quickly thought, but she hadn't, she'd gone just up to the point beyond which the Clapeaus would never be able to free themselves of her.

Madame Clapeau simply needed some time to adjust.

Monsieur Clapeau stared indecisively at his wife's down-turned, joyless face, then murmured towards the Cheffe, "Very nice, very nice," and he who hadn't gleaned from the Cheffe's new aplomb what an influence that sixteen-year-old girl would henceforth have in their lives now glimpsed it in Madame Clapeau's alarm, but he was already conquered, they were both of them conquered, and in a sort of horror and resentment they were enslaved, and they consented to it.

Nervous but still breezy, he added: "So you knew how I love cromesquis?"

Madame Clapeau gave him what seemed to the Cheffe a look of slightly sickened surprise, but also of distant pity, they were prisoners and he was trying to cosy up to the girl, did he think he was going to come to some understanding with the pines, with the girl, with the forces that now possessed them?

The girl had lived with them, beside them, and now she was in them.

They had to consent to that with a modicum of dignity.

The Cheffe spared Monsieur Clapeau the awkwardness of an answer, she slipped away to the kitchen, where, shaken by a delight she'd never known before, pitiless, almost cruel, she opened the little window and craned her neck to press her forehead against the big pine tree's bark, the pine kept silent but the Cheffe wasn't expecting anything from it, there was, she thought with a cool brazenness, nothing it could teach her that she didn't know already, whatever she was thinking the pine kept silent, the bark scraped her forehead.

What the Clapeaus would have been drinking? Yes, I can tell you that, they'd brought their wine from Marmande. They only drank red, always the same, Château-Lehoul, a Graves, they claimed white gave them bad dreams.

I think they were afraid of adding another passion to their passion for cuisine, and so, knowing themselves, restraining themselves in that area because doing so brought them no great frustration, they'd long before resolved never to devote another thought to wine, and above all not to let themselves be invaded by a curiosity about wine, a taste for wine, they'd settled once and for all on that fine Lehoul and forgotten everything else.

The last act of that first dinner at the house in the Landes, although the Cheffe passed over it quickly, finding nothing worth noting in it (but I'd learned to mistrust her shows of dismissiveness when she was trying to distract me from some very particular point, even if, as a matter of integrity, she wasn't overtly ruling out speaking of it someday, how well I knew every oscillation of her cherished face!), was, I believe, marked by the Clapeaus' instinctive determination to give themselves at least a little freedom within the boundaries of their submission, and so a way out of the dumbstruck astonishment, ever so slightly tempered by fright, that they'd been plunged into by the revelation (and their unavoidable, awed acceptance) of the girl's authority, her investiture, that's what they'd wanted, and without knowing it what they'd feared, who could ever aspire to feel suddenly small and needy?

Yes, yes, it's not nearly enough to say they liked the soup and the chicken.

But in their stunned enchantment they couldn't entirely judge and reflect on their dinner, their powers had deserted them, their concentration had dissolved, they'd eaten as they hated to eat, swept along on a pleasure their intoxicated minds couldn't guide and control, hence the remorse they always felt afterwards, sometimes they wished they could be done with food forever.

The peach tart let them recapture just a little freedom in their cage, which is why the Cheffe quite genuinely didn't remember her peach tart as a failure, she'd sensed the Clapeaus' visceral need to move freely again, even if it was in a confined space and under the girl's superior eye, and she didn't mind if they found that in the peach tart, that was acceptable, unimportant, it was only a dessert.

And so she let the Clapeaus treat that almost unsugared peach-and-verbena tart as a bizarre joke.

They would take a special, overheated delight in telling their circle of friends of their bafflement before that ridiculous tart, making something comical of what they depicted as their dismay, thinking they were hiding the thing that had seized hold of them at that moment, the girl's power, the thing that had enslaved them.

But their laughter would ring false, no-one would chuckle along, deep down the Clapeaus were only innocent people, fairly good people, bad liars, their laughter would ring false. Nothing came through but their incomprehension at what had become of them, their inability to find themselves in what they were, even as they consented to be just that.

After expressing open surprise at the peach tart's appearance, they swallowed a few dubious mouthfuls, then, when the Cheffe came back to the table, they forced an indulgent smile and pushed away their plates, so relieved to find themselves no longer dazed and afraid that they suddenly seemed almost euphoric, though timidly so, ready to retreat into their anxious silence should their reaction offend the Cheffe (so deeply did they already fear she wouldn't want to go on cooking for them), and that moved the Cheffe, she wanted to press them to her bosom.

"Odd dessert you've made," said Monsieur Clapeau, feeling more confident.

He laughed to make it clear that wasn't a rebuke, and laughed again to show the girl nothing remotely like a rebuke would ever cross his lips.

Whatever she was trying to do with her inedible peach tart, he wouldn't allow himself to criticise it, and if he gave himself permission to laugh it was on the assumption that this was all a peculiar joke, in any case he would go no further than that in the expression of his bafflement, and even his disappointment, when it turned out there wasn't going to be any other dessert.

And so the Cheffe laughed too, she wanted them to know she was fond of them, felt no scorn for them, didn't side with the dark, secretive pines, sometimes she almost tenderly loved the Clapeaus, in their weakness.

And so she laughed with them.

She tasted the peach tart, thought it was perfect, claimed it still needed work.

She laughed, her mouth full, knowing that outside the pines were disapproving of her, they who weren't so forgiving.

Yes, I asked her that, and apart from a few minor changes it's the very same peach tart, as famous among the Cheffe's dishes as green-robed leg of lamb or foie gras on a bed of black radishes and red beetroot, and the Cheffe always especially liked making that tart, and knowing people wanted it, the same tart that, at the house in the Landes, had set off a very welcome burst of levity in the Clapeaus, she was even grateful to that peach tart for granting the Clapeaus the modest freedom they would have needed to fight off their dependence on the girl as the years went by, yes, it's that same famed peach tart, oh the Clapeaus might have gone completely over the edge, the Cheffe didn't entirely realise it.

The peach tart we'd later come to know was enhanced by thin slices of cold honeydew and a switch to puff pastry, but to the Cheffe it was still the tart from that house in the Landes, the only dessert I ever saw her eat with any appetite, though apart from that the Cheffe was never one for nostalgia.

With that tart she could privately, secretly send the Clapeaus a fond greeting over the barrier of death that separated them, she could give them a wave, whereas she never lifted her hand towards her parents, never gently shook it back and forth before her parents' two little joined souls, it was too painful, that's right.

The Cheffe spent those two summer months at the house in the Landes cooking as well as she possibly could, striving, she thought, to cement her standing with the Clapeaus, though there was really no need, and the Clapeaus spent them driving the girl to every shopkeeper and farm in the area, then waiting in that house whose heart beat in the kitchen alone, that silent, useless, forgotten house, waiting for the girl to call them to dinner.

And while in previous summers the Clapeaus had always found vague pastimes to occupy them and insisted on their children coming to visit for a few weeks, their new devotion to the girl seemed to have traced a circle of fire around the house, they only crossed the threshold to climb into the car with the girl, and in fact when their children told them they were coming a strange panic gripped the Clapeaus, an insurmountable weariness, they continually postponed any visit on the pretext of imaginary water damage in the bedrooms, they wanted passionately to be alone and to throw themselves passionately into the task of knowing and understanding the cuisine the girl was inventing for them, so unlike anything they were used to.

Whenever we talked about it, the Cheffe confessed that all three of them were caught up – a little less so in her case, since her work kept her grounded – in an ecstatic whirlwind that without their even noticing hoisted them out of themselves and never set them down again, exhausting them without their even feeling it, and the awareness of the incredible responsibilities of her work, like the Clapeaus' awareness of the reverence they owed her, would, the Cheffe admitted, eventually have destroyed them if that stay in the Landes had gone on any longer, if they'd remained in that violent, fanatical solitude à trois, their hearts devoured by the house's heart, which beat in the kitchen alone.

Though swept along at a more moderate level of the turbulence, the Cheffe realised as she lay in her bed at night that her efforts each day to serve the Clapeaus dishes that outdid those of the day before in inspiration and taste were enough to temporarily rob her of her sanity, was she sane even now, now that her dreams were invaded by visions of foods and cookware, now that she could be wrenched from her sleep by a trusted voice whispering that the garlic, cream and egg-yolk sauce was boiling?

But the next morning she got up in a state of tranquil impatience, a quiet joy at the thought of going back to work, the cement tiles were warm and rough under her bare feet and the now-familiar pines weren't unhappy to see her, she spoke in low tones, she was happy, and the pines were happy too.

It was in the hours that followed, when the Clapeaus got up and she brought them coffee and all the rest from the little kitchen they didn't dare enter, that she felt the cyclone gradually picking her up again, and she had to resist the intense, unwholesome excitement the feverish Clapeaus were innocently radiating, at times they were just like children she had to look after, she thought, which seemed only right, since they'd given themselves up to her, she was responsible for the

Clapeaus as you're responsible for animals you're the master of, children placed in your care, she'd be accountable for their misbehaviours and mistakes, their sorrows, their furores, since they were no longer fully in possession of themselves.

She soon realised how silly she'd been to think she had to cement her standing with the Clapeaus. Wasn't it the Clapeaus who should be cementing their standing with her, taking every pain not to displease her, weren't they the ones who felt the greatest need, who lived in a state of permanent, insatiable anticipation?

Alone with the Cheffe in the freshly cleaned kitchen, well after midnight, my head spinning with happy exhaustion, I liked to ask her to tell me the dishes she made in that house in the Landes, and I took their names and descriptions back with me to my Mériadeck studio, where they offered me friendly consolation in the always downhearted minutes after I turned out the light.

Which the Cheffe clearly knew, because she ran through the list in a softer, lower, almost sing-song voice, as if she wanted me to hold in my memory not just the names but the soothing power of her voice, so I'd hear her there at my bedside, lulling me to sleep, she was so good to me that I was often tempted to think it was love, the love between a man and a woman, not a mother's love for her young son, and then I stopped thinking it or wondering about it and simply hoped for it, waiting, with patience and loyalty in my heart, for the day when she would send me an unmistakable sign, it never came, or maybe it did but only when my loyalty had faltered, for which I still can't forgive myself, and it couldn't get through to me.

But when the Cheffe saw my curious, harmless gaze in that idle kitchen she gladly granted my wish, and in a different order each time she told me she'd made the Clapeaus roast duck with blueberry jus, fresh salmon ravioli, confit of rabbit, fricassee of fennel and carrots with lavender honey, aubergine-and-pistachio stuffed sea bream, cauliflower fritters in sauce piquante, pigeon with apples and red cabbage, mackerel with garlic, escalope of foie gras on white-fig compote, beef-jowl stuffed mushrooms, lamb sweetbreads with sorrel, prawns sautéed in pepper and ginger, salad of purslane and chicken livers, cream of bitter almonds, goat's-milk custard, using the dinner leftovers for the following lunch, having agreed with the Clapeaus that she wouldn't have to come up with two meals a day.

That arrangement was meant to let Cheffe catch her breath, said the Clapeaus, but the fact is she never did, she confessed to me with a little laugh, she worked so hard to transform those leftovers into surprising new dishes, to make them seem they'd just been made as what they'd become, like mackerel transformed into a terrine with *fines herbes*, pigeon reappearing in a feuilleté, rabbit recast as an aspic with peas, and those morning labours gave her no rest, no, in fact they demanded even greater feats of creativity, the Cheffe told me, still in awe of that sixteen-year-old girl's tireless inventiveness decades after, in the kitchen now at rest for the night, the two of us in quiet conversation, her mind like mine half in the little kitchen in the

Landes I would later come to know, that kitchen I would later enter otherwise than in my thoughts, I never told her about that.

My Lloret de Mar friends spend a good part of their boundless free time cooking complicated dishes, and since I made sure to tell no-one how I once earned my living they take me for one of those men who can't cook a meal to save his life, who's happy eating anything set before him, I think I hinted I was a bookdealer, I don't quite remember. They watch me taste their elaborate concoctions with patronising interest, confident that my palate isn't subtle enough to appreciate their dishes as they think they deserve, so I limit myself to a few happy mmms, I never comment, I'd find it too painful to talk about cooking in Lloret de Mar, my friends don't know me.

Because, that day when I drove to Sainte-Bazeille in search of the house where the Cheffe had once lived, I went on through the summer afternoon to the Landes, and I parked by the side of the road, at the start of a long sandy lane that led towards the house between the flaking trunks of towering pines, the same pines, I told myself, moved, that saw the Cheffe's birth into the world of cooking, those fearsome pines.

I walked to the house, and then, forbidding myself to think so I wouldn't rob myself of the boldness I needed, I turned the knob, the door opened, and I went in, not knowing if the (most likely) vacationers who lived there were home, I made for the little kitchen, my footsteps as sure as if I'd been there before, which in a way I had, I knew that house so well I'd made drawings of it in my notebook of recipes, and now I was finally seeing my model, nothing came as a surprise.

Sand covered the kitchen's tiled floor, the old table was grimy and dust-coated. The huge pine outside the window let through only an ashen light, and then the pine spoke to me and I realised, looking around in panic at the shelfless walls, at a broken lightbulb hanging from the ceiling, that no-one had cooked here for a very long time, the house was dead, as the pine told me in a whisper with nothing kindly about it, suggesting in the same breath that I vacate the premises at once.

I ran out the door, raced down the lane, now all the pines were whispering but I forced myself not to try to understand what they were saying because they didn't wish me well, that I knew, which I explained by my sudden certainty that I'd committed a betrayal, as in truth I'd already felt the day before as I planned that covert excursion, I'd pushed that feeling aside and now it came back as I ran towards my car, I could have wept with shame.

The Cheffe would have been horrified to learn I was out prowling around the scenes of her life, I knew it all along, that's why I hadn't told her, but the pines were right to accuse me, how can you claim to love someone and then betray them with your intrusiveness, wasn't I a man she thought she could trust?

Back in the safety of my car, I thought the pines had gone easy on me, I could have found the door incorruptibly locked when I tried to leave, with wrathful pines blocking off every window: "Alright then, so cook!"

And then the fun would be over, and that would be the end of my little detective act, I told myself as I turned back onto the road, still shaking with a fear so powerful it made me even more sorry and ashamed, but still I sensed, as the pines retreated and then disappeared in my rear-view mirror, that when my tranquillity came back it would quickly revive my consuming, exhausting desire to know every detail and every setting of the Cheffe's life, to know more about her, and to know it better, than she did herself, I studied my feelings to be sure of the perfect integrity of that desire that took up so much of my thought, I wanted to appear before the Cheffe with all my decency intact, unavoidable little secrets notwithstanding, it was hard, it was torture – before the Cheffe with all the trueness of my being intact, yes.

The return to Marmande, in September, put an end to that imprisonment in the little Landes house and in culinary obsession, and the Cheffe was glad it was over, not because she was tired, she paid no attention to weariness, but because she'd been starting to sense, with repulsion, something she always tried to avoid: the threat of a sensual atmosphere taking shape around a rich, succulent cuisine, it hung over the Clapeaus without their knowing it or being responsible for it, just as a cloud of desires hangs over the head of a child or a young animal, ambiguous desires, inescapable, uncomfortable, though irreproachable and profoundly innocent.

The Cheffe felt like the oxygen in that little house was slowly being driven out by the erotic emanations her work aroused and sustained in spite of her, which excited and demoralised her, she couldn't wait to be free of it, the Clapeaus' minds were clouded, they weren't themselves, she couldn't wait to be free of their weakness.

The Clapeaus' handful of social obligations in Marmande woke them from their spell but didn't make them forget how much they owed the girl, or how indispensable her presence had become to them.

And although it tested them terribly, they suggested she go off for a few days' rest at her parents' house, in preparation for which the Cheffe made the Clapeaus several full meals to reheat, and they encouraged her to triple the recipes so she could take some of each dish to Sainte-Bazeille, where Monsieur Clapeau drove her with the saucepans and casseroles carefully sealed away in the trunk, the Clapeaus were as proud of her as if she were their own daughter, they wanted others to marvel at her talents, the parents in Sainte-Bazeille most of all.

The Cheffe brought beef roulades with leeks and spinach, duck-and-almond terrine, chicken bouillon with dumplings, half guinea-fowl and half cheese, along with three dozen smoked-mackerel fritters for her young brothers and sisters – "quite a feast," as I called it, a stupid thing to say, unintentionally condescending, and the Cheffe gave me her oblique little smile, hesitated, then finally told me she didn't find the success she was hoping for in Sainte-Bazeille, that although they didn't say so her parents would have rather she come empty-handed, not loaded down with dishes they must have found excessively refined, and in some obscure way disturbing.

In honour of her visit, they themselves had cooked the kind of simple foods she once loved and still did, vegetable soup, couscous with raisins, jugged rabbit with lardons in blood sauce, they were disconcerted by the elegant eccentricity now coming into their house, the effort expended on those dishes seemed wasted, extravagant, their daughter's work deeply pointless. They said nothing unkind, but their muted reactions, or else their excessive enthusiasm over minor details, like the Marmande pots' polished enamel, clearly expressed their uncomfortable disapproval, I don't know if they disapproved exactly, that wasn't like them, but they couldn't approve of or understand such empty feats, and that bothered them.

And the Cheffe, who a few months before, on the road to Marmande, had felt she was dishonouring her parents' hearts simply by the sophistication of her thoughts, never imagined she might feel subtly tainted when she came home to show them the best part of her, that was how she saw it, the most sincere, the most fertile, the most generous.

It was a terrible shock. What a strange, what a deformed reflection of herself in her parents' quietly evasive gaze!

Her brothers and sisters didn't like the smoked-mackerel fritters, all her dishes were duly tasted and then ignored in an atmosphere of pained bewilderment, and two days later they went back into Monsieur Clapeau's trunk almost untouched, and the Cheffe was relieved to be leaving, sad, yes, but not defeated, she knew the mistake was to think she'd been corrupted, the mistake wasn't hers.

I see a sign of the Cheffe's new maturity in her silent confidence before her mother and father, who in those days and in other contexts could still devastate her with a single surprised or dubious glance, their perplexity at her cooking couldn't get to her now, and neither could their incomparable innocence seem the only way to lead an honourable life.

Not thinking any the less of them, she believed she was entirely their equal, and that discovery first stung her eyes, then entered into her, gently illuminating her from inside.

The Clapeaus told her that while she was away the old cook had reappeared as if nothing had happened, intending to go back to work, and they'd had to let her know where things stood, so astonished to see her again that at first they stumbled over their explanations, but very soon the solidity of their relationship with the Cheffe brought categorical words to their lips, they stopped explaining, they only said that the job was the girl's now, and for them that sentence had the force of a diktat, they believed they'd be diminishing the girl, making her ordinary, if they tried to justify that new state of affairs, the job was the girl's now.

The cook took offence, she didn't dare insult the Clapeaus but she called down a furious curse on the girl, which did nothing to shake them.

But it did trouble the Cheffe, who'd never been cursed before, and she turned ever so slightly harder, she said, as if to protect herself from the imprecation's potential effects, so every word aimed against her would crash against the thin stony shell that would henceforth shield her courage and her will, something hard-headed and gruff came to life in her, she hunched her dense, opaque, resolute body like a little bull.

And so began the second phase of her life in Marmande.

The Clapeaus hired an aged relative of theirs to help out

in the kitchen, a woman with a mild mental impairment, but she neatly handled the jobs the Cheffe once did for the former cook – washing, peeling and slicing vegetables, cutting meat, scaling and cleaning fish, washing and drying the cookware as it was used – and obeyed the Cheffe's instructions with touching seriousness, immediately enveloping the Cheffe in all her piety, the boundless, burning piety of a lonely, backward woman, and the Cheffe learned to give orders and to speak very clearly, because the woman had to work to understand, the Cheffe took that in and never forgot it: make every order unambiguous, never shout or bully, blame only yourself when instructions are misunderstood, the woman had too simple a mind to show initiative, so ask of people only what's within their grasp, and the Cheffe learned that lesson in her kitchen in Marmande and never disobeyed it, she could be curt but she was never furious, she never raged.

One of her great pleasures was going into town to seek out the best products, and she quickly developed a keen eye for the nature and the value of the things she needed, she learned how to ask the butcher for just what she wanted, first by describing the shape, the texture and the taste, and then remembering the names, she learned quickly and forgot little, and so she taught herself through her work, her experiments, which sometimes failed, for which the mesmerised Clapeaus never criticised her, when they even noticed it, nor did they voice any weariness or impatience when they found the same dish on the menu several days in a row because the Cheffe wanted to get it right, she reacted to failure or partial success with no visible dismay, but in truth she refused to give up, she was coolly and fanatically determined, even if in some cases it would have been more sensible to set the recalcitrant recipe aside and then either come back to it with a slightly different intention, catching her stymied intelligence off guard, or else, in time, understand that it was an ill-conceived idea from the start, the Cheffe wasn't good at that game.

Sometimes, once I thought I could see us as friends, seeing the Cheffe so insistent on perfecting a recipe she'd imagined but wasn't happy with, I suggested it might be better to give up than labour to subdue such uncooperative ingredients (because I thought their refusal to obey held the answer to the question of a recipe's soundness), but the Cheffe didn't take any notice, she listened without a word, determined to go on, to begin again as many times as it took, forever if need be, until she could prove to herself she was right.

In her one concession to my opinion, she granted that the dishes she'd mastered only through obstinacy and dogmatism and sheer insistence weren't her best, in fact she still felt a sort of strange rancour towards them and didn't like making them, but she would have liked even less remembering that she'd failed to overcome their resistance, that's how the Cheffe was, she never looked for a fight but if there had to be combat she never backed down.

She served the Clapeaus pig's feet au gratin three times before she was happy with the sauce her theory told her would be perfect, a reduction of sweet white wine and cream blended with fresh bay leaves, after which that sauce never appeared again, and pig's feet rarely, except when Monsieur Clapeau, who'd loved that dish, sometimes asked for them.

The Cheffe preferred to cook from her own ideas but didn't say no to the Clapeaus' timidly expressed wishes, she liked pleasing them, she liked them to drift happily off to sleep while in her little room above theirs she thought over her work, sometimes so excited that she got out of bed, went down to the kitchen, and paced through the room visualising what she'd do the next day, and then, more hazily, what she'd do in all the days to come, and all the years, thinking with almost painful euphoria that a lifetime wouldn't be enough to create the infinitely varied, enigmatic, fertile cuisine she had in her mind, and there were so many ingredients she didn't yet know, and her swarming thoughts invented beautiful, abstract images of finished structures that she wanted her cooking to resemble, she felt that but didn't understand what it meant, it was too soon, she had too little life and experience behind her to pin it all down, she thought about it endlessly but still it was too soon, and she hated being so young, such a novice, she had no reason to fear but she feared it would be too soon forever.

"I was afraid I might never find the way to make the things I was seeing," she told me one day.

And when I asked what they looked like her hands sketched out sibylline forms in space, and she explained, none too clearly, that she was looking for perfect shapes that would amaze even her, as if someone else had created them, someone more talented and better in every way, and all she could say would

133

be "That's it exactly," without being able to specify what the "it" might be, because even the word "perfect" would seem to shrink the emotion she felt, that's what the Cheffe was aiming for, so intently that she sometimes found herself breathless with impatience, hope and fear in that Marmande kitchen, and that's what the Cheffe was still aiming for much later, still and always, in the kitchen of her restaurant, much later, when with her confident hands she mimed those impenetrable spheres, no longer breathless but with sadness in her eyes, I wanted to touch her, I didn't, and then I did, only because, no matter what anyone said, no matter what sorrow I felt myself, she'd found what she'd been pursuing all her life, and so I could gently lay my hand on her shoulder without it seeming I was stupidly trying to console her.

Her pain wasn't the consolable kind, but the Cheffe was happy to talk to me about what she'd been seeking for so long, even as she was silent or deeply evasive on subjects that involved simple, everyday information.

For instance, I would never know just how old she was when she left the Clapeaus' house for a little apartment in Marmande, or if she was married to the man she had her daughter by, or what sort of man he was, although I have an idea, it's only conjecture, and as you see I don't jump to conclusions, but my conviction is firm.

The Cheffe simply shrugged when I asked if she'd found it hard to leave the Clapeaus'.

"I was getting tired of my little room, you know," she answered.

I found the courage to ask if it wasn't a little complicated all the same, back at the end of the Sixties, giving birth to a child with no official father, I could see I was annoying her, and before she launched into her tedious, dishonest routine about her joys as a mother, how lucky she was to have such an exceptional person for a daughter, she shot back, "How do you know whether I was married or not?"

Knowing the Cheffe's disregard for other people's opinions, I've always thought she wasn't trying to tell me she was married, wasn't trying to create an image of respectability she couldn't possibly have cared about, no, she was trying to hide it, or at least to obscure the unbecoming weakness she'd shown in marrying her child's father, a man she'd never loved, never admired, the Clapeaus' gardener, yes, she must have found it so humiliating to think she'd let that trash touch her and penetrate her, had maybe even wanted it and encouraged it, that she couldn't admit it to anyone, not even someone like me who knew nothing about the man and so had no reason to be disgusted or shocked.

Those omissions and that unease of hers led me to suspect the gardener, so I wrote to a relative of the Clapeaus who told me he remembered the gardener marrying the year of the Cheffe's daughter's birth, but he couldn't guarantee that his bride was the Cheffe.

The daughter always claims she was born of an unknown father, but that means nothing coming from someone with such an appetite for legends, such a need to be thought a child whose mother never stopped hurting her from the moment she was born, it means nothing, and I think I'm more to be trusted with my reasoned speculations and discreet, thoughtful enquiries than that crackpot who supposedly knows her own life better than I do, I'm far more to be trusted than that woman who could easily know just who her father is and claim her mother forced her to grow up without that essential information, because she hates her and envies her even today, more than you can imagine.

Why am I revealing all this? Why, when the Cheffe wouldn't tell me about the gardener or her possible marriage, why deliberately go against her wishes, particularly since in this case I can't hide behind the conviction that it was wrong of the Cheffe to cover that up, since it wasn't right or wrong, but simply her prerogative? And how, with these revelations that do nothing to improve my own image, could I possibly be improving the Cheffe's?

I don't know.

I'm telling you all this after I'd promised myself that I wouldn't, and now it's said and I can't erase it, and it didn't just slip out, it came from my mouth with my full consent and in the presumptuous belief that I'm right to say it, not for my sake but for hers, people might call me pathetic and two-faced but they won't think any the less of the Cheffe just because she might have married the Clapeaus' gardener and had a child with him, might have held him in her arms without love but with pleasure, no-one will think ill of her simply because her young, healthy body hungrily, curiously pressed itself to the body of the first man, perhaps, who took that sort of interest in her, who happened to be there just when her flesh was demanding to be taught by and known to someone else, when her body was begging to be told about itself, to be initiated into its own mysterious abilities, no-one will find fault with the Cheffe for going through what we all go through, and in fact I hope it will make her seem more like one of us, more worthy of love, too bad if I come off as a villain.

I'm not convinced those are fine reasons.

I doubt myself, a certain torment is always with me, sometimes I'm not sure of anything, nothing but my unforgivable disloyalty to the Cheffe's memory, and so I argue it out with her all night long, night after night, asking not for her forgiveness but for a sign of her approval.

I try to remember her exactly as she was in our long nighttime talks, and once I've made my case I try to extract the most true-to-life answer from that image of her, not the answer I'd like to hear but the one the Cheffe would most likely have given me, with the small, childlike smile that gave a little bend to her mouth or the morose, dour, cold look that expressed her displeasure, and it's only because I thought I glimpsed a shy child's smile twisting my beloved apparition's lips that I don't regret bringing up the gardener.

I also think it's important to counter the daughter's lies, the way she proclaims far and wide that she has no idea who her father is, that her mother wouldn't tell her the first thing about him, so everyone will think the Cheffe was a hurtful, unstable mother, oh that's so unfair, I can never do enough to combat that woman's warped ingratitude, and what will she have left when she can't defame the Cheffe anymore, when she can't make anyone sympathise with her made-up miseries, what will she have left when she finds herself alone with her putrid soul, who will take pity on her, no-one, no-one, then she'll know how terrible the absence of true pity is, and she'll be sorry she spent all that time seeking sympathy.

So the Cheffe moved into a little apartment in Marmande and gave birth to her child with what I assume was a mixture of pride, surprise and discouragement, since her ambition never foresaw the coming of such a demanding little creature, with so many needs you can't say no to, her ambition never foresaw anyone intruding on its existence, which was in fact growing, expanding with each passing day and every new meal, every deeper understanding, every exercise more expertly mastered, every thought more inventively guided.

I don't know if the gardener moved in with her, but I do know she fell into a loneliness all the more cruel in that she was never really alone.

She had the child with her, she had other mothers around her, relatives or acquaintances from Sainte-Bazeille who sweetly stopped by to say hello and make sure all was well, and although they thought they were doing her a favour they were entangling her in a net of relationships, duties and discussions, every one of them about motherhood, in which cooking never figured as the aim of a quest, of a thought, of a morality, of a hope, or as something you could simply talk about, endlessly and from every angle, or which, once the word was spoken, you could drape in a silence filled with that precious word's rich resonances, but only as yet another wearisome duty of days weighed down with chores, which saddened the Cheffe more than anything else.

How she missed the solitary hours in her little room at the Clapeaus', the moments of transport and intense, fruitful meditation that let her drift off to sleep in the impatient certainty that the next day she'd go further, learn more, maybe even discover or invent some new way of putting foods together, she often saw herself in that room in her dreams, and the next morning she hesitated before she went back to real life, before she put her feet on the floor of a room never visited by creative fervour, a room that was only what it was, not a vast, living, encouraging vessel for her untrammelled mind, her blossoming intuition.

She still tried every night to devise new combinations of spices and fish, fruits and meats, harmonious or jarring juxtapositions of colours on a plate, but, knowing she'd have no chance to do anything with them the next day, she began to think the spirit of cooking had tired of her, was little by little slipping away from her, that she'd let it down by manifestly preferring the child, depriving that spirit of so many of her thoughts, and now maybe it was going off to find a more deserving heart to lodge and prosper in, manlier, tougher, she felt depleted, unreal, all her grace gone, but she wasn't sorry she'd had the child, she always insisted, and I don't know if that was true, I don't know if she'd convinced herself she had to say that and feel that, that the child meant more to her than anything, there and there alone she showed a sort of cowardice, a fearful or superstitious obedience to the way things are supposed to be, which didn't stop her from feeling utterly pointless.

The Clapeaus came to see her, bringing a present of a little black woollen dog that the Cheffe lovingly preserved, she showed it to me one day, it had a red satin ribbon around its neck.

The Clapeaus admired the baby, very amiably and at great length, and the Cheffe sadly realised they were hoping that if they stayed bent over the cradle mouthing platitudes they could hide their dismay at the new feelings the Cheffe was arousing in them, now that she was a young mother, estranged from her kitchen and its thrumming solitude, sitting with arms folded next to her daughter, on the alert for any appeal the child might make, slightly lost, with nothing to say, and the Clapeaus couldn't have sworn they'd ever had a conversation with the Cheffe before but they were certain that when she was with them her lively, jubilant body radiated such lyrical vitality that they never noticed her silence, only her vast, intense calm, and to be sure the Clapeaus didn't disavow the thing in them that had humbly bowed down to the Cheffe, that had submitted itself to her force and her grasp of their devotion to good food, but when they looked at this phlegmatic young woman they didn't recognise their celebrant, the girl they'd granted such power, whose devouring influence had wholly monopolised the kitchen, forbidding them to cross the threshold, and with what ardent modesty they'd acquiesced!

No, the Clapeaus disavowed nothing.

But the Cheffe saw their confusion, maybe even their sorrow, she saw how they glanced at her body slumped in a chair, banal, passive, ponderous, and she saw the indomitable spirit slipping free of that useless body, the spirit that for a time had honoured her with its presence and love, she was sure the Clapeaus also saw it dancing through the apartment, whose air the infant's despotic existence seemed to thin and whose every corner it seemed to colonise, and then there was no sign of the spirit's scintillations, it was gone, and the Cheffe felt such shame that she let out a sudden, sharp sob.

And since she'd never learned how to talk to the Clapeaus, her distress took the form of a dull, bored, almost rude taciturnity.

There was no charm left in her as she silently, gracelessly went through the motions required for her daughter's care, seeming to have forgotten the Clapeaus were there but in fact terribly aware of their dismay and their helplessness, she'd once been inside them, she still was, their blood flowed through her heart more naturally than her own blood had flowed to the heart of her child.

The Clapeaus told her they'd hired a cook, wanting to give the Cheffe some time to tend to her baby and then find someone to watch her during the day, assuming she was willing to come back to them. They scarcely spoke of the new woman, telling her with a gesture that there was no comparing her to the Cheffe, and, not wanting to pressure her, maybe uncomfortable to be urging her to entrust her child to another, they kept their despair to themselves.

But the Cheffe knew perfectly well how they missed her,

she could see it in a strange restlessness that made their legs twitch as they sat, or put a damp gleam in their eyes, as if they were exhausted and feverish at the same time, and they waited for her answer, hoping they wouldn't seem to be, they waited for her to tell them she'd be back, to tell them a date, that glum, torpid girl they felt as if they'd never had in their house, whom they clung to all the same, not knowing what else to do, not yet ready to face the possibility that they might have lost their Cheffe.

She didn't answer. She put the child back in her cradle and sat down, inert, unreachable.

With a brief grimace of anguish, the Cheffe told me she was certain they'd seen the one justification for her authority and sovereignty in the kitchen undulating away from her, and she thought it pointless and cruel of them to act as if they hadn't, to pretend the situation was less desperate than they all knew it was, she was exhausted and she only wanted for them to go away, let her sleep, she was empty and insignificant and never again, she was sure, would she dare show herself to the Clapeaus.

At long last they left, as downcast as she was, trying to convince each other she'd been unsettled by the child's coming and would soon get a grip on herself, but clearly sensing, since in their way they knew the Cheffe intimately, that something vital had turned its back on her, something that wasn't directly connected to the child, something that once let the Cheffe be the perfect intermediary between the Clapeaus and magnificence, that let them stop hating what they were.

The Cheffe's cooking, the joyous gift she'd made of her entire soul, had cured them of their tortured hypocrisy, they'd become better people, and every day they'd striven to prove worthy of her, every day they'd tried to do no wrong and to think fine thoughts, and their nagging shame had abandoned them.

Now it was with a sort of grim resolve that they ate the unexceptional food cooked by the replacement, they ate a great deal, with an ordinary pleasure that diminished them in their own minds, they could see themselves slipping, limp and horrified, without the Cheffe there they lacked the strength to stay on the plane of spirituality she'd unassumingly led them to, a plane of joyful, accepted mystery.

She pitied the Clapeaus, the Cheffe confessed to me.

Because the thing that had turned away from her, leaving her so sad, so tired, so drained of any desire to live, had also sent the Clapeaus back to a place where they no longer wanted to live, back to the pragmatic, demoralising universe of their old, untransfigured obsession.

I'm trying to tell you of that time as precisely as I can, but the Cheffe's account was heavy with equivocations and an obvious hope that I wouldn't draw certain conclusions she would have found troublesome, again and again she told me how she loved the baby from the moment of her birth, what joy she found in looking after her, etcetera, which I don't dispute, how could I, but which I must nonetheless hold up against the lethargic despair she slumped into after the Clapeaus' visit, a despair whose every symptom the Cheffe couldn't stop herself from describing, she didn't really want to and she did all the same, with a pained astonishment and an emotion that thirty years after the fact seemed to expect from my friendship an unguarded expression of sympathy, as if my friendship owed that to the very young woman who felt so alone, so adrift in her Marmande apartment, even though she was never really alone and had to endure that punishment as well, the punishment of never being visited by the one principle she cared about but only by people she had nothing to say to.

I didn't refuse the Cheffe my understanding, I used it to implicitly tell her, with a squeeze of my fingers on her wrist, with a prolonged gaze, that it wasn't my friendship she could ask anything of, it was my love, and the Cheffe must have seen that, and I was sure a patient, persistent love would eventually overcome any trivial reason for rejecting it, the age difference, a lack of time and desire, in any case she knew my love demanded no sacrifice, and especially not the sacrifice of a diminished devotion to cooking.

There I think I can say I succeeded in a way, the Cheffe welcomed my love, accepted it, and returned it when she could transform it into something bigger than the two of us, when in short she felt that the spirit of love had invaded her.

I'm the only one in our little Lloret de Mar crowd who hasn't had relatives visit from France. My friends regularly receive their children, their grandchildren, a brother or sister, and then the parties on the terraces aren't so relaxed, so casual, so spontaneous, and in a strange reversal it's as if wild youth were playing host to sober maturity and daren't show itself in all its unbridled licence, and afterwards we laugh about that, their children would be shocked to see us as we are in Lloret de Mar. I told my friends that my daughter was coming to see me. They clapped and whooped, which is how we express our elation in Lloret de Mar. I feel anxious, I don't want her to come but I can't keep her away, on what grounds? But I really don't want her to see Lloret de Mar.

She told me she went out ever more rarely to walk in the streets of Marmande with the child, and then gave it up entirely, in the end she developed an absurd but unconquerable horror at the thought of leaving her apartment, even though she was sure it didn't like her, didn't wish her well, was in fact plotting with the world around it to make her feel even sadder and more out of place.

When I asked her who, in that case, did the shopping, she tersely answered that the child's father brought them more or less everything they needed, though I didn't know if that meant he was living with her or came to visit and then went away.

She spent her days in a chair by the crib, only getting up to feed and change the baby, and although she assured me she was still lucid enough to look after her daughter, I thought she clearly didn't have it in her to play with and smile at the girl, to press her to her for reasons other than logistical, in a word to love her in a way that the child could actually feel, because the modicum of energy required for tenderness had wholly abandoned her.

I know what you're thinking: the secret disinterest the Cheffe had walled herself up in must have affected the child's personality, so we should see the animosity she would later inflict on her mother, her tireless, whining insistence on sabotaging her, as simply a consequence of what she'd endured in her first months of life, when her mother sitting beside her wasn't really there at all, when her mother's hands touched her skin but didn't seem to remember that skin, when her mother's eyes turned away, impersonal and distant, from the face anxiously looking up at her, or stared back without seeing her, with no emotion but a vague, cold perplexity, until the child began to wail and, mechanically recalling that sounds coming from the object before her meant she had to do something or other, she gave her a bottle, or maybe her breast, she didn't tell me, or changed the nappy she'd just changed, that didn't need changing, she'd lost all ability to see what had to be done, but she did something, clinging, unmoored though she was, to a very tenuous, mechanical sense of her responsibilities.

I know that's what you're thinking, and the Cheffe herself wasn't immune to that simplistic idea of personality as a mere matter of causes and effects, for as long as she lived she accused herself of shirking motherly love for a few weeks or months, I'm not quite sure, and if you ask me her mistake was that she never hid her guilty ideas from her daughter, never hid the awful thought that she'd failed her terribly, even if she never told her just how, I don't believe she ever breathed a word of that to anyone but me.

But she filled her daughter's head with the thought that she hadn't always been an ideal mother when she was very young, and although after that everything she did fervently, selflessly sought to make up for that failure, more out of love than in hopes of washing away her misdeed (she could live, however unhappily, with her misdeed, but she couldn't live without proving her love to her daughter), although she did infinitely more for her than many parents whose children would never dream of reproaching them for anything, her daughter clung to that semi-confession for all she was worth, she saw it as a rationale for her self-centredness and lack of enterprise, and with a sour contentment she nestled into the stinking folds of self-pity, no doubt she would have shown more drive if the Cheffe had simply loved her and forgotten to feel guilty, and there she was wrong, alas, she was gravely wrong.

So yes, that thing she couldn't possibly remember, that dark time in both their lives, must have had some effect on the daughter, but why a bigger or more decisive effect than the care the Cheffe devoted to her for most of her existence?

"You shouldn't think that way," I told her. "Whatever trifling damage you might have quite involuntarily done to that child when you yourself were barely an adult, you should set it aside and remember all the good you tried to do for her, more than you had to, and what came of it, your own exceptional self erased simply to prop up that insignificant woman."

I was angry then, things were going downhill at the restaurant, I came to work angry and left the same way, that's what I told the Cheffe as she continually accused herself of hampering her daughter's development thirty years earlier, not wanting to understand that her mind had more urgent things to be troubled about.

My friends press me to tell them exactly when my daughter will be coming to Lloret de Mar, and although I always do my best not to seem like a weirdo I find I can't answer, I force a quick smile, I'm sure my daughter is very nice and I'm not proud of myself. But the prospect of her disturbing my precious, secret tranquillity in Lloret de Mar, even a little, almost makes me nonsensically want to flee Lloret de Mar, to wash my hands of it all.

The Cheffe pulled through those hard days in Marmande all on her own.

Late one springtime afternoon she opened the window to hang baby clothes on the line, in the emotional numbness she now vaguely thought of as normal, even more or less pleasant, and the light, breeze-swept air brought the smell of baking meatloaf to her nostrils, the Cheffe recognised it, greedily breathed it in.

A violent sensation clutched her stomach, not hunger but a sudden longing, forgotten and now suddenly rediscovered in that enticing scent, to make the most aromatic and most tender of all terrines with her own hands, or more precisely to once again be the young woman whose memory now came flooding back, the young woman she could see in the Clapeaus' kitchen, bent over a bowlful of pork, veal, onions and a generous dash of *fines herbes*, and the motions of that young woman who was once her filled her with an odd jealousy, she yearned to slip into that body and go back to those motions, recover the thoughts animating those skilled hands, those industrious, precise hands that had forgotten nothing, she wanted to retake possession of what was once hers, what she'd earned, deserved, the immense, quiet pleasure of those motions, the intelligence of those careful hands, that delightful, enviable image of herself as a young woman who needed no-one but herself, a worker forging her own joy, her own tranquil pride.

And she felt an anger at the body she was living in, heavy and shapeless, its hands blinkered, she was violently sorry that she'd permitted the dulling and disappearance of the faithful instrument she now so clearly saw again, and she cruelly missed the company of her passion, her own little soul, liberated, lightened, alert, and the deep, sweet solitude she could find even when she wasn't alone in the kitchen, now forbidden her whether the child was there or not, imprisoned in a stupor that barred her from looking into herself, she felt sadness as well.

Again she inhaled the scent of meatloaf, with a starved woman's longing. She closed the window, collapsed onto a chair and began to weep, frightening the baby with her sobs.

"Oh, you wept," I stupidly repeated when the Cheffe paused, the words just slipped out, I'd never seen the Cheffe weep, not even in the bleakest depths of her difficulties.

"Yes, yes," she said, with the quiet, suddenly distant impatience I always heard in her voice when I said something stupid, and she looked at me with a dubious stare, as if she were wondering how far she could trust such a halfwit, and although that stare made me deeply ashamed I didn't hate it when she looked at me like that, I felt a gruff intimacy between us, and it didn't displease me.

The day after she wept, the Cheffe felt herself coming back to life – back, that is, to herself.

That resurrection took the form of a restlessness so powerful that the Cheffe feared she might be consumed by exhausting, sterile rapture and wondered if she'd ever regain the dense serenity that in the Clapeaus' kitchen enveloped and eased the fever that came with her work.

For the first time in ages she went out for a walk with the child, and springtime astonished her, she felt her bare forearms faintly shivering, she felt their pale down standing on end, she was astonished by springtime, she had tears in her eyes and her body was awakening, determined to be hers again, her hands quivered with repressed vitality on the handle of the baby carriage.

Over the next few days she packed up their things, hers and the baby's, gave the little apartment a thorough cleaning, then demanded to be driven to Sainte-Bazeille by the child's father, possibly her husband, that man I haven't been able to form a clear image of, except − because this is how the Cheffe chose to portray him, the few times she spoke of him − that of a sometime companion, who came back into her life only to do her various favours, evidently with no sign of gratitude from the Cheffe, which only confirms my idea that she didn't love him, felt little respect for him, and quietly blamed him for a situation she never wanted.

She left the child with her parents. Yes, yes, she left her in Sainte-Bazeille, firmly intending to take her back as soon as she could.

Then she got on the train for Bordeaux, where she'd never been in her life.

When I asked why she didn't simply go back to the Clapeaus' she said nothing for some time, not because she didn't know how to answer but because she was trying to find the words, I could see her attention turn away from my face and descend into her, cautiously, as if it were afraid it might startle the truth that was hiding there, still loath to be flushed out. Finally she looked back towards me, gave me a strange, insistent stare (and as I shivered with fatigue in the just-cleaned kitchen I found myself wishing, absurdly, that I could lose consciousness and so escape the tyranny of her gaze, and so run no risk of disappointing her with a yawn or a shocked look, she who so rarely felt the need for sleep, and never the desire) and told me the sacrifice she'd resigned herself to when she left the child with her parents obliged her to undertake something far more ambitious than a return to the Clapeaus' kitchen, she told me her only hope of enduring what she saw as a desertion, however temporary, and the thought of the child's unhappiness, even if that too was short-lived, was to risk her own security, her own comfort, because it would have been unthinkable that the only price she had to pay for abandoning her child was running to the shelter of the Clapeaus'.

"Don't exaggerate, you weren't abandoning her," I stopped myself from saying, crossly, and as if she'd read my mind the Cheffe added, "The baby and I had never been apart, you understand."

But no, I didn't want to understand.

I was deeply put out to hear the Cheffe explain the decision to go to Bordeaux not by her entirely legitimate ambition but by some amorphous need to suffer, to have it as bad as the child would supposedly have it in Sainte-Bazeille, where I'm sure she very soon felt perfectly at home, I didn't like seeing the Cheffe flatter herself like that, or disparage herself, I wasn't sure which, in any case I didn't like seeing that stubborn, unyielding will to become a real cook, an artist of the kitchen, whose aspirations demanded a clientele less limited than the Clapeaus, reduced by her own words to a dim, banal feeling of guilt over her child, I didn't like it that thirty years later she still couldn't admit she wouldn't have let anything or anyone keep her from the city, from exploring and learning her talents, once the breath of cooking consented to visit her again.

Yes, the Cheffe was always like that, she didn't exactly minimise the scale of her intentions or the steadiness of her resolve but she kept them quiet, maybe she didn't know how to make it clear she wasn't looking for money or fame.

She was trying to answer, as meritoriously and melodiously as she could, a call that honoured her, a call that had to be heard and respected, she was trying to bring about the fruition of the thing put inside her like a seed, which was a gift of good fortune, and an enviable fate.

Yes, I'm trying to say it for her.

That's why she claimed she only went up to Bordeaux so she could bear the thought of her need to get away from the child, but I didn't understand that when she told me, and it irritated me.

That child took up too much room in the reasons she gave me, just as the thirty-year-old daughter was beginning to occupy too many of our thoughts in those days when the Cheffe talked to me in the slumbering kitchen, her still brimming over with her tireless energy and me wobbly with exhaustion but still dreading the moment when I'd find myself outside, heading home to my Mériadeck studio, only in the Cheffe's company did I ever feel comfortable, interesting and wise, only there was my existence as good as another's, as coherent, as complete.

When she got to Bordeaux the Cheffe took a room in a run-down hotel near the train station, then, dressed in her best dark-blue cotton skirt and a sky-blue, full-waisted blouse, her chestnut hair combed back and bound tight behind her head, she walked to the centre of town through the hot, soot-black streets, regularly asking her way with an unshakable, almost aggressive confidence that concealed a preference for silence.

She walked into a restaurant she liked the look of, and that was the first time the Cheffe had ever set foot in a restaurant, she'd drunk an occasional cup of hot chocolate in a Marmande café, but that was all.

She said she was looking for work in the kitchen, she didn't have a degree but she knew how to cook, and those words, repeated in every establishment whose door she pushed open that day, always met with more or less the same reception, a discreetly mocking surprise not at the words themselves but at the brash self-assurance of this young woman with the serious, stolid face, who was making not a request but a fair offer of her services, as if she were trying not to take undue advantage of the obvious fact that she was the ideal candidate, her face was perhaps only middlingly pleasant and attractive, bent as it was on not trying to charm, and her voice was blunt, plain, with something mechanical and efficient in her tone, her arms hung straight down her slightly stiff torso, her fists faintly clenched so her hands wouldn't quiver in their eagerness to get down to work.

She looked at people a little too straight on with her gentle, imperturbable brown eyes, eyes that expected nothing, hoped for nothing, were simply doing their job of looking, and when the "no" came they serenely turned away, neither disappointed nor pleading, and seemed to carry away with them nothing they'd seen.

Some who said no might have misread the very particular way she stood before them, dense, almost massive even though she wasn't, so perfectly contained in her solid flesh, her short muscles, that she sometimes seemed to stand there for longer than she did, her thick, heavy body refusing to hear that no and go away, her gaze as steady as ever, but that was an illusion, a misperception, the Cheffe turned around as soon as she heard there were no openings, her certainty that she would be hired never shaken, no weariness slumping her very straight back.

She walked the streets like that for two or three days, quietly obstinate, neither anxious nor bored, on the contrary, she never entered a dining room, whether crowded or dead, without a happy excitement shooting through her, heightened by the mingled aromas streaming from the plates when she came in at lunchtime.

She looked all around her as she waited to be dealt with, attentive, methodical, meticulous, she judged the look of a sauce, the presentation of a salad, she was severe, often disapproving, nothing seemed quite beautiful enough, nothing entirely thought-through.

The idea of the customer being used to such drab inadequacy, not seeing it, even believing that what he was brought conformed perfectly to what a beautiful plate was supposed to be, that idea simultaneously saddened and stimulated her, with the placid, neutral, almost distant self-confidence that was hers alone she told herself she'd work hard, when she ran a restaurant ("when I have a place of my own," she thought), to develop and refine the customer's tastes, to endow him with the capacity to judge the food more exactingly, whatever the consequences for the cook, but she knew her own pleasure in working would feed on that customer's high expectations, she already knew the complaisance of praise too easily given would leave her far more disgusted with herself than with the over-eager customer.

It was on Rue du Cancera that she finally found work, in a little restaurant that had opened not long before.

The owner had knocked around France and Belgium, making use of his pragmatic detachment, his dry, mirthless humour and his supercilious benevolence to manage various joints, as he put it, before he finally opened his own on Rue du Cancera, with the goal – proclaimed with a studied twinkle in his eye, a practised facetiousness – of taking it easy while others toiled to make him rich, those others consisting of a cook and two apprentices, the owner thinking it made him look good to imply they worked harder and better than he ever could, which wasn't true, the Cheffe soon realised, since he owed his restaurant's growing success as much to his own constant, alert, hospitable, professionally cheerful presence and energy as to the quality of the food, but he liked to think he was essentially an idler, he considered it more elegant.

One of his apprentices had just quit when the Cheffe walked through the door.

Seeing that slight, silhouetted figure appear from the sunlit street and then stand motionless amid the tables, its momentary stillness deceptively suggesting something sluggish and heavy and unsuited to hard work, his first impulse was to send her away with a polite, gentle, inflexible refusal, but he prudently reined in his impatience to be rid of that stranger he couldn't quite make out in the narrow-windowed dining room, and, his thoughts still full of the apprentice's sudden departure, he came forward, considering the navy-blue skirt, the pale blue blouse, the severe, neutral outfit that seemed to faithfully conform to the body that wore it and to precisely, forthrightly, seriously represent the character of the woman who'd chosen it, even if she didn't know it herself.

Then his eyes saw the Cheffe's eyes tranquilly, imperturbably looking back at him, and at once the brief misgiving he felt on seeing that silhouette almost riveted to the floor vanished, he saw the intensity, the initiative, the selflessness in that peaceful gaze, everything that gave freely of itself but never lost its self-possession – the very way the Cheffe's body completely occupied any space was itself a product of her self-possession, she never shrank, never scattered, wherever she happened to be.

Maybe the owner noticed that too, because he immediately forgot his plan to show her the door, and later he wouldn't remember he'd ever had it, he would always say he was determined to hire the Cheffe from the first words she uttered, when in reality he asked her to repeat those words, he was scarcely listening when they first issued from that very still, very intrusive backlit silhouette.

"Alright," he answered, hurriedly, as if he didn't want to give himself time to think, and also curtly, almost angrily, as if he were furious at himself for not giving himself time to think.

Once he'd said yes, and since there was no unsaying it now, he fell back into the affably impersonal tone he essentially never abandoned, the Cheffe said, you couldn't imagine him talking any other way, but neither could you imagine anyone talking like that in private, so you vaguely imagined him as a man who never left his restaurant and had neither family nor friends, no-one would have been surprised to hear he laid out a mattress in the dining room and spent his nights there, the one place he felt at home, the one place he could be himself, restaurant work being all he knew.

His name was Declaerk.

When I asked the Cheffe to describe him she closed her eyes, so many years had gone by, and her delicate face with its long closed eyelids took on a meditative look that brought a silly little laugh to my lips.

"You weren't in love with him, were you?" I said, immediately shocked at my boldness but rankled to see that the Cheffe didn't vigorously protest as she usually did when I said something foolish, she only shrugged, murmuring, "Really, he was twice my age," and there was nothing reassuring about that answer, it said nothing one way or the other, but there was something demoralising, because the Cheffe herself was twice my age, and I hoped she no longer saw that as a bar to a romantic relationship but especially to genuine love on the part of the younger one, before she loved me back I wanted her to believe in my love for her, believe it was real, even fated.

And so I answered, a little tartly, "That doesn't prove anything, you know," and the Cheffe gave me a noncommittal smile, the kind you give someone whose odd, uninteresting ideas you don't feel like discussing, her eyes still closed, her pink-tinged lids so smooth and so delicate I could see the mobile bulge of her eyeballs behind them, like two uncooked eggs, I thought she was luxuriating, almost drowsing in the possibly wistful remembrance of Declaerk's physical appearance, until her voice seemed to startle her awake when it spoke again, saying, "He could eat whatever he liked, he never gained weight."

Coming from the Cheffe, that remark had an odd moral connotation, as if Declaerk, along with a handful of others granted the same privilege, lived in a state prior to sin, and so went unpunished for excesses that others, less graced with innocence, paid dearly for.

The Cheffe looked on overfondness for food with the deepest indulgence, as she did all sorts of weaknesses or eccentricities, she never condemned them, and – depending on the person's age – either ignored or chided anyone who did, but at the same time she showed a fervent, naive respect not for those who ate very little but for those who by some miracle stayed thin, so she had questionable idols of her own.

I would never be one of them, I wasn't fat, but neither was I built to be thin, though that wasn't what bothered me about the Cheffe's uncritical wonderment: it was that I thought it gave a taint of condescension and disloyalty to her goodwill towards healthy eaters who put on weight, those who weren't quite fine enough to hang on to their youth, but I was probably making too much of it and no doubt I was simply jealous, that's my way, always jealous and never thin, and too sensitive, easily offended by everything that in one way or another drew the Cheffe's approval or respect, yes, I often made too much of things.

And so I remembered the mention of Declaerk's magical thinness better than the rest of her description, which nonetheless conjured up in my mind a caricature of a type from those days, a poseur with shaggy hair brushing his neck, a fine blonde moustache, tight jeans over excessively slender and definitely bowed legs that he must have thought attractive, narrow shoes a size too large, and shirts with long stiff collars that he ornamented with garish, hand-width ties, the Cheffe explained that he was bold enough to come to work in jeans but not so wild as to go tieless, to me the interest of that portrait lay in the idea it gave me of the Cheffe's tastes in men, because I couldn't help thinking that this Declaerk, even twenty years too old, clearly appealed to her, even if the Cheffe always quietly denied it, but with a half-heartedness that convinced me she was hoping I wouldn't believe her, hoping I would persuade her she'd been drawn to that guy as if she weren't sure she hadn't, as if she wanted that to be how it was and was waiting for me to prove it to her.

After a long internet search I recently found a photo of Declaerk standing behind the counter of his restaurant, taken to illustrate, among other things, one of the first articles on the Cheffe that appeared in the local press, the article called him the man who'd given her her start, and portrayed him so fulsomely that you might think she would never have become a cook had he not had the goodness to take on that ignorant, inexperienced young woman, I couldn't make out if he'd told the story that way or if the reporter had put that spin on what might have been his narrowly factual account, but at the same time it clearly came out, from certain expressions that could only have been his, that he never forgave the Cheffe's going into business for herself, he even hinted that she'd stolen some of his recipes, which amused me enormously, and which I found so sad that I felt a sort of compassionate, posthumous sympathy for this Declaerk, I couldn't decide if his professional bitterness hid a sentimental and sexual rancour or if he was sincere in his idiocy, if he genuinely thought he'd been robbed.

I studied his face with a magnifying glass for hours.

I didn't know just what I was hoping to see or learn, I was waiting for something about the Cheffe to be revealed, some side of her I had no way of knowing, just as I'd hungrily, feverishly studied her daughter's face when I met her, looking for something that I would never have, her undeniable, stupefying link to the Cheffe, the emotions of the Cheffe's that had been projected onto that face and were now held fast by it, however it hurt me to imagine that cunning, vulgar face containing emotions felt by the Cheffe, the purest and happiest as well as the ugliest, my own loving face was the guardian of no such treasures.

So, if the Cheffe once felt the desire to sleep with this Declaerk, I not very reasonably hoped I might, in that dull grey photo I hadn't zoomed in on to keep it as sharp as possible, detect or uncover some echo of that desire, its explanation, and also a paradigm of the Cheffe's erotic proclivities, and the answer to that mystery, the mystery of womankind and of her especially.

But I found nothing I could learn from, even dimly, I didn't feel changed or aquiver as I did every other time my investigations afforded me a sudden leap from ignorance to understanding.

Declaerk asked the Cheffe if she'd be willing to start that same evening and she accepted at once, adding that she'd rather not go home, rather spend the next few hours visiting the kitchen, learning all about the dishes they served, to which Declaerk smilingly replied that they weren't hiring her to cook but only to wash dishes and help with the prep work.

She said nothing, she consented with her whole unmoving, contained, amenable body, she gave that disconcerting impression of agreeing and obeying with all her being, her limbs and face perfectly still, even as she kept herself at a slight remove from docility, like a little donkey that lets the burden be placed on it but inside itself can't be forced into anything, from what I could tell that's just how her parents were, she didn't realise how like them she was.

Declaerk vaguely waved towards the kitchen, saying that Millard, the chef, would tell her everything she needed to know as soon as he came in, in the meantime she could certainly take a look around if she liked.

No sooner had he spoken those words than that passive body, that cumbersome body he'd earlier thought too lethargic, abruptly flitted away, whisking almost inaudibly over the floor, and by the time Declaerk had bestirred himself, walked around the counter and entered the kitchen behind her, the Cheffe was already exploring the cabinets with a discreet, almost hushed attention, she pointlessly slid her hands back and forth over the stainless steel countertop, almost caressing it, Declaerk would say in the interview, she seemed absurdly happy, though her face was serious, almost solemn, her hands trembling visibly.

The dour Declaerk of the article seems to be trying to make the Cheffe's emotion faintly ridiculous, even as he paternalistically preens himself on having allowed her that joy, but I'm sure he found nothing to smirk at as he wordlessly watched her test the edge of a knife against her thumb, stroke the butcher block with her hungry palm, methodically pace from one corner of the kitchen to the other on her quick, silent feet, her heart soaring but restrained, deliberately held in check so it wouldn't reveal itself so soon and so entirely to the man watching her in silence, though she didn't even seem to see he was there, or to care, not for a moment did Declaerk think of laughing at her.

At the very most, he quietly thought she was strange, but that didn't bother him, he'd been around, he'd come across specimens weirder than this.

Wanting to say something, and perhaps prompted by the shadow of an apprehension, he repeated with a chuckle that he wasn't hiring her to cook, for that he had Millard, who was excellent, she had only to do exactly what Millard told her, and the Cheffe, smiling for the first time since she had opened the restaurant door, patiently nodded, reassuring and distant, disciplined, unreadable.

She asked if he'd mind describing the menu.

A little taken aback, he handed her the big, stiff sheet, and she sat down on a chair and laid it on the table without looking at it, her eyes serenely fixed on Declaerk, waiting for him to come and read the names of the dishes, not that she couldn't have done it herself, if she concentrated she could grasp the meaning of what she deciphered, but she wanted to hear the words from the mouth of someone who knew what they stood for, in whose mind the precise image of each dish appeared as soon as the name was spoken, she thought that by probing him on what he was seeing she could construct a schematic reflection of that image in her own mind, and then she would enter Millard's kitchen fully briefed, and she'd feel at home from the start.

At the same time, she knew she took such a deep pleasure in listening to the language of cooking that she furrowed her brow and hardened the bow of her mouth so Declaerk wouldn't see it, wouldn't know it, in the article he would say, no doubt stupidly thinking he was taking her down a peg, that she was illiterate, that she had common sense and intuition but no intellect, and neither would he know that the Cheffe would take no offence when she read those words, would in fact be mischievously delighted that a description so far from the truth would protect her against any irrefutable claim to know who she was.

I knew the Cheffe better than anyone.

But she sometimes misled me, she didn't lie but she didn't correct me when I misunderstood her, and what right would I have to complain that she wasn't always sincere, she didn't owe me anything, you never owe anything to people who want to know your secrets, even out of love, and she wasn't quite sure of me even if she'd placed a considerable part of her trust in me, she didn't think love was any guarantee of decency, and even if today I'm trying to treat her as honourably as I can, that's most assuredly not what she thought of as decency, and I know it.

What an idiot that Declaerk was, I told myself when I first read that article, I laughed to find him so stupid, that popinjay the Cheffe might have sexually desired, but I realised he wasn't saying what he really thought of the Cheffe, he was only trying to taunt her, to hurt her and belittle her, in his bitterness towards that woman who'd left him and outstripped him in every way, richer and better known than he ever was, so was he really as stupid as he seemed, I wouldn't dare say he was, the only thing that's certain is his resentment, that and another sort of pain, set off by the memory of the Cheffe, but I don't know enough to understand what it is.

He stood behind the Cheffe and read the name of the first starter, and was about to go on when she broke in, wanting to hear more about those crab croquettes in hollandaise sauce, and when he didn't understand she added that she'd like an idea of their appearance, and how many on the plate, and of course what was in them, but on that last point Declaerk knew next to nothing, for which the Cheffe mentally faulted him.

She often told me it was a conscientious restaurateur's duty to know every ingredient in a dish, it wasn't enough to taste and to judge, you had to be able to answer the customer's most unlikely questions with precision, and for that you had to know every bit as much as the cook.

He told her what little he knew, that it was crab meat with some sort of binding agent, breaded and fried and served with a sauce that was, well, what we call a hollandaise, he couldn't think what more there was to say, so he went on to croustade Ile-de-France, ham charlotte, gratinéed asparagus, shellfish vol-au-vents, quickly and tersely so the Cheffe wouldn't ask questions, which she was no longer tempted to do, realising he didn't have what it would take to fill her with the rich, limpid visions that would fertilise her imagination, and so she simply listened, eyes wide open so he couldn't suspect she'd rather have them half-closed, monkfish-liver terrine, wild boar à la Bordelaise, leg of lamb Cabrières, fillet of veal Riviera, how she loved that language! – it was almost painful, as if Declaerk's voice were pressing too insistently on a very subtly receptive spot of her brain.

When Declaerk was done, the Cheffe had the feeling he was faintly embarrassed, was vaguely wondering if such a situation, him bent over this mysterious stranger and reading to her over her shoulder, might make him seem ridiculous, he stood up straight, cold and brusque, curtly told her he'd take her on a trial basis, and that sudden severity reassured her, she felt at home with plainness and austerity and didn't want to feel his unease for one moment longer.

For my part, when she was near, I always worked to rein in my emotions, my tendency to underscore perfectly intelligible sentences with dramatic faces or broad gestures, and above all I tried to be sure, often in vain, that my skin, my scent, the invisible emanations of my being didn't confront the Cheffe with a moist, warm wave of emotions she had no time for, and I was sorry I wasn't naturally and effortlessly tightlipped, puritanical and radiant, yes, I regretted that even as I consoled myself with the thought that what seeped out wasn't the worst part of me.

In Millard's kitchen the Cheffe found herself faced with a thing she despised, she discovered that she despised it, because she'd never been exposed to such an environment, neither in Sainte-Bazeille nor at the Clapeaus', where a certain gentility of tone and manner always reigned.

That thing was the obligation, as she worked with Millard, to endure an unending chatter, inelegant, sniggering and slimy, as much from Millard as from the apprentice, a skinny, giggling, obsequious boy, which in the early days so tortured the

Cheffe's ears that it made her dizzy, her head relentlessly spinning and buzzing.

About the same age as Declaerk, Millard looked at the world around him with a gaze at once indignant and waggish, given voice all day long by a directionless string of double-entendre complaints and imprecations, without which, said Millard, he would suffocate, he would go off and hang himself, so it had to come out, whatever he thought about absolutely anything, no matter how moronic, he went on to say proudly, he had to throw it out for the judgment of his fellows, which is to say the apprentice, who served as a chorus with his interminable tittering, and the withdrawn old waiter, and, when he visited the kitchen, Declaerk, who didn't even pretend to listen and felt no obligation to answer, and the Cheffe, whose pained silence spurred on rather than quelled Millard's eloquence, so she took to murmuring an occasional *hmm*, which didn't encourage him but didn't offend him, she was ashamed for them and herself, she kept her head down, focused on her work, blank, dismayed, she was ashamed and didn't quite see why.

She grew to hate Millard's vitriolic reflections on the state of the world, on French politics, on the Bordeaux city government, so much so that she started to fear them, alarmed at the force of her hatred, realising she didn't know much about anything he was talking about and nonetheless sensing that she had to fight off Millard's influence, that there was something ugly in the way he furiously mocked everyone on all sides, the way he delighted in the ugliness or illness of an elected official, of a customer, the way he howled in malignant joy at the bankruptcy of another restaurant, and Millard seemed to her fearsome and very small, monstrously powerful in her life and tiny outside his kitchen, and that disparity worried her, shook her, wasn't that a sign of her own weakness, her own insignificance? That she was so disturbed by Millard, that she hated and feared him and so let herself be distracted from the undivided emotions she wanted to feel for cooking?

It became so bad that her ear was almost relieved when it heard him launch into one of his favourite routines: vile remarks aimed at her.

She could tell they were coming from the way he theatrically turned his back to her and sidled towards the apprentice, whereupon, in a voice loud enough for her to hear but pretending to be a whisper, he threw out a preliminary joke about women in general, followed by observations on the presumption of women who had the gall to work in a kitchen, and beneath the boorishness and impertinence the Cheffe glimpsed something serious, upset, sincerely aggrieved, which in a way reassured her, as did the very care Millard took to disguise his genuine distress beneath that clownish insolence.

She understood him then, she stopped fearing him, and she hated him less.

Disturbed by the prospect of women entering his profession, the potential of their alien, abstruse, humourless ways hampering the carefree exchange of manly banter and confidences, he thought he had to say so out loud, and had also to hide his real anxiety, he wanted to be only obscene and irreverent and unintimidated by anything, and so he joked even more disagreeably, in a mean, bloodthirsty, all-consuming need to make his opinion known to the world without coming off as a man whose cocksureness could be shaken by that very thing, and the Cheffe wasn't far from recognising, in that obsession, a tenacity not unlike her own, Millard's provocations stopped bothering her.

When I asked, not entirely convinced, if she didn't find it intolerable all the same, hearing him call her "the gash" or address her as "chicky" or "babe", she answered with an apathetic shrug, saying that to her that was more or less the natural order of things, an acceptable price to pay for her admission to Declaerk's, where she did, after all, learn the ins and outs of her trade.

I put that detachment down to the Cheffe's usual refusal to feel sorry for herself, which sometimes led her to sugarcoat the truth of things, or remember them less precisely than I demanded, but I managed to locate the apprentice who worked in Millard's kitchen back then, I went to see the old man in his retirement home in Toulouse.

We had a cup of coffee in the dining hall and I must admit it moved me to lay my eyes on the long, bony face of that man who'd known the twenty-year-old Cheffe, the Cheffe I've never seen a picture of, the Cheffe no-one has ever been able to describe for me with the kind of detail that makes a portrait useful and true, not even her sister Ingrid, she couldn't remember anything of any importance, nothing I hadn't already imagined.

I began by asking the apprentice what the Cheffe looked like, I wasn't prepared for what he immediately named as the most memorable thing about that young woman, and although I didn't doubt his word I put on a sceptical air to give myself time to take it in.

The Cheffe, he told me in his profoundly indifferent old-man voice, had eczema all over the back of her neck, or more precisely red, rough patches he assumed to be eczema, and evidently they itched, because when she occasionally left her post in the course of a day he'd noticed she would head not for the bathroom but out to the courtyard the kitchen gave onto, where she took off the scarf she always wore and vigorously rubbed or patted her neck, clearly not letting herself scratch so she wouldn't inflame the lesions or make them bleed.

When I asked how he could have known what the Cheffe was doing in the courtyard, my feebly dubious tone trying in vain to shake his blasé, vaguely bored certainty (he didn't care if I believed him or not), he answered that from March onwards the door to the courtyard was almost always left open, because the narrow, low-ceilinged kitchen was stiflingly hot, and since the courtyard wasn't large either it wasn't hard to see what went on there.

He didn't think anyone ever had mentioned it in front of the Cheffe, no, but he and Millard sometimes talked about it with sneering disgust, pretending to be afraid she had leprosy, deep down they pitied her a little, because they couldn't imagine even the ugliest, loneliest man ever wanting to touch that scaly skin, they imagined her rejected, humiliated, they weren't without feeling, they pitied her a little, even if they didn't much like her.

Why not?

Oh, he didn't really know, no particular reason, but it annoyed them having a woman in the kitchen, they sort of held that against her, and besides she had no taste for jokes, she never smiled, and he, the apprentice, didn't care for stand-offish girls when they weren't beautiful, only the pretty ones had the right to be aloof.

And in what way, I then asked, with an emotion I'd stopped trying to hide, was she not beautiful?

He stiffly spread his bony old arms and sighed, his way of saying he had nothing more to tell me, and in any case he was tired of all this, so I left him a little brusquely, I couldn't decide if I was shaken by what he'd told me, something I never suspected and came within a hair's breadth of never knowing, or if it was above all his dull, closed-off disinterest that got to me, *just as I'm irritated sometimes — not often, fortunately — to my own surprise and my sharp displeasure, at my Lloret de Mar friends' complacent incuriosity, even though that's the very foundation of my pleasure at being with them, I would never have tried to work my way into their little circle if I suspected they'd ask about my old life, and consequently about the Cheffe. Happily, those fits of pique soon subside, calmed by a drink or two, alcohol keeps me quiet and friendly and strengthens my very grateful affection for Antoine, Jean-Pierre, Virginie, my Lloret de Mar friends who don't care who I am outside Lloret de Mar any more than I care about them, like children we don't even know or bother to remember each other's last names.*

What I concluded from the apprentice's account was that the Cheffe must have had a case of psoriasis severe enough for the itching to often force her outside, however briefly, but knowing that the Cheffe hated leaving her work, and that furthermore she must have wanted at all costs to give Millard and Declaerk the highest possible opinion of her conscientiousness and devotion, I thought her suffering must have been far worse than they assumed from those occasional retreats to the courtyard, that she could only bring herself to walk away when the burning became too much to bear.

I wasn't surprised she never spoke of that to me.

But I was surprised – no, more than surprised, deeply disappointed and angry with myself – that beneath the Cheffe's stories I'd failed to detect a possible secret of a very different sort from the ones I'd imagined, like her physical desire for Declaerk or her probable marital history with the Clapeaus' gardener, and I kicked myself, with the torment of a thing come too late, for my lack of attention and sensitivity, and I found no consolation in the unlikely hypothesis that no word, no expression on the Cheffe's face, in the hard white glow of the newly cleaned kitchen's fluorescent lights, had ever revealed a trace of the illness that must have poisoned her existence, that thought didn't console me, I didn't believe it.

No doubt vaguely urged on by a magical hope of curing the Cheffe across the divide of the years, or at least of imaginarily spreading a balm of tenderness over her ravaged skin, I set out to learn all I could about psoriasis, I consulted dermatologists for a full description of its characteristics and origins, *a habit now so thoroughly ingrained that I questioned Bertrand or Bernard when I heard him tell a hospital joke while we were picnicking* on Santa Cristina beach, even though I never ask anyone anything in Lloret de Mar, he admitted he used to be a doctor, and I couldn't help pushing him to tell me all he knew about psoriasis, I pay my debt to the Cheffe by convincing myself that today I would know how to care for her, soothe her, I gently touch my lips to her poor inflamed neck. I almost asked Bernard or Bertrand, "Do you think, knowing what I now know, I could have helped the Cheffe if I'd been with her when she was twenty and had that terrible disease?" I almost asked him, "Do you think I could change a past I had no part of, do you think I could make the Cheffe never have been stricken by psoriasis? Suppose in my thoughts I pressed my loving lips to her burning skin: could that help?"

And I obviously looked into the ailment's psychological causes, I was tempted to connect it with what the Cheffe told me of the hardships she faced trying to keep her daughter beside her, or at least what I could worm out of her, the Cheffe clearly having little wish to remember that painful side of a time – her apprenticeship at Declaerk's – that in other ways exhilarated her, a time she was always happy to hold forth about, on the subject of cooking and cooking alone, she wanted to remember only what went on within the walls of the restaurant, and nothing that happened outside.

But hadn't she brought her complicated outside life into Millard's kitchen all the same, in the eloquent, humiliating, stinging form of a skin attacked by an illness that disgusted the others?

As soon as the Cheffe saw that her work was acceptable and she'd be staying on at Declaerk's, she went off to bring her daughter back from Sainte-Bazeille. The child might have been one year old.

The Cheffe didn't quite know how she was going to manage, she only knew she had to take back her daughter as she'd vowed, but without weakening in her resolve to advance quickly in her work, she was so anxious to make those two obligations fit together that she raced to Sainte-Bazeille to stop herself, I imagine, from wondering if she wouldn't do better to leave the child where she was, as I said she felt guilty.

She brought the little girl back to the hotel where she was still living, then the next morning took her across the street to a neighbour's, a woman raising two or three children alone, who'd agreed to mind the Cheffe's daughter while she was at work.

And the Cheffe worked late into the night, and then she was with the child when she went home, and then she took her to the neighbour's the next day, and so on for several weeks, no-one at Declaerk's knew she had a child and she meant to keep it that way.

With all that arranged, what stopped working for her, why did she take the child back to Sainte-Bazeille before the end of the year? That was my question when she very matter-of-factly told me the story, knowing this wasn't the first I'd heard of it, since by then the daughter had begun speaking out, airing her grievances, her litany of recriminations against the Cheffe, particularly the vicious, recurring accusation that the Cheffe couldn't stand having her around once she got her first job.

The truth, she told me, was that she soon learned the neighbour was a woman of low morals and bad hygiene, and the Cheffe feared for her daughter's health as well as her language, so she had no choice but to take her back to her grandparents, however hard she found it to admit that she'd failed.

And, brushing the air before her away with an irritable little flick of the wrist, she exclaimed, "I didn't even know there were such things!" when I expressed my surprise that she hadn't tried to find daycare for her daughter, or another neighbour to mind her, and I let the matter drop there, pleased, secretly convinced that she'd realised she couldn't devote her every thought, her every moment, every moment of her thought to cooking while at the same time tending, in a tiny hotel room, to a child just learning to walk and talk, and so she'd resigned herself to the only choice possible and took her back to Sainte-Bazeille, where her grandparents looked after her properly, as they did everything, I was convinced and pleased, I didn't know about the psoriasis.

But surely I wasn't wrong to suspect that the Cheffe couldn't bear the child's babbling or wails invading her thoughts, couldn't endure the terrible impossibility of reflection that came with a baby's presence in a cramped space, or that she was afraid the stupor of Marmande might fall over her again, from which Sainte-Bazeille was supposed to protect her and the child alike, she didn't say anything about it, there was no need.

If the Cheffe wanted only to learn her trade at Declaerk's, make a start in her career like the tittering apprentice, then she could have done her job and looked after the child at the same time, but she had another goal, not just higher but of an entirely different order, and when night came she desperately needed a solitude with a silent heart, a place to commune with the thing that had recruited her, the thing that had summoned her.

But I was wrong to think that the Cheffe had retrospectively inflated her sadness and shame at having to part with the child again, yes, I was wrong to think she'd artificially reconstituted that grief from what she'd seen in her grown daughter, the vain disaster her daughter had become, because I didn't know about the psoriasis and I'd pictured a far more unflappable, independent, and resolved twenty-year-old Cheffe, who loved the child as much as she could, to be sure, who loved no-one more, but who was also capable of forgetting the child the moment she found herself in Millard's kitchen.

Maybe she was, but her uneasy conscience was not, and even in the hottest days of the year the Cheffe hid the back of her neck with a scarf, how could I not have known about the psoriasis?

The Cheffe had been dead for two years when I met the aged apprentice in his care home, where with a lingering trace of cool, objective revulsion he described that young co-worker he didn't find beautiful frantically rubbing her neck in the courtyard, the Cheffe was dead and that unpleasant old man wasn't, and I'd missed the chance to show the Cheffe my sadness, my boundless sympathy for what she'd gone through back then, standing behind her I would have stroked the back of her neck and perhaps, beneath my fingers, made out something still faintly rough, and the Cheffe would have felt my compassion, how could I not have known?

I still can't forgive myself.

My Lloret de Mar friends want to cook an elaborate dinner to celebrate my daughter's visit, they don't think I could manage it myself, they only see me buying little ready-to-eat dishes at the Lloret de Mar supermarket. Their thoughtfulness, the fondness they seem to feel for me, a fondness far deeper than I'd imagined, deeper than I could ever reciprocate, touches me more than I'd like to be touched by anything in Lloret de Mar. They asked what sort of food my daughter liked and I couldn't tell them, I felt a moment of panic and irritation. I wish everything could be the way it used to be in Lloret de Mar, I pray for something to stop my daughter from coming, nothing serious of course, something to make her change her plans, but with that reckless prayer am I not running the risk of bringing misfortune down on her innocent young head?

Little by little, seeing Millard at work day after day, the Cheffe came to feel a solid respect for that man she so little respected in every other way.

She who had never separated talent from goodness, she who saw an indisputable link between the Marmande cook's small heart and her stunted abilities (was she afraid she herself might end up only an insignificant cook if her love for her daughter wasn't great?), she was troubled to see that in Millard an inventive, resourceful talent coexisted harmoniously with a blinkered, trivial, vacuous personality, neither in any way affecting the other, the two of them together producing a Millard who was very happy to be alive, sure of his worth as a cook but blind to his failings, a first-rate professional and a detestable person.

His worthiness never faltered when he went to work on a dish, and he took a strangely humble pleasure in the customers' praise passed on by the waiter, as if he'd never expected even so simple a reward as a compliment for his labours, his ambition always to do the best that can be done.

His cooking duly conformed to the practices and tastes of the time, but he added a personal, aesthetic touch to the classic recipe of, say, pike *quenelles* in Nantua sauce, snipping a few sprigs of flat-leaf parsley into the pink béchamel, casually observing, in a tone that tried to sound self-mocking, that there was too much pink in that sauce, it needed a fresh colour for contrast, but he approached his work with great seriousness, and generally strove, without seeming to meddle with it at all, to lighten – if only for the eye – the floury thickness of a roux or the layer of fat floating atop a broth, he used all the green parts of the vegetables, he never said anything of it, he wasn't comfortable explaining his instincts.

And with a surprise that never faded, the Cheffe saw that man's lips spewing words and sentences of inexhaustible idiocy, full of an ill-will that rarely rested, even as Millard's sure hands obeyed the ingenious instructions of a mind unhobbled by idiocy or ill-will.

How could it be, the Cheffe wondered back then, and was in a way still wondering when she told me about it thirty years later, that Millard's ugly soul never got in the way of his hands' diligent labours, or that those hands didn't flounder helplessly on the counter, unhappy or embarrassed to find themselves guided by so hateful a mind?

For her part, the Cheffe feared that any failing in the conduct of her life, any lazy habit of mean-spirited thoughts, would cost her forever the favour that had been granted her, she kept a close watch on herself, tried not to let herself get away with anything.

Because Millard had the greatest respect for his craft, he always spoke politely and precisely to the Cheffe when he assigned her a job.

Thanks to that same seriousness, he soon saw that the girl was quick and capable, talented, already proficient in many tasks, and although every day he reflexively called for the girl to be replaced by an apprentice of the other sex, although each morning he viscerally longed not to see her walk into his kitchen, he never let those emotions interfere with the scrupulous, loyal idea of her held by the professional inside him, who soon stopped limiting her to prep work and entrusted her with jobs requiring what he called a good hand.

He discovered that what she didn't already know how to do perfectly – puff pastry, meat glaze, a delicately stuffed fish – she learned the first time he showed her, and every term he used she remembered, but she lay low all the same, out of prudence, strategy and discretion, pretending she had no ideas of her own, taking great care not to get a fat head, as Millard was quick to say of anyone who expressed an opinion in his presence.

I've had the outlandish idea of renting an apartment in Rosamar and telling my daughter that's where I live, she'd never see Lloret de Mar or my friends, the two weeks of her visit would quickly go by, I'd never take her to Santa Cristina beach or any of my Lloret de Mar friends' other meeting places. I'd tell them my daughter ended up cancelling her visit, they'd soon forget the whole thing, they'd forget I have a daughter at all. That thought cheered me up, suddenly it all seemed so simple.

Hearing Millard's approving if gruff and laconic reports on the Cheffe's work, Declaerk raised her salary. In the article, he would use that elegant gesture as a pretext to denounce what he insisted on seeing as his employee's disloyalty, insinuating that the Cheffe was an ungrateful girl, even trumpeting the kindly things she always said of him or Millard as proof that she couldn't be trusted, why did she leave if she was so happy there?

That article's readers must have clearly seen that Declaerk simply refused to accept that the Cheffe had earned her independence, and hadn't been prodded into it by some disenchantment, he thought he was protecting her, he said, when all along he was only preparing her to walk out on him.

The Cheffe must have known Declaerk had spoken ill of her, but I never once heard her criticise him, never heard one sharp or ironic word about that man who so vaingloriously exaggerated his role in her education, who gave the ridiculous impression that out of pure fineness of spirit he'd taken on a completely lost girl and for all her many failings helped her along, she understood even his bitterness, she was sorry to see him show himself to be so vulnerable, so needlessly hurt, she would have taken his side against any attack, no matter how justified.

For him, for the smallness and spite he revealed in that article, she felt the indestructible forgiveness you might feel for your indigent parents stewing in their resentment as the wave of a success they can't understand sweeps you far, far away over a silvery sea, and a stupid jealousy whose spur I wasn't too proud to obey made me suspect that a lingering carnal attraction, the nostalgic memory of a special desire for that man and his trim body, lay behind an indulgence that might have been simply a sort of filial attachment.

Yes, I was jealous, I couldn't imagine the Cheffe being so faithful to me, it was stupid (I was jealous of the saintly slimness of a man like Declaerk!).

He never got over the Cheffe's announcement, after eighteen months with him, that she'd found a place to rent, a long-closed old bistro, far from Declaerk's.

She wanted to open a restaurant of her own, she gave Declaerk fair notice, several months in advance, she innocently hoped for his approval and encouragement, even his advice, and possibly a loan, she told me, laughing at that very young woman's naive effrontery.

She was surprised by Declaerk's stony-faced reaction. He said nothing more of it for several days, then informed her he'd found a replacement and he never wanted to see her again, never hear another word about her, she could file a complaint if she dared.

Coming from him, that was little short of a curse on the

Cheffe, and I like to think it came back to bite him far harder than she had any right to wish, she obeyed his furious command and never again turned to him in any way, but he heard about her, oh how he heard about her, with a stinging pain it gives me some pleasure to imagine, though the thought of it inspired only sadness in the Cheffe.

She long hoped to see him walk into her restaurant as she'd walked into his decades before, not looking for work of course, but to show her he'd forgiven her and all his anger had faded, and then the Cheffe would forget she'd done nothing she wanted forgiveness for, she would be infinitely relieved, at peace, she would gratefully welcome his pardon, as if she were guilty of something, thinking there was a cause even higher than justice, the cause of reconciliation.

But Declaerk never appeared in the Cheffe's restaurant, and if he agreed to answer a journalist's questions on his one-time employee, a request that must only have stoked his resentment, it was probably because he hoped to discredit her, he didn't understand, he refused to understand, that she was awaiting him with a magnanimous heart, a wide-open heart, she would have laid all her weapons at his feet before he'd spoken a word, even if she was unmistakably the stronger of the two.

I didn't like to see her relinquish the authority that was rightly hers, sacrifice her legitimate self-regard for the sake of Declaerk's misplaced pride, I saw in it something feminine that should never have been, that eagerness to make peace at any price with someone who had no idea of the good fortune granted him, the grace bestowed on him, but when I said so the Cheffe only chuckled and answered, "I felt sort of bad for him, you know," and I told her I couldn't accept her feeling the tiniest bit bad for a man whose emotions towards her were envious and ignoble, I told her it was precisely the excessive indulgence of women like her that encouraged the shameless misbehaviour of men such as him, and the Cheffe didn't answer, which I think was her way of telling me I was right but so was she, for reasons I couldn't understand.

And it's true, I still don't know if the Cheffe sympathised with Declaerk because there'd once been vaguely something between them and she'd backed out and angered him, or because, more generally, she felt sorry for envious people, because she felt guilty for being the object of such an emotion even if she'd done nothing to cause it, that's how she was, horrified at the thought of very unintentionally engendering something hurtful, of ugliness spreading by way of her.

And so the Cheffe was shown the door at Declaerk's in a brutal, humiliating way whose force she nonetheless felt only fleetingly, only glancingly, bent as she was on seeing her project through, she no sooner found herself in the street than she was already sailing far away from Millard and Declaerk in her thoughts, and the memory of her firing was already fading, like a trivial incident in the course already plotted out for her, the faint sketch of a destiny she could see with her imagination's wide-open eyes.

She hurried to the rental agency for the space she had in mind, toured the premises, very excited to find them much as she'd hoped when she peered through the wide corner windows, it was a busy intersection, not far from Place de la Bourse.

Inside she found a dining room measuring all of forty square metres, a kitchen of fifteen, and lavatories in need of repair.

Yes, the same restaurant as now, the Cheffe later bought the two adjoining shops and expanded, but she never moved.

The floor was laid with those beautiful terracotta tiles you've seen, with a green cloverleaf motif on a pale blue background. The bankrupt bistro's furniture stayed: dark oak tables, straw-seated chairs, and in the kitchen all the requisite butcher blocks, sideboards, cabinets, baking dishes and casseroles, everything but dishes, glasses and silverware.

The Cheffe told them she'd take it, begged for a little time, took the train to Marmande and rang at the Clapeaus' door.

They weren't surprised to see her, she told me, in fact they seemed to be expecting her, which I saw as a luminously clear sign that she'd recaptured the silent, commanding hold she once had on them, that her power to provide what was for them the highest of all pleasures once again radiated from her to the receptive Clapeaus, who, I thought, surely hadn't known she was coming, no, but on seeing the Cheffe at their door found themselves struck by a certainty – that it was inevitable this girl would come back into their lives, that their lives couldn't be overturned and remade as they were after the Landes without the author of that transformation regularly, ritually reappearing, because chance had no hand in all this, the Clapeaus must have told themselves day after day, missing the Cheffe without grief, calmly, grateful for what had been given them, knowing they hadn't seen the last of it, living in a patient, wistful state of suspension, enduring it.

A half-hour later, when the Cheffe took her leave, she was carrying a generous cheque.

She'd scarcely spoken a word, and neither had they. From the first moment they understood what she needed, just as she understood, thanking them, that they didn't want to be thanked, that the very thought of it horrified them, they were visibly squirming and it wasn't an act, so the Cheffe held her tongue, tucked the cheque into her little purse and immediately bade them goodbye, not for a moment thinking to make some semblance of small talk, neither she nor the Clapeaus.

She would soon repay that debt, and although the Clapeaus were opposed, although they'd even written to her several times urging her to stop sending cheques that they never cashed anyway, she would insistently go on making those payments, knowing full well that the Clapeaus believed with a sort of terror that they weren't on an equal footing with her, that she owed them nothing, that by taking from her even something as uncompromising as a repayment cheque they were sullying their passion, not living up to their idea of themselves, subtly taking a dangerous risk – but for the Cheffe that was the Clapeaus' concern, their very honourable obsession, while hers was owing nothing to anyone.

And so she signed a lease for the restaurant as well as the shabby little apartment above it, paid several months' rent in advance, bought table linen, china, silverware and stemmed glasses, along with a simple mattress that for years would be her only furniture, she'd keep her clothes stacked on pallets, her own comfort didn't interest her.

When I later grew close enough to the Cheffe that I dared stop by in the winter for a visit, I found that, although her apartment was no longer fitted out with only a mattress, she seemed to have filled it with things in obedience to a societal obligation whose codes she didn't quite understand, taking so little interest in them, and caring so little about the opinion of the few people she allowed in, principally friends of her daughter's, when she was living with her.

For example, I was amused to see that the Cheffe had crammed two armoires of two different styles and two sorts of wood side by side in the entryway, or that she'd laid down a thin Oriental carpet just next to a geometric contemporary rug of rough wool, and I also observed that the Cheffe moved through the apartment in a furtive, tentative, very slightly vexed way, as if on waking from a dream she'd found herself just where she hadn't wanted to go, a place she furthermore didn't know very well.

Once she'd bought everything she needed, she had a sign painted in red letters against a cream background, with a *trompe-l'œil* effect so that the letters seemed to have been cut thick and then glued to the wood. As you know, she called her restaurant La Bonne Heure.

I rent a car for the day and drive to Rosamar to reserve an apartment I'll tell my daughter is mine, and here I am walking the streets of Rosamar, so like the streets of Lloret de Mar that at any moment I expect to run into Jean-Claude or Jean-Luc or Marie-Christine or

Nathalie out doing their high-priced, sophisticated shopping in the best grocery stores, but no, I'm in Rosamar, where I don't know anyone and no-one knows me, which is why I could conceivably have my daughter visit me here, but now I don't want to, my head is spinning in despair, my legs go weak, and I drop onto a chair on the terrace of a café exactly like my usual in Lloret de Mar. I don't see how I'm ever going to get through this. Suddenly the sun is my enemy and the sky seems too big, I miss Bordeaux in the winter, the dark, high-walled streets of my childhood and the cottony silence, the sounds imprisoned by the fog over the grey, veiled Garonne, in Rosamar as in Lloret de Mar the weightless light gratingly amplifies every metallic clank, every idiotic cry of joy in those places devoted to the pleasures of people like me, how will I ever get through this, get through what exactly, where's the danger, what could my daughter do or say that I feel so incapable of enduring?

When the Cheffe was asked how she'd settled on that name for her restaurant, she always found some way not to answer, something like, "Well, it's the perfect name, don't you think?"

And it was indeed one of the best restaurant names you could possibly come up with, cheerful, simple, easy to remember, but the Cheffe had chosen it long before, back when she was working at the Clapeaus', thinking of a memory she cherished even if it sometimes clenched her throat with an indefinable sorrow.

Because when she was a child scarcely a day went by that she didn't hear her mother merrily proclaim "*A la bonne heure!*" for one reason or another, whether she was happy to see her daughter home from school or rejoicing at the promise of a well-paid job or glad of a light breeze that cooled a hot day, any occasion at all that wasn't overtly unpleasant and could thus easily become the source of a sort of happy gratitude, the very root of the pleasure of being alive for the Cheffe's parents, her mother let that expression spring from her lips, never mechanically, but rather like something risen up from the most open, most sincere part of her sincere, open heart.

When the Cheffe told me the secret of that name, she also told me she'd revealed it to her daughter a few years before, and since in all the interviews that woman very freely gave before and after the Cheffe's death I never once saw her bring up the story of La Bonne Heure, I think it's safe to assume she was deliberately keeping it quiet so as not to portray her mother as a sensitive, even sentimental woman, she wanted to convince the whole world that hard and calculating was all the Cheffe could ever be.

She tells any journalist who asks that she has no idea where the name comes from, her mother must have stumbled on it by chance, which is of course meaningless and to my mind perfectly expresses the very special nastiness of that woman who should have realised that by revealing the name's sense she would be paying homage less to her mother than to her grandmother in Sainte-Bazeille, with whom she'd spent her first years, whom she'd loved more than anyone, said the Cheffe, but how does a creature as self-centred as her feel love, that's what I can't help but wonder.

Once she'd scrubbed down the dining-room walls, the Cheffe decided she'd leave them painted that bold royal blue, with a dark woodwork she generously waxed, and that undersea atmosphere, muffled and reflective, where every move seems to take place more slowly and more serenely than outside, went against the reds and golds that still prevailed at the time, it was a daring decision, and by way of a very yellow lighting the Cheffe sought to erase the feeling of coldness that might come from those blue walls' subaquatic solemnity, it was a daring decision, the Cheffe made it all on her own, like everything else she did, and she never regretted it.

The walls at La Bonne Heure are still blue today, and I've often thought that the generally decorous behaviour of that restaurant's customers, their propriety, their tendency to keep their voices low even as they feel marvellously at ease and never watched over by a censorious staff, still come from that blue, imbued with its own solitude and gentle austerity even before it was imbued with the Cheffe's uncompromising cuisine or the reserved ambience she imposed by her mere presence, visible or hidden.

It seems people always say this sort of thing to build up a legend, always the same, no matter the endeavour in question, but it's an understatement to say that the early days of La Bonne Heure were hard.

"I never thought it was going to be easy," the Cheffe would say, dismissing that subject and the emotions she felt in those very difficult beginnings.

She opened La Bonne Heure on April 3, 1973, with a menu she'd had printed on sky-blue paper.

On that menu were crayfish pie, lamb's-brain fritters with

anchovy sauce, veal *quenelles*, baked tuna, lavender-honey-glazed roast beef, the peach tart from the Landes, a vanilla parfait topped with coffee syrup, and, although she was planning to hire someone for the dining room as soon as she could, she wasn't afraid to greet the customers herself and wait at the six tables, at lunch and at dinner.

The first week she had only a handful of customers, who left very happy, she modestly told me, and their numbers didn't grow as the weeks went by, nothing guaranteed that she was going to make it.

She closed only for Thursday lunch, she got up at five every morning, washed the table linen in her apartment's bathtub, then went off to the Marché des Capucins, pushing a little cart, caught up, she told me, in a relentless, even furious rapture that almost erased any sensation of tiredness, that gave that sensation no chance to awaken, that made her look on the need for rest with a boredom not far from anguish, though she slept well, she sank into a narrow, cool grave and never turned over or moved or dreamt, climbing out the next morning feeling like the events of the day before were long past, that her life was just then beginning, untouched by care, that La Bonne Heure was going to open for the first time that noon.

It might have been the same unrelenting, imperious fever that swept her off to Sainte-Bazeille one Thursday at dawn, she was a galloping horse with no bridle, fiercely confident in her instinct, she ran to Sainte-Bazeille, ran into her parents' house, came out still running, unhearing, unreasoning, burningly sure of herself, carrying her soon-to-be three-year-old daughter.

If she chose to come for her daughter just when looking after the child would most complicate her life, if she chose that very moment to take her back once and for all, as she announced to her parents, I believe that was a deliberate escalation of her struggle, an example of the furious but completely optimistic go-for-broke spirit she had back then, secretly convinced that she had to risk total disaster, as a mother, a cook and a restaurateur, or give herself the chance to succeed brilliantly at all three, but in any case she couldn't undertake the adventure of the restaurant without incorporating her daughter's care into it, she'd never rejoice in the success of the one if she avoided her responsibility for the other, yes, perhaps there was something manic about it, but it was exactly that combination of nerve, heedlessness and a consuming sense of her responsibilities that made the Cheffe what she became, a great artist.

Talking to you, thinking about the Cheffe, I sometimes forget that through the circumstances of her birth her gifts found their outlet in cooking, because no matter what she might say I consider her an artist, if things were different she would have made her name as a painter or writer, or who knows what, but the Cheffe didn't like me thinking that way, she didn't believe there was anything special about her, any particular talent, only the good luck to be organised, hard-working, intuitive, and to house within her, with no guarantee that it would last, the little spirit of her craft – "That's exactly what I'm talking about when I talk about art," I would answer, and the Cheffe would frown, she didn't trust highflown words, didn't like fancy talk, as she called it.

Now, simply knowing that I can always take my daughter to Rosa-
mar, I can accept the idea of having her in my real home, Lloret de Mar.
The spell broken, I came back from Rosamar telling myself I would
have had to live a lie with her for two weeks, forever fearing we might
run into someone I know, inventing a different life for myself, different
habits. There's no point in fighting it, and I realise I'm almost relieved
— my tranquillity is at an end, something unpleasant is coming, but
it's the unpleasantness of reality, not of lies. I know the unpleasantness
is coming, so there's no reason to fear that it might, what's done will
be done, I feel unburdened before anything's even happened, and this
evening like every evening I'll find myself on a terrace, drinking and
eating and talking with my Lloret de Mar friends, and they'll kindly
ask me for news of my daughter, and I'll tell them she'll be here in a
week, her name is Cora. Oh, that's a pretty name. Yes, maybe it is,
I'm not quite sure, I've rarely spoken it, Cora, her name is Cora, and
that summons up so very few memories, Cora might be a pretty name,
her name is Cora, I had nothing to do with it.

The Cheffe enrolled her daughter in nursery school and
added her daily care to the packed, arduous list of things she
already had to do every day – easier, she said, than all the many
things she'd done up until then, even if the time she managed
to make for her daughter by racing through certain chores
even faster than she once had, washing the linen or cleaning
the kitchen, say, must sometimes have seemed to her not time
enough, which filled her with a painful sense of failure, of dere-
liction, and the child who slept on the mattress beside her,
hearing her own heart less clearly than her mother's, that child
less aware of her own thoughts than of her mother's absorbed

that regret and senselessly, cynically exploited it, as children do, becoming a capricious, mean little thing, skilled in blackmail and extortion, such that when they saw her again the Cheffe's parents would be astonished at how little they recognised her, they who'd never had the slightest trouble with the child.

The Cheffe pretended she found it perfectly normal to be ruled and intimidated by a three-year-old girl, so long as it happened outside the restaurant and didn't get in the way of her work, and her daughter understood that, she realised she could push the Cheffe around as roughly as she liked so long as she didn't threaten La Bonne Heure's well-being.

And since she was slyly intuitive, cunning, calculating, since she grasped that her mother would have mournfully taken her back to Sainte-Bazeille before she let tantrums and scenes hamper her work, she only bullied her mother when they were alone in the apartment, she always behaved herself in the dining room or kitchen where the Cheffe sat her down to draw or look at a picture book, I'm convinced that her hatred for La Bonne Heure was born of and fed by those seemingly harmonious hours when she was sentenced to watch her mother come and go with no hope of affecting her or commanding her to obey the aimless but strategic summons of her omnipotent young presence, she would hate the restaurant, yes, but that didn't mean she loved her mother any the more.

That the Cheffe had to do battle each day to build La Bonne Heure's reputation, that when she went back to her apartment late at night she had to grapple with a child determined not to go back to sleep after the few hours' nap she'd just awoken from, in a sense determined never to go back to sleep again, just as she was determined never to stop crying, all that came back to me on those nights when, drunk with exhaustion, shivering, I listened in gratitude and resigned despair, convinced I would never go home to rest, while in her sweet, steady voice, discreetly tinged with self-effacing humour, the Cheffe told me of all she went through in the early years, not easy but instructive, she said, of La Bonne Heure.

I myself don't think life with the girl taught her anything at all, unlike the creation of La Bonne Heure, which taught her – unsparingly, but with loyalty, coherence and a logical hope that her hard work would one day be repaid – much of what the Cheffe later used to make of herself far more than the owner of a fine neighbourhood restaurant.

No, she learned nothing from life with her daughter, that child of such scant grace, apart from the least laudable aspect of her own character: an eager, desperate submissiveness to the sinister whims of people far, far beneath her who nonetheless looked down on her, like that girl, whose glowing opinion of herself was built on the certainty, never contested by her mother, by the way her mother treated her, that she was by far the sharper and cleverer of the two but alas luck never came through for her, the same luck that had mysteriously proven so generous to her mother.

As the weeks went by, the Cheffe's paupiettes of rabbit with sorrel, transparent fillets of olive-oil-marinated sole, or gratin of Provençal vegetables attracted a more copious clientele of regulars, who more and more often filled up the six tables, keeping others from discovering the place.

The Cheffe had her young sister Ingrid come up from Sainte-Bazeille to wait on the tables and help with the shopping, as well as look after the child after school, she was sixteen years old, the Cheffe's daughter still likes to say Ingrid took the place of her mother, another fiction, a lie, or maybe a false memory.

Ingrid was an old woman when I met her, and I knew it made her more uncomfortable than amused to so often hear that the Cheffe's daughter never mentioned her without calling her "My beloved Ingrid" or "My dear aunt" when she felt no friendship for the daughter back then and saw to her care so impatiently that the Cheffe often had to rebuke her, had to ask her to be nicer and more indulgent with the little girl, and the aged Ingrid assured me the Cheffe's daughter had no grounds to claim she still loved her to this day, they hadn't set eyes on each other for twenty years, maybe twenty-five, in short they'd never got along from the start, for which Ingrid felt not one shred of guilt, not even when I asked her what it meant to say that a young adult of sixteen did or did not get along with a four-year-old child, wasn't it her job to be kind and loving, to earn her niece's respect and appreciation?

And that hard-faced old Ingrid shrugged her shoulders, exactly like the Cheffe often did, and told me that's just how it was, she'd felt no affection for the child, who in any case didn't lack for it, since her mother loved her and stupidly spoiled her, no, she'd never managed to find the child interesting, she was a weight and a weariness for the Cheffe, and for her too, Ingrid, who was beginning to develop a taste for cooking through her contact with the Cheffe and would have preferred to work only in the restaurant instead of spending her days with that child, that's how it was, a weight and a weariness.

But her sister the Cheffe loved the girl with a passion, there was no doubt about that, which is why the elderly Ingrid was mystified by those declarations of love for someone who'd treated her without warmth and those vicious, bitter, incongruous allegations against the Cheffe, who'd enfolded her in all the tenderness she was capable of, that girl who never gave anything back, such a weight, such a weariness.

Ingrid came from Sainte-Bazeille in the middle of summer, and with that the Cheffe carried out the plan she'd devised when she found herself turning ever more people away.

For the moment renting the space next door was out of the question, so she bought four new tables and set them out on the pavement, wide and sunny at that intersection, then put in a navy blue canvas awning, sitting beneath it with the bright August sun vainly trying to get through you felt a heavenly coolness, limpid and majestic, a kindness freely given, and she also pared her menu down to the dishes she most loved – crayfish pie, cold Chantilly pigeon with spices, terrine of duck and spinach, transparent fillets of sole, green-robed leg of lamb, beef with honey, Landes peach tart, pistachio cream – along with summer specials that changed every day according to the market.

I believe she was the first to surprise a dithering regular with dishes she picked out herself, perhaps adding some special touch, even leaving out ingredients or condiments she knew he had no fondness or taste for, as people do with friends they invite to dinner, the Cheffe didn't pretend to be their friend, she wasn't forward, she could even be distant, but she got to know people quickly and observantly, and in perfect sincerity she wanted people to feel at home in her restaurant, as if they were visiting a strange, slightly cold friend who never opens up about herself but knows a great deal about you, and who, in her reserved, almost unfeeling way, works to please you well beyond anything you can imagine.

You don't dare call her a friend, so unyieldingly does she seem to resist any intimacy, so skittish is she about any manner of closeness, and yet she treats you as only a friend could, unfailingly thoughtful, perpetually attentive, she seems to care far more for you than she cares for herself.

Some of the Cheffe's customers ate at La Bonne Heure for more than thirty years, several times a week, and although they could never call themselves the Cheffe's friends, although they never managed to have her over as a guest or meet her outside the restaurant (she didn't go to Arcachon, she didn't go to Paris, she didn't go to town hall receptions or the theatre or opera, she never went anywhere she was invited), the only words they could have found to describe their bond with her were words that evoked a longstanding, unshakable friendship, even if as they paid their bill they always felt like they still owed her something, felt like they'd never had the chance, since she turned down every invitation to parties or weekends, to repay her with anything other than money (and not much of that) for the pleasure she offered them, the lengths she went to for them, never saying a word about it, never showing it, so maybe the inequality she deliberately imposed on that exchange proves she didn't know how to be a friend.

I do think I can say we were friends, she fought it, but the need she came to feel for my presence, attention and boundless love won out in the end, I was her friend and without saying so she asked me not to leave her alone through those nights when I stood in the kitchen, thighs twitching in exhaustion, and listened as she told me of the long years before I was there, offering her my solicitude and thankfully, fondly sacrificing my sleep for her, which she humbly accepted, she was grateful, knowing I'd never use a word she said against her, and so she conceded that you can owe someone even as you remain on the pedestal where that person wants you to be, and then the debt would be erased the next night, when everything would start all over again, all debts forgiven, I was her friend, she'd never had that before.

My Lloret de Mar friends are as fond of a drink as I am, and it's obvious that the happiness we feel when we meet up every day resides partly in the pleasure of drinking together, in that way we know each other, trust each other, because we've found we can all hold our liquor, as they say, and in our merry, frivolous little gatherings no-one stirs up trouble or creates any awkwardness by proving a bad drinker, aggressive or obnoxious. And yet yesterday my Lloret de Mar friends thought it best to give me a tactful warning, we were all gathered on a terrace I'm not sure wasn't mine, so how can I remember exactly what they told me, I can't come up with the words but I do recall the meaning, because it shook me, drunk though I was, my Lloret de Mar friends told me I've been drinking too much for some time, I should take it easy, my health was going to suffer, couldn't I go back to being the well-balanced guy I was just three or four weeks ago, and anyone listening to my Lloret de Mar friends from outside would have found that perfectly hilarious, we're all serious alcoholics but we can spot the person who's going too far. I'm that person, their warning shook me, I don't want to alienate my Lloret de Mar friends, my only family, they've noticed how nervous I am about Cora's visit, I feel embarrassed before them, nothing ever troubles them, they receive their own children with perfect equanimity, they're just where they deserve to be, in the paradise they've forged for themselves, it's a good and simple way to live.

Soon La Bonne Heure's blue-tinted terrace was such a success that the Cheffe had to hire extra staff in the kitchen as well as the dining room.

She still turned away more than she took in, which irritated her as a matter of principle, because to her a restaurant was a place where without premeditation everyone should be able to find a chair to catch their breath on, a clean table to put their elbows on, good food to comfort them, and out of respect for that principle she believed she should never have to tell that modest demand it can't be met, never have to postpone her hospitality, never, without a thousand legitimate excuses and the very best reasons, have to put off the thing that cannot be deferred, the thing there can be no good reason for not producing without delay: the gift.

No, of course, the Cheffe didn't give her meals away, strictly speaking, though I can tell you she always kept her profit as modest as she could, even for the wine she charged just a hair more than it cost her, she'd put no work into it so she thought she had no right to make money on it.

As the years went by the Cheffe turned towards an ever simpler cuisine, not, I don't think, in the sense that she unwittingly followed the dictates of the time and conformed to the dogma of a "nouvelle cuisine" she never quite felt a part of, but in the growing and in the end almost exclusive importance she placed on the quality of each ingredient, from the priciest cut of beef to the humblest sprig of parsley, from the finest fish to the tiniest grain of salt that would season it, even as she insisted on presenting a generously filled plate, restrained in its appearance (no more than three colours), but on which the concern for perfection was literally nowhere to be seen, nor any other concern for that matter, apart from the concern of bringing immediate pleasure to any eye longing for beauty and anxious to know whether hunger would be sated and tastes pleased.

Many people came for a blowout at La Bonne Heure and never suspected, since the prices were modest and the plates bounteous, that every dish was made with the best ingredients the Cheffe's painstaking research could dig up, whether it be the oil the beef or aubergine was browned in or that very meat and that vegetable, which the Cheffe no longer inevitably brought back from the Marché des Capucins but ordered from a stockman in Bazas or a grower in the Lot-et-Garonne, from farms she'd scouted out during the winter months and judged worthy of La Bonne Heure without worrying too much about prices, which is to say never raising her own on the pretext that she was paying more for her products, she adapted.

And so she came to offer a deeply thoughtful cuisine, highly refined in its appearance, preparation and cooking, conceived precisely to erase any memory of labour, of duress, of punishing hours, but nonetheless a cuisine that almost anyone could approach without knowing anything about it, expecting nothing more than a full stomach.

The favourites at La Bonne Heure in those days? Apart from the famed green-robed leg of lamb and the Landes peach tart, veal cutlets with *fines herbes* breading were often ordered, as was cabbage stuffed with andouillette de Troyes, Bresse chicken with tarragon and Nyons olives, new turnips glazed with cane sugar, little Ratte potatoes with their delicate skin fried whole in goose fat, Webb lettuce with roast beef juice and dried fruits, terrine of duck and Corsican tangerines, all of them dishes that as a child in Bordeaux I heard people talk about like food for fairies or ogres, and it never once entered my mind that my mother could have put my coat and shoes on me, taken the bus that crossed the river over the Pont de Pierre, clasped my hand, and walked into that restaurant without having to prove she was a secret aristocrat, a fallen princess, that restaurant whose reason for being revealed itself, as I didn't know at the time, in people like us, my mother and me, who sometimes went out to eat in restaurants where the food was somewhat unpolished and mediocre but sold for a price she found manageable, for the same money we could have had a feast at La Bonne Heure, surprising, delicate, wholesome dishes, my mother never even considered it, to her that was all fairy tales, she didn't believe in such things.

The Cheffe rented the shops on either side of the little corner dining room, had wide openings put in to make three contiguous rooms, had the walls painted that same royal blue, with a dark, polished wainscoting up to the tops of the chair backs.

Noon and night, the dining rooms were never less than full, and as before there was no choice but to turn people away, but even then the Cheffe refused to take reservations, anyone could sit down at a table if there was room, and there, on the spur of the moment, find repose, and the freshness of the blue and green floor tile in its cold purity, and when autumn came the Cheffe lit the little bottle-green porcelain heating stoves.

My future co-workers, the people the Cheffe had hired before me, told me she seemed to glow back then with a constant joy, undimmed by everyday anxieties or fatigues, they told me her face seemed to be permanently smoothed, bathed in a silent, indestructible happiness, as if pulled tight by her chignon and by enchantment, and they also told me, as the aged Ingrid confirmed, that that face only furrowed, just a little, when the Cheffe's daughter appeared or simply let her voice be heard from the next room or the street, high-pitched, demanding and plaintive, and then the Cheffe slightly hunched her shoulders, and, like a dog that doesn't know what to expect from its mercurial master, listened with a discreet apprehension, veiled but visible to those who worked beside her day in and day out, an apprehension that disappeared as soon as her daughter went away or her voice fell silent or when that changeable girl walked into the kitchen with a smile on her face, almost excessively friendly and cheerful and so utterly unpredictable that it gave the Cheffe a sort of jolt, she turned strangely timid, and towards her daughter turned servile in a way that was painful to see.

Yes, the very independent, very solitary Cheffe had unwillingly but not unknowingly or acceptingly made herself the slave of her daughter, a girl of unappealing features and limited intelligence, and I think she felt guilty, absurdly, that she hadn't passed her fineness of mind and appearance on to her daughter, I think above all she submitted to her daughter's undeserved authority because her daughter had no hope of impressing anyone in any other way, and the Cheffe vaguely imagined she was hiding that from her, shielding her from that indisputable truth by offering herself up to her despotism, not, then, so that it wouldn't be inflicted on others but so that her unhappy daughter, because that must have been how she saw her, could at least grow up with the certainty or the illusion that she had, in spite of everything, some sort of strong point.

And all through those years, all through that burgeoning of La Bonne Heure's reputation, the Cheffe seemed to have no other real concern than shoring up her daughter's belief in a preposterous idea of herself, than each day convincing her daughter of the persistence and boundlessness of the motherly love she poured out for nothing, which didn't stop the daughter from continually testing that senseless love by treating the Cheffe in a way that made everyone around them cringe, and the Cheffe's strange, longstanding fear of that child who was so unlike her was joined by another sort of fear, that she might see her upbraided for those public scenes, which, the Cheffe was lucid enough to see, painted an unflattering image of her daughter, even more than of herself who endured them, she would have endured far more of them if they could be blamed on her alone, and if people could have some reason to love and admire her daughter, but that too was only a fairy tale, the Cheffe couldn't believe in it.

Yes, that was her one torment, her one sorrow, and the only thing that ever troubled her face, a face as if each day burnished by an abrasive, inflexible joy, in the twelve or so years that La Bonne Heure peacefully flourished and finally became, virtually uncontested but nevertheless humble and elegantly unimpressed, the finest table in Bordeaux.

What did the daughter look like?

I didn't meet her until she was twenty-five, as was I, since as it happens we were born in the same month of the same year, but what struck you about her when you first saw her must have been there since she was a child, and I don't think I'm wrong to imagine that for the restaurant's workers the mark left by the fingers of the cruel, ironic or vengeful angel who on the night of her birth chose to make that girl a botched, parodic twin of her mother could already be seen on the teenager who came into the kitchen radiating boredom and disgust to make some inevitably hare-brained, impossible or ridiculous demand on her, just as I myself saw that pitiless, indelible mark a few years later: her daughter had inherited the Cheffe's stocky frame, her solid body, which couldn't enter a space without seeming to accumulate around it an equal quantity of dense, stagnant air, but the astonishing grace of movement and the warm brown gaze that in the Cheffe immediately erased that impression of heaviness hadn't been granted the daughter, there was something aggressively immovable about her stout form that was off-putting to look at, and her eyes were dull and narrow, they seemed dead even in the heat of her tantrums.

There came a time when I thought I should judge the Cheffe's daughter less harshly, when I sometimes told myself she seized any excuse for outbursts and recriminations only in the hope of illuminating her eyes with the life she was lacking, of which she had only the appearance and never the emotion, the sensation, whose taste was unknown to her, so that that fire, lit at long last, would spread to the rest of her, and she would, she hoped, feel the emotion of being alive and no longer just the colourless experience of knowing it, I'm not sure how true that is, how true that was, because I long ago gave up trying to understand the Cheffe's daughter, but in any case she looked like her mother in the most mocking, incomprehensible way, and there, yes, perhaps, you could feel some sympathy for her, because, she must have wondered more than once, who was fate trying to punish by ridiculing her like that, was it the Cheffe or was it her, and in the latter case why?

I'm not entirely deaf to reason, I take my Lloret de Mar friends' advice, at least about driving, and I'm perfectly sober when I set out for the train station in Blanes to meet my daughter Cora, so sober that, this late afternoon in June, I see everything around me in a blazing, prophetic light, I hear something eloquent and insistent from the yellowed palms, the swollen clouds, the potholed roadway, but nothing they're saying gets through to me, precisely because I have no alcohol in me and my imagination has run dry and I know that if I were to stop off for a drink in that roadside hotel over there the meaning of their silent bellowing would unveil itself to my anxious heart and then I wouldn't be nearly as anxious, since alcohol generously brings a comforting touch to everything I see, and everything that upsets me. That howling and thundering was only trying to greet me and accompany me on the road to Cora, that roaring was meant to praise me for going and meeting Cora, for welcoming Cora to Lloret de Mar, my only home, for introducing Cora to my Lloret de Mar friends, who expect us this evening on Anne-Marie's terrace, my kind, loving friends, so genuinely eager to make my daughter's acquaintance.

I was nineteen when I started as an apprentice at La Bonne Heure, fresh out of training college, with a diploma the Cheffe didn't even glance at when, one springtime mid-afternoon, she met me in the dining room, sat me down opposite her, and asked me a few standard questions in a voice at once clear, commanding and soft, regularly running a slow, tranquil hand over her glistening hair, so flattened down and pulled back towards the little chignon that it almost seemed she was stroking her bare, polished skull, I'd never seen such a face, a face that to my eyes, as I felt but couldn't yet put into words, seemed the archetype of all human faces, unmarked by sex, age or beauty, I thought that face painfully perfect, and as I turned my own face towards it, a face so muddled by timid youth, by uncertainty and ignorance, I feared I could never live up to the moral rigour that must very naturally belong to someone whose dignity had given her such an incarnation – a face impossible to weigh on any common scale or judge by any ordinary standard.

The Cheffe might have seen my panic, my doubts and befuddlement, my vague longing to flee, every bit as urgent as my wish to die if I wasn't hired.

She gave me a kindheartedly ironic little smile.

She had to force herself, she didn't approve of sarcasm in critical moments, she was only trying to make me "come down", as she liked to say, by which she meant that I'd too quickly and needlessly scaled summits of emotion where there was no air to breathe, I was suffocating, and that was of no use at all, not to me or to anyone else or the work.

So she gently mocked me with her slightly wry smile, obliging me to smile back, and I took my eyes off her face for a moment, I'd stopped thinking of running away, though in my heart there remained the trembling certainty that my life couldn't go on if I wasn't hired at La Bonne Heure.

What could I do anywhere else, and who with, and what good would experience do me if I didn't acquire it from this face and this voice, in this ultramarine sanctuary, so still at that hour that I thought I could hear my own blood flowing through my clenched, hopeful body, that I could feel it pounding between my eyebrows and imagine the flesh there visibly throbbing, would the Cheffe feel sympathy or disgust at that, how to know?

All the same, I'd "come down" just as she wanted, and I

could answer more or less calmly when she asked what made me think of applying at La Bonne Heure in particular, I could tell her, sincerely but with a lyricism I was painfully aware of, that since my earliest childhood I'd often passed by that restaurant's windows, mysteriously tinged with blue from inside by the glow and the wisdom of a supernatural colour, I'd always thought fairies must be at work in there, conjuring up the mysterious, wondrous plates I saw being set down on the tables of the terrace once April came, oh that was all true but what was that truth next to the one I didn't know how to tell the Cheffe: on first seeing that photo in *Sud-Ouest*, the best-known, virtually the only one that anyone knew, with the Cheffe displaying an inexplicable cheeriness in the midst of her crew, I'd made a vow to do everything I possibly could to work at La Bonne Heure as soon as I got my degree, not for the cheeriness, and not for the hair inconceivably liberated and floating soft and feathery around her face, but for something in that face, however unreal its expression in the photo, something I immediately thought was speaking to me, silently hailing me from the wellspring of a companionship I'd never known, now revealed to me by the prosaic mediation of *Sud-Ouest*, a kinship I immediately understood and accepted, the Cheffe knew I existed and was calling me to her, that's what her face was telling me.

And in the blue serenity of the dining room I discovered that the Cheffe was nothing like the woman in the photo, her hair was severely tied back and her face suffused with an alert, quiet joy, but certainly not cheeriness, and I marvelled to think that that's just what I'd seen in the photo, the Cheffe's real face reaching out to me, I'd been called on and I understood, now her face was telling me that too in the beautiful, cool dining room.

So how could I fear I wouldn't be hired?

I hurried to shut myself up, to what seemed the Cheffe's relief.

I recognise my daughter straight away, even after all this time, I'm so moved that I almost turn and run for the car before she can see me or recognise me, but her eyes land on me from the far end of the platform and I see she's spotted me as quickly as I spotted her, how can that be when we don't know each other in any meaningful sense? I frantically put on my sunglasses, and so in a dark-blue light Cora's face grazes mine, Cora's cheek touches mine, she's as tall as I am, her shoulders are broad, her face strong, I might almost be meeting an old friend because physically we're strangely well matched, I'm not the sturdy father embracing his delicate slip of a very young daughter, I'm letting a solid young woman put her cheek to mine and I don't have to bend down at all, she's tall and strong and her skin is blue, the tinted lenses of my glasses are telling me. This is Cora, so this is what she looks like, my eyes close for a moment, so this is Cora.

When, years later, having become her closest friend, I dared to tell the Cheffe that at eighteen I'd heard the call she sent out to me by way of *Sud-Ouest*, that I'd felt her hand, seemingly motionless in the photo, tracing a sign on my apprentice-cook forehead, and, I thought, on mine alone, she gave me a long, perplexed stare, shrugged and breezily told me, in essence, that a friendship's origins and precise, private motivations don't matter much, friendship is proved and justified every day by words and deeds, and what had brought me to La Bonne Heure one springtime afternoon was of no importance fifteen years later, when that friendship was demonstrated, strengthened and expressed through daily collaboration and long nightly talks in the silent, deserted kitchen.

"And what about love?" I asked, in the same bantering tone. "Suppose it wasn't friendship," I said, "but love that let me hear your voice in the photo, suppose it's love that keeps me here today, leaning against the hard corner of the counter, drunk with exhaustion but unable to imagine any greater pleasure than hearing you talk to me in the slumbering kitchen, confiding in me and me alone, knowing your words are falling into a greedy but loving heart, greedy because it's loving, and respectful to a fault? What about love, then?" I asked her. "Isn't it too easy, isn't it too cautious forever calling it friendship?"

But the Cheffe, who was never tender or sentimental, who with no trace of bitterness coolly and tranquilly refused to believe in the love between a man and a woman, the Cheffe wouldn't play along with me. "Call it whatever you like," she said, "as long as everyone agrees what they're talking about, that's enough."

But did we agree, exactly? And were we talking about the same thing? What did it mean to her if I was her friend, what did she feel for me, her employee on top of everything else, how deep was her trust in me?

Cora doesn't talk much, I'm glad, I was afraid she'd ask questions I wouldn't want to or know how to answer honestly. And so we drive in a strange silence, like old friends, like aged relatives who e-mail each other every day or so often talk on the phone they have nothing to say. I take the opportunity of the occasional right turn to steal a glance at her profile, she has a kind of confident, decent air that intimidates me, I mumblingly ask after her mother, although I couldn't possibly care less. And Cora, that tall, commanding young woman who is my daughter, sweeps the air with her dismissive fingers and tells me she didn't come all this way to talk about her mother, I could have found out how her mother was doing if I wanted to, she says, pointedly but not unkindly, as if to tell me I can skip the small talk, it will be easier for both of us. She's wearing a long, full dress, mauve, decorated with big blue flowers, her bare shoulders are very tanned, you can make out the sturdy bones beneath her flesh, muscular as the flesh of some swimmers, Cora sits up very straight. I then understand my daughter isn't here to pour out her feelings or vent her anger or make some sort of demand, I sense that she's here simply to size me up.

I remember my first months in La Bonne Heure's kitchen as the hardest time of my life, which doesn't mean the most unpleasant or the unhappiest, but I worked so hard, I took such care to watch what I said and did so not even the most trivial detail could displease the Cheffe (not that I paid any attention to whether she was listening or watching, even alone in my studio I was always trying not to displease the Cheffe's gentle, uncompromising face), that I saw every new day as an arduous uphill climb, and the reward wasn't to glide down the slope when day was done, because there was no slope to glide down in a euphoric rush of freedom, there was only the knowledge of another climb to come the next day and every day after, which is why I didn't sleep much back then, even though I wasn't yet, far from it, the friend the Cheffe so freely confided in, I didn't get much sleep, I tried to come up with ways to prove myself the next day, ways to show I was hard-working and perceptive, I wondered how I might become, without artifice or deceit, the man the Cheffe would have to prefer to all others, oh how little I slept in those days!

And in so doing, and at almost the same age, I was unknowingly creating myself just as the Cheffe created herself in her little room at the Clapeaus', inventing or improving recipes deep into the night – in my case, I was trying to inventory every aspect of my behaviour and compare it with what I thought I knew the Cheffe wanted, there were four of us working in her kitchen, I was the youngest, and the most desperate to be noticed.

I tried to do the simple tasks I was assigned so swiftly and flawlessly that it couldn't go unnoticed, even if nothing was said of it.

I saw the Cheffe sometimes glancing intently my way.

It's true that she was hard on me. She didn't care about the things they'd drilled into me at college, my talent for carving potatoes or mushroom caps, for tying green beans into elegant bundles with thin slices of bacon, all those techniques I was so good at disgusted the Cheffe, and it wasn't because she was jealous, as her daughter insinuates, it wasn't because the Cheffe never had the benefit of such teachings, it was simply because she had no time for tricks aimed at prettifying the food, aimed at dressing it up even if that means stripping it of its basic qualities, she didn't think food had any need to be adorned or remade if it had nothing to be ashamed of.

The Cheffe made it clear to me that fripperies were not welcome in her kitchen, that displays of virtuosity would get me nowhere, she knew what I'd been taught and was quietly, patiently waiting for me to quit looking back at it, to quit thinking I had to pull out all the stops to justify my presence at La Bonne Heure, I wasn't competing with anyone here, she was quietly, patiently waiting for me to see that.

My co-workers looked on me with the detached, smirking but tactful indulgence of people who'd gone through the very same thing and knew there was nothing they could tell me: like them, I had to go on to the end of the road I'd been sent down by my anxiousness, my eagerness to make a good impression, my very young man's vanity, I wouldn't have been able to hear anything they would have no doubt clumsily told me, I would have seen any suggestion that I hold back as a sign that they feared for their own standing and were trying to lead me astray.

And so I insisted on showing that I could sculpt a turnip into a rose, deftly scoop perfect balls of potato or melon, the Cheffe was hard on me, even if she never said much, she was hard on me, yes.

With a flick of her finger she sent my turnip rose flying into the dustbin, told me she'd never asked me to carve the potatoes in that ridiculous way or waste so much melon to make little balls nobody cared about, and she finished by smiling, without warmth, to let me know it wasn't serious, that smile skewered me with shame and despair.

Much later, when I asked why she'd been so hard on me in my early days, why she hadn't simply told me just what she wanted, which I would have tried to give her with all the fire and devotion she knew was in me, why, in short, she'd left me to find the way into her thinking, her morality, failing which I couldn't possibly work with her, when it would have taken only a few detailed sentences to guide my hungry, groping ambition, when I asked her why she'd been so hard on me the Cheffe answered in surprise that she had indeed hoped I'd discover on my own what I had to do, and almost who I had to become, if I wanted not to *deserve* my place at La Bonne Heure, that's not how she saw her restaurant, but to decide whether, given those conditions, I'd be happy there, and she couldn't very well have said that in just a few sentences, she was surprised at my question.

And at the same time she admitted she was irritated by my visible ambition to please her, to be the only one who pleased her, and she must have been trying to get that across to me.

"And I ended up becoming your favourite all the same," I answered, with what I hoped would be playful affection. And the Cheffe answered gravely: "Yes, you got me after all."

Coming from her, was that a declaration of love?

But I did become the Cheffe's favourite, through persistence and sacrifice and because my co-workers, who were in truth every bit as talented as I was, had no such goal in their hearts, I succeeded because there was nothing I longed for so much, and because that ambition was within the reach of the methodical, observant, passionate boy I then was.

That "you got me" hurt, particularly because the great sorrow of my life, when she said those words, was precisely that I sometimes felt I didn't have her at all, or had no more of her than one of her indifferent, faraway brothers or sisters, who seemed to keep up a relationship with the Cheffe only so they could go on asking for money now and then.

I'd never "got" the Cheffe, I'd never had her, I sometimes told myself, she was misleading us both by saying such things – but on her thin lips those words might have been words of love.

No sooner have we reached my apartment than I take Cora to Anne-Marie's terrace two floors up, that's how we do things in Lloret de Mar and I see no reason to change just because I'm being visited by my daughter, my one child on this earth, and in any case I don't think she's longing any more than I am for a tête-à-tête this first evening, it would be awkward, although Cora seems so serene, so assured that she could probably get through a mediocre dinner (everything I put in my mouth has been processed and inevitably tainted and ruined by the food industry) in the sad little kitchen of an apartment complex for middle-class retirees. Cora seems relaxed, outgoing, I see her mingling with my Lloret de Mar friends on Anne-Marie's terrace, on which she's complimented her, just like you're supposed to (what a beautiful terrace, what a beautiful view of the pool, what a beautiful life, what a beautiful long wait to die), standing out in her long hippy dress among the other women, far older, almost naked in their short, clinging beach outfits, Cora's here, I sip my sangria, slightly numbed and self-conscious. And Bertrand or Bernard tells me, "She looks just like you," which so shocks me that I drop my glass on the artificial

stone floor of Anne-Marie's terrace, I wasn't expecting that, that my
daughter might look like me, this tall, solid Cora who owes me nothing
and to whom I've given so little. "She has your eyes, your mouth, your
nose," *he goes on, and I hurriedly bend down to pick up the broken*
glass to hide my embarrassment, my shame and my panic, what is
someone who so looks like me going to want from me?

The Cheffe's daughter? No, she wasn't living with her
mother when I came to La Bonne Heure, somehow she'd
managed to pass the baccalaureate and was supposedly taking
some kind of business course in Quebec, where she had insisted
on transplanting herself with every possible comfort, my co-
workers told me, and where the Cheffe did indeed house her
luxuriously from afar, by which I mean she never made the
trip herself but spent so much money on her daughter that
the photos she sent her mother to grudgingly admit that her
living conditions weren't too appalling told all the strangely
numerous people the Cheffe showed them to (her employees,
longstanding customers) that that perpetually disgruntled and
dissatisfied girl actually lived in outrageous luxury, little justified by the inevitably mediocre or even disgraceful grades she
occasionally passed on to the Cheffe, for which the Cheffe's
daughter always had an airtight explanation, there was no logical connection between herself, her work, her attendance,
her abilities and those disappointing grades she owed solely to
the obtuseness or irrationality of incomprehensible teachers,
and the Cheffe believed her, pretended to believe her, sensing
she had neither the ability nor the courage to question claims
founded in an experience so entirely unknown to her.

I soon realised that the Cheffe never spoke of her daughter without cloaking her in a legend, a legend she tirelessly wove by telling everyone over and over what a clever girl she was, as if she knew her handiwork was being almost as insistently covered up by a very different legend, one constructed without cruelty or ill-will by her employees who actually knew the girl. They drew me so dreadful a portrait of her that I doubted it could be true, I thought the Cheffe's vociferous praise and pride more believable, particularly because my youthful naivety refused to let me see how someone as wonderful as the Cheffe could give birth to the horrible person my co-workers described.

But when I did meet her daughter it cast a new light on the Cheffe's joyful, unshakable, creative, almost whimsical mood in my first years at La Bonne Heure – she was happy because her daughter was far away, splendidly poised, the Cheffe pretended to believe, on the cusp of a glittering career that would never bring her back to Bordeaux, it was only because she finally felt free of intimidation and blame that she radiated that quiet, burning, tenacious joy, not exactly happiness, I wouldn't have called the Cheffe happy, I didn't know, but something somehow bigger and better than happiness, a joy that didn't confine itself to her but touched all of us, enveloped all of us, and by way of us grew all the greater.

Because the Cheffe's joy planted in each of us who worked beside her each day something that wouldn't easily be rooted out, something perhaps not even life's daily parade of trials and sadness and frustrations could overcome.

Once I finally understood that there was no point in showing the Cheffe all the gimmicks and flourishes they'd taught me at college, once I dared let her see me as someone who'd learned nothing and would thus let his fervour, his tirelessness and his perfect receptivity teach him all he needed to know, and only the best of it, then I saw my co-workers breathe a sigh of relief and I realised, looking back, how tiresome they'd found the spectacle of my blindness, anxiousness and presumption, and I saw the change in the way the Cheffe treated me, I was a new person, one she liked far better than the old, who was immediately forgotten, it was so foreign to the Cheffe's nature to remind anyone of old ways and past failings, to wave the skin you'd shed under your nose, even as a joke, once the moulting was complete.

She'd never lost her temper with me, but her patience was so enormous, and sometimes so undeserved, that it could bring tears to my eyes, no-one had ever shown me such kindness, not even my mother, who gave me a feeble, lazy, half-hearted upbringing, eager to put it behind her, the very opposite of the Cheffe, who never seemed to weary of teaching me, never wished she could be done with it.

She never tired of showing me how she made her cooking as simple as she could while creating an impression of tremendous elaboration, of an idea long and deeply reflected on, the result being the product offered up in a state not far from naked.

The stark-naked product was unacceptable, neither pleasing to the eye nor enticing to the tongue, so the Cheffe's art consisted in doing just enough to it to make it seem resplendent and delicious but still perfectly recognisable, incorruptible, proudly and serenely displaying its sometimes odd appearance.

"I hardly touch it," the Cheffe liked to say, with no trace of coyness, and all her finesse, all her intelligence was in that "hardly", the very essence of her work.

For example, the green-robed leg of lamb came from her wanting people to taste exquisite Pauillac lamb and Belleville sorrel in their most honest form, refusing to hide the sorrel's roughness behind cream and butter. To that she added spinach, she liked a trinity of ingredients, then slow-braised the lamb in its wrapping of bitter greens so the meat's fatty juices mellowed the sorrel and the lamb turned out at once supernaturally tender and so strongly flavoured that the contrast — a young, dark-tasting meat — disconcerted the eater's first mouthfuls, the Cheffe thought that was funny.

As the years went by, I saw her invent all the dishes that made La Bonne Heure famous.

That was the sunniest, most absorbing time of my life, and I think it was the same for the Cheffe — she was free, she serenely, passionately followed the path blazed for her by her fearlessness, and the very young man that I was padded after, knowing just how far behind her to stay, marvelling, critical, grateful.

One night, unable to sleep, I found my feet taking me back to the restaurant, where I saw a light on in a street-facing kitchen window.

I thought the Cheffe must be working inside, I tapped on the pane, she let me in as if there were nothing odd about it, and I just as casually sat down to watch her, trying to make out what she was thinking and hand her some dish or utensil before she could reach for it.

We didn't speak, and even if, much later, the whole nights I spent in the kitchen listening to the Cheffe's stories would satisfy my need for friendship, trust and forgiveness far more than I could have hoped, more than I thought I deserved, I would still feel an irreparable nostalgia for those hours when time stood still and silent amid the clicks, clanks and rustles of the work, my exhaustion held at bay by the minute attention I paid to the Cheffe's every glance, every move, and dawn appeared in the window without our noticing it at first – the Cheffe would murmur regretfully, "Already!" and then my eyelids could droop and twitch, I felt fulfilled, heroic and modest, and the Cheffe looked up at me with the face of a sweet, happy child, a lock of hair slipping over her forehead, no-one else ever saw her like that.

"What do you think of this?" she asked me once, handing me a piece of crabmeat she'd poached in absinthe.

I thought it would be even better if it weren't cooked quite so long, the Cheffe agreed, her crab with glacier wormwood was born in the course of one of those nights when I came to join her in the kitchen, maybe a year after I started at La Bonne Heure, we kept that up for several years and tacitly agreed not to tell anyone about it, and as a matter of fact when I tapped at the window we pretended to find it all so ordinary and uncomplicated there was no reason even to say anything to each other, sometimes I'm afraid it might all have been a dream, which would be a heartbreaking, sterile thing, since those nights in that fragrant kitchen, that kitchen throbbing like an enthralled, impatient heart, those nights when the Cheffe created before my eyes, those were real, they existed, I think my deep emotion at the memory is proof enough.

Giving me a taste, she would ask for my thoughts on her walnut-crusted young rabbit, artichoke-heart fritters, broccoli stem fries, black-tomato ravioli, sardines gratinéed with bear's garlic, I was present, yes, at the conception and refinement of those celebrated dishes forever associated with the name of La Bonne Heure, in those sleepless nights when, drunk on fatigue and, if I may, the ever more inescapable love I was feeling for the Cheffe, I sometimes thought I'd never sleep again, which was a good thing, a necessary thing, the annals of cooking and partisans of love would bear me out: how can you go home and sleep when the ethereal, intent, silent, lyrical Cheffe made of the kitchen a place where her nightly dreams unfolded under her control, took shape in her hands, with no need to spend hours lying down, with no danger that the dream's benign visions might metamorphose into something horrific or burdensome?

Because the Cheffe did spend her nights dreaming, but her dreams were concrete, productive, she was awake and aware, but still those were dreams taking shape in her hands in those undulating nights, as different from other people's nights as a parallel world from the everyday universe.

I tell myself I'll take Cora for drives in the country around Lloret de Mar, show her the scenery like any other houseguest, and then the days will go by and Cora will get back on the train and nothing ambiguous or dangerous will have had time to happen between us.

But Cora has no interest in sightseeing. I tell her my plans, she smiles, lets me talk, "That's not really my kind of thing," she says quietly, her voice apologetic but firm, polite, my daughter has manners, by what miracle did that happen? I don't dare ask why in that case she came here to Lloret de Mar, I'm feeling agitated, I walk from the kitchen to the living room, Cora's presence stops me from pouring myself a 10 a.m. glass of wine, I'm agitated, anxious and tired, what does she want from me, this tall woman who doesn't want to go out for a walk? Do I? Absolutely not, I can't stand those slow ambles through Lloret de Mar's dull little streets. But then what will we do?

If the Cheffe didn't like being called out to the dining room at some customer's request, if more generally she wanted nothing to do with the eater once he'd finished his meal, I myself loved nothing so much as discreetly slipping out of the kitchen to hear the people talk over the dishes we'd served them, to study the effects of our work on their faces, I've always liked watching others eat something I helped to make, or sometimes something I made all on my own, I liked that more than I liked eating it myself, and to me the taste of the dishes was more interesting and instructive when I imagined it being judged by a palate that wasn't mine, just by looking at him I could become any one of the customers: his lips, his tongue, his teeth, I understood his every organ, I deeply respected his biological functions, in every way one with my own.

And whatever a customer's personality, whatever his reputation, whatever I might vaguely feel about him, I never gave that a moment's thought as I watched him eat, I only tried to feel in myself what was happening in him.

Yes, those were the years when La Bonne Heure became a haunt for all Bordeaux's V.I.P.s.

There was no question it was happening, but the Cheffe was slow to face it, not because she had some grudge against the upper classes (she never forgot what she owed the Clapeaus), but because she didn't want to see that even if she didn't take reservations and kept her prices within reach of any budget the chic, well-heeled crowd was driving away everyone who wasn't like them, not that they wanted that or dreamt it was happening, but simply by the inertial force of their authority, of their innate right, of everything that was exclusive and closed about them, everything cliquish and disdainful, the Cheffe knew it, yes, but she was slow to face it.

And when she did admit to herself that she was now only cooking for a certain type of customer, she felt a loss that would play a considerable role in the decisions she later made.

Because she feared nothing more than so thoroughly mastering her craft that she could get along nicely without the grace that was bestowed on her the summer she turned sixteen, without the inspiring fervour that had lifted her far above herself, that had allowed her to look on herself with surprise and a twinge of terror, that was what she was in danger of losing if she cooked for people who couldn't understand her, people who couldn't imagine Sainte-Bazeille or her happily backward, broke parents, people who would only feel scorn or condescension for Sainte-Bazeille, for her parents.

The Cheffe didn't want to be spared that scorn, that condescension, she didn't want to abandon Sainte-Bazeille and leave it exposed to those stares, she wanted no special privileges, and she didn't want to compromise herself.

In the end, she didn't care if she was scorned, so long as she was scorned along with Sainte-Bazeille, but she would have been ashamed to be pardoned, her alone, on the grounds that she was a magnificent cook.

She knew how to cook, she knew how to create, how to inspire a craze for her restaurant, and she was proud of that, but that pride was hollow compared to her need to feel possessed and grateful for it, with a gratitude that nothing would ever make her forget or neglect.

So how could she make humble gratitude for what she'd been given coexist with the knowledge that her gift now served only to please a privileged clientele, people who in a sense didn't need her or Sainte-Bazeille, people who would have no great difficulty finding their pleasures elsewhere?

The first time the mayor of Bordeaux and his wife came for lunch at La Bonne Heure – they had their picture taken in the dining room, they proclaimed their delight to anyone who would listen – the Cheffe stoutly, almost rudely, refused to go out and greet them, and she stood clutching the counter with both hands, as if to stop anyone from dragging her out to meet those two people who, claimed the mayor, had never eaten anything like this, it was amazing, it was incredible – but wasn't there anywhere else that crowd could go to find the agent of the inexpressible revelation they were looking for?

How, the Cheffe wondered, to remain decent, detached, rigorous and honest when you're working for those people, not that you want to be but you are, those people who in their naivety, in their undeserved eminence, so quickly won you to their side, so soon corrupted you?

They could be demanding, they could be difficult, even more than others, more than the undiscriminating Sainte-Bazeille, but any praise coming from them should, thought the Cheffe, be a cause for concern, should make you tremble, make you feel very slightly ashamed.

I'm troubled to learn that my daughter, this woman so visibly taller and heavier than I am, whose name is Cora for reasons I don't know and by virtue of a decision made without asking my opinion, this Cora doesn't seem to be looking for a father, not even a relative. She talks to me, sometimes she asks questions, as if chance had thrown us together as roommates, her questions are always friendly, always impersonal, and I get the feeling there's nothing about me that interests her but if we knew each other a little better we might get along. I'm not her father, I'm a guy she's just met, she's waiting to see what will come of it with genuine but, for politeness's sake, discreetly exaggerated curiosity. We go out to eat in little restaurants on the beach. I don't want to cook for Cora, I wouldn't be able to pretend I don't know how, and I'm not ready to start cooking again. Cora shows no surprise, at that or at anything she's seen here. She's so different from her mother I can scarcely believe it.

Even if, more and more, she was questioning her fidelity to her own choices, we had some beautiful years at La Bonne Heure, the Cheffe and I.

She couldn't have failed to see how I loved her, and even if that didn't interest or move her in any way I believe she grew attached to me in spite of herself, precisely because she felt no love for me and in some way wanted to make that up to me, as if my love were a present, an offering, even a sacrifice, and as if even as she declined it she thought it her duty to thank me.

She often sought out my eye when she spoke to her gathered employees, which gave me the wonderful feeling that I'd been quietly singled out, and in those days that was all I needed to be happy, hopeful and confident, since her silently choosing me was, I thought, the first step towards her accepting my love.

Yes, those were beautiful, very hard-working years.

The Cheffe had begun to make money, and although it was only later, when she took to confiding in me, that I realised what she was doing with it, even back then I noticed she never abandoned her sober, almost ascetic habits, less out of duty than because she didn't want much of what there was to buy, she had no taste for clothes or jewels or any sort of gewgaws, and she found furniture as boring as rugs, paintings or cars, and since she'd never learned to want distraction, much less fun, she looked at outings and amusements the way you might gaze on the extraordinary native costumes of peoples you can't imagine belonging to.

In short, when she wasn't cooking, the Cheffe did nothing but think about cooking – and look deep into herself to find a sincerity that forced her to ask herself unflinchingly if she wasn't betraying her own rules, if with all her ingenuity she'd managed to hide from her own eyes the death of the impalpable, flickering spirit inside her. "I have to be able to feel it in here," she used to tell me, rubbing the space between her breasts.

Then I learned that the Cheffe was sending huge sums to Quebec, to her daughter, and it's true that her daughter was always nagging her for more, but even if she hadn't been, the Cheffe would have showered her – smothered her, it sometimes seemed – with gold for the clear purpose of keeping her quiet in her distant Quebec, where the daughter had supposedly started a mysterious public relations firm, and where the mother could justifiably hope she would stay as long as the money from La Bonne Heure kept coming, keeping even the least profitable, most preposterous business afloat, and so the Cheffe heaped jewels and trinkets on her daughter to keep her where she was, to stop her coming back.

Still, she did miss her daughter, not the real, exhausting, insatiable, whining, vicious creature she was but the character the Cheffe pretended to believe in, so talented and so loving, she missed that girl, the made-up girl, almost real when the Cheffe was talking to someone who hadn't met her daughter and showed a friendly interest in her, then she could blind herself with her own creation, and for the space of a few sentences, a few falsely modest answers to admiring questions, keep the wool pulled over her own eyes.

The Cheffe would gladly have bankrupted herself if it meant she could deprive her daughter of a reason to come back and torment her in person – she was indeed hurt by the daughter's letters and later her e-mails, but she could bear that, it weighed on her, it saddened her, but it didn't destroy her.

For that matter, she would have bankrupted herself for her parents if they'd let her, although with something very different in mind: she wanted them as near her as possible, living as close as possible to La Bonne Heure, in a beautiful house she would buy them, but as I've already told you the car was all they would take from her, the car they were killed in, did they sense it was time they were dead, and discover the perfect modus operandi for the crime?

It was a morning in autumn, as we were getting ready for lunch, that the telephone rang in the dining room.

Unusually for her, the Cheffe went out and answered it.

When she came back I understood that a great sorrow had come to her.

She looked at us with that odd smile of hers, that delicate twist of her lips, but her eyes were far away, there was an angry crease in her forehead but she was trying to smile, she wanted to see us happy, she gracefully lifted one hand to her forehead, blushed faintly, looked away, and told us that *Le Guide* had awarded La Bonne Heure a star that morning in 1992.

And she dissolved into tears, shocking no-one but me, my co-workers naturally blaming those tears on happiness and surprise, and then, going to her and encircling her with their arms but not daring to actually embrace her, they congratulated her loudly and earnestly, and their pride was the very image of the affection they felt for the Cheffe: deep, serious and devoid of any real understanding.

Maybe even the Cheffe was deluded, maybe even she thought she was weeping from an excess of happiness.

But I saw at once it was nothing of the sort, I don't think she was capable of fooling herself long enough to bask in that honour with no second thoughts getting in the way.

She reached one arm out towards me, invited me to come and take my share of the delight, the sudden, well-earned fame she deserved and never sought, the Cheffe didn't network, had no friends, no connections, she reached out to me and I came forward, telling myself I'd have to show I could not rejoice and applaud her but come to her rescue, because the deep, paralysing, boundless shame that everything in me sensed she'd been feeling from the moment a stranger's voice on the phone had honoured her work was something she couldn't bear alone, without someone beside her who genuinely knew and understood all that, who knew and understood her.

Because a great sorrow had come into her life.

The Cheffe managed to hide what she was feeling from everyone who congratulated her, and although she could never answer with the warmth and sensitivity expected of the only woman of her generation with a star, although strange words sometimes sprang to her lips, such as when a journalist spoke of the pride her poor parents would be feeling if they were still with us and in a desperately impassioned voice she shot back, "Oh no, they wouldn't have liked this at all, they would have been sorry for me!", still, she generally kept up a good front, and it was only to me, only to my eyes, which knew and understood, that she showed her real face.

That first night I stayed behind after the others had gone, and she told me, "It's all over."

And her face was transformed by sadness, shame, disbelief, I scarcely recognised her, but the gestures were hers, the delicate hand drifting dreamily up to her forehead, the quick, gliding footsteps, so light that they made no sound, her face had changed, and I stood silent, afraid I might say the wrong thing.

I saw her shame, even if I didn't quite understand it, even if I thought it perverse and misplaced.

"If they're rewarding me, that means I've slipped," the Cheffe told me.

"But why?" I whispered, with a little edge of revolt, almost annoyance, I don't think the Cheffe heard, and just next to my sadness at thinking or knowing she couldn't simply enjoy an unexpected pleasure there rose up in me the rampart of distrust, doubt, impatience, and I thought I had to take care not to let the tangled gloom in the Cheffe's heart spread to me, I thought I had to take care not to let my love so corrupt me that I too would become incapable of pleasure.

Joy was one thing, I grumbled to myself, and pleasure was another, and why should pleasure always have to take a back seat to joy?

But I was very young, I understood the Cheffe only up to a point, which at the time I thought was the furthermost, it was much later that I started down the road that my twenty-five years stopped me from seeing stretching onward, it opened up before my eyes, before my feet, which hesitantly consented to go forward, and I caught up to the Cheffe late, when she had given up hoping to be rescued or heard, and so I missed my moment, my chance to be needed by her, I could only be useful, bringing her repose, relief and intense, unspoken love.

Eventually I understood that the star confirmed something the Cheffe had begun to feel not long before, a sense that she'd compromised her standards.

She hated the thought that her cooking pleased and charmed people, not that she hoped or imagined it repelled them, since so many came back to La Bonne Heure again and again, but the Cheffe needed to think that her regulars were returning to a place where they'd come face to face with a mystery.

Often she was perfectly happy to see a plate angrily sent back to the kitchen, she balanced on that rugged crest where one small misjudgment, one act of carelessness, one excess of exuberance might send her dishes tumbling into the abyss of the unacceptable or the ridiculous, but she balanced on that crest, drawing the eaters to her by her inflexibility, even if it sometimes made for an experience that wasn't exactly appealing – because that wasn't and couldn't be all there was to it.

Given all that, the Cheffe didn't see how it mattered if she accepted or turned down the star, either way she'd been judged worthy of it, and that meant she'd failed.

Still, she played the game, as you know, answering questions from the occasional journalist, thanking *Le Guide*, though always in her own way, evasive, guarded, tight-lipped and ambiguous, and there were many who decided she wasn't very bright, her thoughts were slow to stir, she had no vocabulary.

No-one ever knew she was being gnawed by shame.

And that, I guarantee, is what she meant by "It's all over," because she couldn't have foreseen what was coming, she had every reason to think it couldn't happen, since the money now pouring into La Bonne Heure more copiously than ever went straight off to Canada, the Cheffe bedecked her daughter with finery, like a lavishly adorned young elephant.

My colleagues and I did our jobs, never looked up, with an enthusiasm and a devotion that had little do with the fat raise the Cheffe bestowed on us, and she worked with her usual deftness and efficiency, but also, I sensed, with a new sadness, a disillusionment that she tried to mask by smiling more than she used to, at anything, mechanically.

The star brought us so many new customers that the Cheffe had to relent and begin taking reservations like everyone else, and as it happens I'd seen fit to encourage that, telling her it was simply a question of respect for our regulars, because otherwise there were days when we'd have to turn them away or force them to wait, and there the Cheffe agreed, she agreed to all my suggestions, but I could see it was with a lost, down-cast gait that she walked down the road of inevitable changes, and that her intuitive, penetrating mind, her uneasy sixth sense, violently refused everything her reason was urging her to accept.

Which is why I was deeply surprised, not long after she'd taken my advice and replaced the little straw-seated chairs with standard dark-wood bistro chairs, to hear her announce that she was closing La Bonne Heure for three days to repaint the walls and replace the lighting, she wanted to take out the fixtures with the bronze-green metal branches and put in hanging lamps of white opal glass.

I praised the idea, closely watching her face, her gestures, which seemed to me tenser than usual, while the Cheffe smiled, even laughed with no real call for it, she who was so reserved, and her beautiful brown eyes jumped too quickly from one of us to the next, as if taking care not to fully meet our gaze.

I thought it strange it should put her so on edge to tell us she was having La Bonne Heure repainted, in that same deep blue what's more, and putting in new lamps, until I saw what was really behind it when, almost by the by, the Cheffe told us she was going to have to raise her prices.

There too, I vigorously approved, I told her I had been thinking the same thing but hadn't dared bring it up.

"You know I don't like this," she murmured, "you know there's not one thing about this I like."

And when I protested, too brightly, resolutely upbeat, hoping to convince her to find a little pleasure in it all, telling the Cheffe fewer obligations came with the star than reasons to be happy, the Cheffe suddenly turned grave, became herself again, she lost that ridiculous smile, she gave me an unsteady, almost desperate stare and said, "It's not that . . . not just that. My daughter heard about the star, she's coming back."

"Oh, well, that's good," I said, cautiously.

"Yes," said the Cheffe, "it's good news, isn't it?"

And I could tell from her voice that it really was a question, she was genuinely asking, as if she weren't sure of the answer, and as if my thoughts on the matter would carry an unquestionable weight in the view of all this she'd have to come up with.

"Very good news," I told her, with all the conviction I could muster.

The Cheffe seemed ever so slightly relieved, and almost grateful to my answer for extricating her, at least for a moment, from her confusion and guilty misgivings, from her thoughts forever circling, alone, forlorn, far removed from any wholesome good sense, around the question of whether the sorrowfully loving mother she was had the right not to rejoice with all her heart at such news, whether the fine mother she claimed to be could allow herself to think of that imminent return and tremble.

Not long afterwards, one of our waitresses came into the kitchen, went to the Cheffe and murmured something close by her face, whereupon the Cheffe put on her vacant little smile, which lingered on her lips even though her eyes showed only dread when she understood what the waitress was saying, and that inert smile seemed to replicate itself, to spread, to hang like an echo on the girl's hesitant lips, none of us liked to upset the Cheffe, and now the waitress was realising her words had sent her into a panic.

Then a stranger came into the kitchen, and I immediately thought she was the most beautiful, most extraordinary person I'd ever seen.

I'm still mystified, still dumbfounded by the memory, so soon would I find the Cheffe's daughter a person entirely without charm, beauty, originality, that's why I still can't understand what she was radiating in that one single moment that fooled my gaze, that anaesthetised my intuition, unless it was her cool determination to charm, the mobilisation of her cruellest, most dishonest, most aggressive faculties for the purpose of subjugating us all.

She was dressed in a strange motley of fabrics and styles, a mismatched jumble of ideas, tastes and seasons that became just the opposite, perfect coherence, when you realised that every one of those fabrics, rough or silky, thick or transparent, shimmered in one way or another: the long red satin skirt, the sweater of coarse wool woven with silver threads, the thick tights of a shiny dark green, the pink plastic belt, even the little-girl red velvet hairband in her permed hair, everything sparkled in a tasteless, childish, almost disorienting way, since, in spite of the youth clearly visible on her smooth, fresh face, she was dressed like a middle-aged lady trying to pass for a teenager, whose look's idiosyncratic logic vaguely evoked an obsessive, off-kilter mind.

My memory of her first appearance in our kitchen is the memory of an illusion.

Here she was at last, the Cheffe's daughter I'd heard so much about, she was splendid and stunning, my love for her mother leapt towards her, immediately wrapped itself around her.

However deceptive, even monstrous, that first impression is something I'll never forget, even if two days later I cast it off completely, because the lie was there first, and the truth took its place but didn't erase it.

That's why I later hated her all the more.

She came towards the Cheffe in a shriek of joy and a crackle of fabrics, I saw she had shoes like a little girl's, silvery Mary Janes with steel soles that clattered metallically over the tiles, she bent down to put her arms around the Cheffe, she wasn't actually taller but she pretended she had to stoop so you'd think she was, and so, deceptively, she seemed – illusorily tall, in truth bulky and wide – to swallow up the Cheffe, to smother her in the pink mohair of her enormous sweater, in her hair, which, now freed from the band that had fallen to the floor, slipped over the Cheffe's face, perfumed, chemical, asphyxiating.

And the Cheffe stood motionless, locked in her daughter's arms, for many long seconds before she extricated herself with a gentle push, still silent but now looking into the strange, full, heavily made-up face hovering over hers, and I saw in the Cheffe's eyes an expression I never could have imagined: adoring and vanquished, tender and defeated, timid, ill at ease, but still, it must be said, vaguely happy (though tinged with a very clear "in spite of it all" that to me made it tragic).

What dumbfounded me was not that I'd never seen the Cheffe look like that, but simply that she could look like that, I'd always seen her in perfect control of the face she showed the world.

Not wanting to embarrass her, and anxious to hide my own turmoil, I quickly looked away.

The Cheffe's daughter liked to claim I was jealous of her, and as she told it that jealousy infected me from the very first day, from the moment she embraced her mother in front of me, since that simple gesture was forbidden to me, despite the many liberties I'd insidiously permitted myself.

I've always refused to answer that woman's sordid allegations.

But, on the subject of jealousy, and since that emotion might, why not, have gripped the impassioned young man that I was, I can in all humility tell you I never felt any such thing towards the daughter, and what actually tightened my throat at the time, as I looked back at my knife and the red peppers I was slicing, was something very different, something entirely new for me, it was a sense of impending disaster.

Those coming miseries were written in the Cheffe's loving, downtrodden eyes, those eyes had already seen them, and maybe the Cheffe already knew of them too, the steel soles of those ridiculous Mary Janes couldn't pound the tile floor without meaning something, foretelling something, and it would have been cowardly or stupid to refuse to understand that prelude, and the Cheffe wasn't cowardly or stupid, she was wise, perceptive and in her way fatalistic.

Because already everything had changed, and the Cheffe, who as the irreproachable boss of La Bonne Heure had never walked out on any of us, her assistants, her employees (she left us to ourselves when she thought or sensed that's what we wanted), the Cheffe who was always there when we came in and still there when we went home now followed her daughter out of the kitchen, slinking and docile in the spectacular wake of those rustling fabrics, she didn't look back, didn't say a word, and we didn't see her again until evening.

And when we did she simply congratulated us on having

so capably handled the lunchtime rush. She was distant, un-settled, pensive, sadly smiling and gentle, and when my eyes questioned her she looked away with neither a moment's pause nor, it seemed to me, any trace of regret, as if our bond were a dream I alone had dreamt, or as if – now that thanks to her daughter she was herself again – she were extracting herself from it as she would from an unseemly or immoral liaison.

My colleagues pretended they'd seen nothing, and maybe there was nothing to see when you didn't live in the heart of the Cheffe's heart as I had for years, but I couldn't help think-ing her attitude towards them had changed, the Cheffe seemed to be weakly and hopelessly struggling against an indifference, a detachment that put an edge of weariness on her most every-day words, her orders, her thanks.

"I'm going to show you something," Cora tells me. She takes a big dark-blue box from her bags, delicately sets it on the table, and I want to turn away, because I know what it is, I know that kind of box, and even as I'm thinking it Cora tells me just that: "You know this kind of box." And they're magnificent steel-handled knives, I can't help but caress them with my fingertips, I give Cora a questioning look, she picks up her knives one by one and holds them towards me so I can feel their weight.

The daughter didn't put in an appearance that first evening. I could hear her walking back and forth over my head, in the apartment, hammering the floor with her steel-soled Mary Janes as frantically as a penned, frightened mare, but nothing was holding that girl captive, in her obstinacy, egotism and hardness she was in fact a creature freer than most.

Late that night I went out to nose around the kitchen windows as usual, and just as I feared I found them dark.

But the apartment windows were blazing, the casements open wide, though no hum of voices drifted out, in fact the silence seemed so deep, so solid that I could picture them up there, the mother consumed, the daughter at rest and on guard, the girl soundlessly breathing, staring and plotting, the two of them perhaps sitting face to face with nothing to say but perversely united as they waited for two very different things.

I wanted to call out to the Cheffe, take her off to my studio in Mériadeck, away from that girl from Canada who neither resembled nor, I was sure, understood her in any way.

I lingered a while under the windows, paralysed by the knowledge of my powerlessness, my pointless youth, my irrefutable absence from any familial connection with the Cheffe.

And evening after evening I kept coming back (as if my perseverance, founded solely on hope, might somehow gain the power to change reality) to see which of the Cheffe's windows were lit, and to my dismay the kitchen's never were, whereas from the three rooms of the apartment above poured a light so pale and bright that the street was coldly ablaze with it, and I thought the windows were open only to spare the Cheffe an immediate, total, white-hot incineration of her freedom and genius, in silence, in the vast watchful silence that convinced me someone was up there.

Never again, after that, would I go back to my cherished place late at night in the kitchen alongside the Cheffe.

Because when I did once again spend whole nights in the

kitchen, it would be to hear the Cheffe talk, not to watch her work, that trust would never be granted me again, that openness, and I've always bitterly regretted it: no caution or calculation ever showed on the Cheffe's face on those nights when she spoke only to herself, and I'd seen that, and she'd loved me enough to let me.

As for what lay behind her daughter's sudden return to Bordeaux, for truth's sake I must confess that a time came, much later, when the daughter told me about it with what seemed a sincerity beyond question, when I was tempted to believe her word over the Cheffe's, the daughter claiming, in that very brief time when we were more or less friends, that her mother called her home on winning the star, whereas the Cheffe would later tell me that her daughter came back without being asked, and with no other goal than to shatter her confidence.

I knew having her daughter far away was a comfort to the Cheffe, and I knew about the money she sent to Quebec to keep here there, as if to bury her under the weight of riches she literally couldn't dig herself out of, so I never should have trusted the daughter's claims, but how to describe the sort of innocence or objectivity that briefly illuminated her dull eyes when she told me, with no ulterior motive I could make out, that her mother had asked her to come back when she was recognised in *Le Guide*, so I believed her immediately and in spite of myself and later had to struggle, reconsidering my first impression, to question those words that didn't fit with the rest, with what I knew of the Cheffe and what she herself had told me, that she'd never suggested her daughter come and join her.

And when, not for the moment her overt enemy, I asked the daughter why her mother had wanted her home again, she answered very plainly, with that openness I couldn't manage to find feigned, that the Cheffe thought it would be sensible to make use of her daughter's knowledge in marketing and business consulting, the skills she'd acquired at an expensive college in Quebec, she'd earned a diploma, she showed it to me with some pride.

I held back from laughing at her, stopped by the exceptional sweetness I saw on her often hard, bitter face.

But I didn't believe for a moment that the Cheffe was hoping to raise La Bonne Heure's profile, with the help of her daughter or anyone else, and although I knew perfectly well how we can sometimes be disconcerted by some aspect, unsuspected for lack of opportunity, of the character of someone close to us, close in life and even closer in dreams, I found it simply impossible to picture the Cheffe as a businesswoman determined to capitalise on flattering and promising circumstances such as recognition by *Le Guide* – particularly because she was ashamed of that honour.

No, that I absolutely could not believe.

Besides, the fact that the daughter assured me she'd come back to put her marketing skills to use for La Bonne Heure, the fact that she made that claim with such serene, open vanity (she who was ordinarily neither serene nor open) will show you just how irrational and shockingly shameless she was, her illusions were so powerful that they could be disarming, even convincing, in spite of everything and in spite of myself, back in those days when the enmity had subsided, when she and I were seeking the warmth of a temporary peace, a truce.

Once we parted ways forever I realised nothing she'd said could be trusted, even if she was perfectly sincere, even if she was trying to stick as close as she could to reality in the most commonly understood sense.

But there survived in me the ineradicable memory of that moment when I'd been convinced by the look on her face, so I could never entirely shake the idea, the ridiculous suspicion, that the Cheffe had indeed asked her to come back to Bordeaux, had even, in a way, cried out for her help.

We next saw her, the daughter, two days after her return.

Her second entrance in the kitchen was so unlike the first that I almost didn't recognise the slow, heavy young woman scuffing her gigantic trainers over the tiles, with no trace of a shimmer in her dress or her aura, as if for the crucial moment of her arrival two days before she'd expended all her resources of flamboyance, bravado and intimidation, or as if she'd decided there was no need for such stratagems now that her mother had been *caught*.

The Cheffe gave her a businesslike greeting, weighed down by a term of endearment that jarred in this working kitchen, something like, "Hello, my darling, how are you?", which she seemed to have to work hard to say, and which she said cautiously, hesitantly, with the deep discomfort of someone forcing herself to violate her natural reserve but who, to protect her own tranquillity, to avoid giving offence and suffering the punishment, has no choice but to speak those words.

The daughter grunted a vague reply. Her cold little eyes scoured every corner of the kitchen, looking for something to fault, something to criticise, even some reason for outrage, and though at first I didn't understand what that meant it was soon made clear by a laconic "Lot of stuff's going to have to change around here," murmured with a glance in my direction, looking for my approval, seeking the unity of two like-minded young people (we're exactly the same age), which I wouldn't give her – I immediately looked away, appalled by that arrogance and also badly shaken to see the Cheffe's dazzling daughter, whom I had spontaneously enveloped in my love and admiration, now showing her true face, true in the literal sense, stripped of the artifices that let her make such a resplendent entrance the first day.

A poisonous atmosphere of menace and fear hung over the forty-five minutes she spent in the kitchen.

The Cheffe's nervous, humble, deferential demeanour influenced my co-workers, who answered the daughter's ignorant questions quickly and anxiously, and although she asked me nothing, perhaps wanting to keep me on her side, I felt as wound up and angry as if she were putting those idiotic questions to me, the questions of a woman with no idea what she was talking about who thought she could hide her ignorance by snidely taking people to task over insignificant details, looking at them with a smug, disdainful or sardonic smile, pushing up a lock of hair that had fallen over her ear, with the same gesture as the Cheffe, then slowly exhaling through her nostrils, so common, so bereft of elegance that I found her revolting.

When she was gone the Cheffe's shoulders relaxed, she stood up straight again. But the look she gave us seemed different, veiled with insincerity, sadness and resignation.

I alone dared to look back, she lowered her eyes, smiling mechanically, the smile drifted away from her lips, floated out of reach of her mouth, her quivering chin.

Nothing made sense to me anymore.

How could she give birth to a daughter like that, why did the Cheffe obey her in a way I thought couldn't be explained by motherly love, and hadn't she made up for the terrible mistake of bearing such a daughter by sending virtually everything she earned to Quebec, hadn't she paid enough to be free of that torture?

And if the Cheffe was now being made to endure the consequences of some act or attitude I knew nothing of, why did that obligation take the ignoble, sneering, ambitious form of a daughter who had nothing to teach her?

For all her visible distress, I thought the Cheffe wasn't being honest, I couldn't understand her, I could feel my youth, and I hated that I was so young, and that I understood nothing.

From one day to the next, the Cheffe entrusted her daughter with the outrageous authority to make any changes she liked to La Bonne Heure, even though that daughter's only experience was class projects, purely theoretical, in which she had shown no great talent (she had had to take the final exam three times), involving businesses of an entirely different nature – lending banks, a correspondence foreign-language school, a consortium of dental offices – and even though that daughter had no interest in cooking, even loathed cooking, as she admitted to me one day, seeing it as nothing more than an odious chore, redeemable only if it was dressed up with luxuries, she said herself she ate only in big restaurants and prided herself on never cooking, never wasting her time with that crap.

Hearing the judgments she handed down like the precious illuminations of a dazzlingly inventive mind, I soon realised she was willing to enjoy a dish only so long as she didn't know what she was eating, didn't recognise or think she recognised a shape, taste or smell, only so long as its very name said as vaguely as possible what it was made of, which is why she immediately resolved to rechristen all the Cheffe's dishes with circumlocutions she considered infinitely more enticing, to stop confronting the customer with words like tuna, chicken or tomato, preferring phrases I can barely bring myself to repeat here, phrases some of you might have the misfortune of remembering, and which, to the surprise of many who assumed it was the Cheffe's idea, soon invaded the menu of La Bonne Heure: November Germon, Prince of Bresse, Tomatina Carpaccio . . .

The Cheffe agreed to it all, pathologically cooperative, and I saw the sad, beleaguered look drain from her eyes, replaced by an expression of flat acquiescence, a look of grimly pleased dejection that put a new sort of joy on her face, paradoxical, almost cynical, as if with every passing moment she were saying to us, "So here we are," but where were we exactly, and why, in that opaque atmosphere thick with antagonism, vanity and disdain, should she assume we were bound together, to varying degrees but unbreakably, like galley slaves united by the chain and their shared awareness of their fate?

Because the Cheffe never seemed to doubt what we felt for her daughter: admiration, fear, reverence.

And I think it was because I was caught up in the Cheffe's eagerness to see us fear and adore her daughter that I silenced all my misgivings and tried to recapture the wonder I'd felt when I first saw her walk into the kitchen, the powerful sense, immediate and unambiguous, that she deserved my affection and my devotion every bit as much as her mother.

"She's not going to accuse me of denying her daughter," I cynically told myself at first, but in the end I stopped aiming even for that, swept away on a tide of tangled emotions that produced only one insistent, fanatical thought: to obey the Cheffe's will even if I couldn't understand it, even if that will disappointed and diminished me, infuriated and disturbed me, even if it forced me into a fraudulent friendship with her daughter, because later it would all turn out to be justified.

Still, I'll admit it, in the early days I approved of some of the daughter's ideas, even approved with enthusiasm, I'll admit that today, not without shame.

"My mother's falling behind," she said, "we've got to innovate." She never missed a chance to mention that the Cheffe had no degree, unlike her, who had learned things the Cheffe's limited understanding couldn't conceive of or entirely accept, but which the Cheffe nonetheless needed to know, if, as the daughter put it, she wanted her place to have class.

The daughter thought we needed new china, for instance,

which didn't seem to me a bad idea, and a few more tables, she thought we weren't getting all we could out of the space, and she also found the sound of conversation and tinkling silverware tedious as well as unchic, she wanted music piped in, and there too I agreed, all the more enthusiastically because I didn't like the idea and didn't want the daughter or the Cheffe to see it.

She picked out some elaborately overdesigned china. Once again, I pretended to admire the basins that replaced our shallow soup bowls, even though on first sight they made me think of miniature urinals, and the oval plates, the slate slabs for serving cheese, I admired it all even as I found it vulgar, pretentious and impractical, as I stood before the Cheffe whose face showed no reaction, and who, when as a pure formality her daughter asked what she thought of it, answered, "I'm sure you know best."

But the day the daughter announced that she'd decided to delete the prices from the menus given to women accompanied by a man, as she insisted all the best establishments did, I let out a bitter, furious laugh and slammed down the knife I was holding.

The Cheffe gave a little cry of protest, of reproach, childishly putting her hand to her mouth, then looked at me severely, not, I'm convinced, to chide me for overstepping my place but to tell me that no-one was to express such an attitude towards her daughter as long as she herself made no objection, she was right, I saw that and mutely begged her forgiveness. I gently picked up my knife.

A certainty then came to me, cold and sharp, a certainty

that brought me closer to the Cheffe: we were headed for disaster, knowing it and accepting it with a consent that was as cold, grim and fervent as it was mysterious and senseless.

It was easier that way, I told myself, and, darkly relieved, I felt my indignation fade, I caressed my beloved knife in apology for treating it so roughly, without a trace of lingering antipathy I looked at the daughter's hard face, telling myself she would soon lose the power to send me into a rage or drag me away from my secret, time-honoured, inexpressibly precious connection with the Cheffe.

Finally, the daughter decreed that the prices were too low, and we had to raise them considerably.

I saw the Cheffe recoil at the idea, whose brutal arrogance shook her resolve to submit without question to her daughter's commands, she protested that she'd already had to raise the prices not long before, but then, seeing the daughter sternly cross her arms, the Cheffe threw me an alarmed, hunted glance and in a tone of hopeless entreaty cried out to her daughter, "We really have to?" and the daughter nodded with an exasperated sigh.

The Cheffe forced out a laugh, dredged up with heartbreaking effort from an almost completely drained store of frivolity and irreverence, and then, on the brink of tears, murmured, "Anything you say."

And she fled the dining room, leaving me alone with the daughter.

Opening her little eyes wide, the daughter gave me a look miming a beleaguered, sarcastic alliance, the two of us obviously united against the Cheffe, and I played along, raising my eyes heavenwards, wanting to die.

The daughter had new menus printed up, she insisted on an expensive violet paper with the words in pale grey, you had to work to decipher them through the curlicues.

As the weeks went by, as I got used to concurring with all the daughter's dangerous whims and not dwelling on them afterwards, I learned to maintain a relationship with her that was no longer founded only on my desperate desire to please the Cheffe and not too cruelly heavy with fear, anger and disgust, I could joke with the daughter, and even, for as long as it lasted, I could manage not to remember the reasons for a fear, anger and disgust that had grown more remote and abstract inside me, like feelings you remember from childhood, and the Cheffe was there, faraway, smiling wanly, erased, I didn't step aside, I went on bantering with the daughter, the Cheffe was there, behind my back, broken and opaque, I didn't step aside to let her in, I was obeying her mystifying wishes but the strength was all on the daughter's side.

The Cheffe and I lost all our closeness.

We kept our thoughts to ourselves when we happened to cross paths, almost staring at our shoes, cold and polite.

I avoided any camaraderie that might give my bewildered co-workers the impression I was on their side, that we were fearing the same fears, because I would never take their side against the Cheffe, and because I had to be on the daughter's side to stay with the Cheffe I had no choice but to distance myself from my co-workers, even if they were right to deplore all these changes and to fear numbers falling at La Bonne Heure, which is exactly what happened, as you know.

The daughter hated La Bonne Heure, she hated everything that made the restaurant a success, everything the Cheffe had invented in her delicate, tender inspiration, the dark blue of the walls and the awning, the clean, simple china, all that, yes, the daughter hated it blindly and violently, everything her mother had chosen, loved, lavished her thoughts on, and she hated, I'm sure, though she didn't know it, the mere fact of La Bonne Heure's existence.

How else to explain why the first complaints of the regulars, who now ate from fussy china to the sound of music turned up a little too loud, encouraged the daughter to harden her ideas in the ice bath of absolutism, as if those justified grievances fit perfectly into the plan she'd devised to demolish her mother's La Bonne Heure and remake it in her own image, her own way, so utterly unlike the Cheffe's?

Because the daughter rejoiced in those complaints.

A customer asked for the music to be turned down, the daughter refused, he promised he'd never be back. "Good riddance," I heard her whisper exultantly, and when I asked her why, she told me she didn't like that guy, didn't like all these people acting like they owned the place.

"But those are the people who made La Bonne Heure," I answered, in the light, amused, confidential, almost flirtatious voice I now used with the daughter, as a familiar despair reddened my cheeks, my forehead, the back of my neck.

"They're the ones who loved the Cheffe's cooking from

the start," I went on in my pretend voice, my insolent, slightly cynical voice, which I thought particularly appealed to the daughter, like a reflection of her own.

She muttered that they'd have to get used to things or go and eat somewhere else, that's how it was and that's all there was to it.

The daughter had made the dining room the seat of her omnipotence, she'd laid off and taken the place of Delphine, whose job was to greet the customers, to show them to a table and make sure the meal went smoothly.

And so she gracelessly piloted her intrusive body between the tables, spoke to the customers in a voice both superior and overfamiliar, not to mention too loud, and she was forever interrupting conversations to ask if everything was fine, if they liked the food, then walking off before she could hear the answer.

Thanks to her, a tense and at the same time strangely careless atmosphere hung in the air at La Bonne Heure, an atmosphere of apathetic decline.

Oh, I used to tell myself, the Cheffe was perfectly happy to have a good reason never to come out into the dining room again, how could she who so hated showing herself even to a discreet, mannerly audience possibly think of going out and greeting the new clientele her daughter's management gradually began to attract as the months went by, as she slowly undid everything that had made the quiet uniqueness of La Bonne Heure?

She was perfectly happy, I seethed as I looked at the Cheffe working mechanically in the kitchen, outwardly impassive, and to us kind in an aloof, cursory, reflexive way we took no pleasure in, I least of all, since when we very occasionally came face to face I gave her a sort of questioning, helpless, naked stare, and the look she returned was exaggeratedly, artificially hard, indifferent, which hurt me even as I felt sure it was her way of trying, in her distress, to protect me.

Yes, La Bonne Heure's new customers were exactly what the daughter was after, rich and crass, not worried about the price so long as, in an atmosphere they could consider classy and relaxed, they ate dishes with names so allusive as to have no meaning, but nothing too out of the ordinary – and the daughter took all the Cheffe's most demanding dishes off the menu, the ones without which the Cheffe found cooking only a pale pleasure, nothing she needed in any way, the daughter kept only the dishes least dear to her mother's heart, wood pigeon with quince confit, fat leeks stuffed with partridge salmi, almond and pistachio cream, which the Cheffe had left on the menu in a spirit of magnanimity towards customers discouraged beyond all possibility of pleasure by her insistence on rigour.

And to that too the Cheffe acquiesced.

One morning, brushing past me, she whispered, "You ought to leave."

"Why?" I answered, shocked.

"You know perfectly well," the Cheffe told me, giving me the wry little smile that was hers alone, which since her daughter's return she'd replaced with the imitation smile that seemed to waver in front of her lips, she raised a hesitant hand, quickly caressed my cheek, then walked off with her lively, light gait, which now also seemed false, studied, as if with each step the Cheffe were fighting the temptation to drag her tired feet over the tiles, or even collapse in a corner and abandon herself to a will other than her own – since it was indeed that will, not its absence, that made her obey the daughter's every command, and hadn't the Cheffe shown the mighty force of her will from childhood on?

So yes, I left, right away, and I had no trouble finding a good job at Le Select, near the Grand Théâtre.

I didn't think I was following the Cheffe's advice, I was angry, in my paradoxical way I thought I was insulting her – I was so angry!

And I thought I could find no better way to hurt her than to take her at her word, since, I told myself, she was surely counting on the fidelity of my longstanding, absolute love to make me refuse a suggestion she was probably only giving me because she thought it was her duty.

I was sure what she'd told me to do was the last thing she wanted.

But I did it anyway, so abruptly that we only had time to exchange a few hurried words, and I didn't properly say goodbye to her, I just went away, not caring whether my disappearance might interfere with the work, whether I could be replaced at such short notice, I was so angry, so stirred up, my anger lifting me high above any thought of regret, that was new to me, and I didn't entirely dislike it, it let me see myself as heroic and implacable.

But once I'd been hired at Le Select and fell into the routine of a cooking untouched by the Cheffe's spirit, then my galvanising anger faded away, I reflected in despair that I'd been disloyal to the Cheffe, and it wasn't enough to tell myself again and again, as I tried, that she'd driven me to it: that very reasonable argument collapsed as soon as I measured it against the tests real love has to face, the tests true loyalty has to face – and what is love, much-vaunted love, without the discreet and even invisible loyalty that has to come with it, what does love, that pleasure and asset for every heart, mean without an indelibly faithful spirit, known only to the person who feels it?

I'd betrayed the Cheffe, since I'd deserted her the moment she suggested it, and in my self-pity I'd let my anger – at her for not trying to explain herself, at myself for not understanding her – become the uncontested master of my will.

For that, I told myself, I would never be forgiven.

Heading home at night from the huge kitchens of Le Select, where I worked under a dutiful, insignificant chef (the food they served there was stingy and pretentious, tiny cubes of raw fish, ordinary chicken breast portioned like caviar, minuscule praline tartlets), I often detoured past La Bonne Heure and invariably found it locked up, because it now closed far earlier than it used to, and the apartment windows were dark, the whole face of the building was hostile, condemning me for my desertion.

It felt like another desertion when I turned away to go home, and another desertion when I set off for Le Select every morning, and still another when I got down to work on tasks devoid of ardour or moral sensibility or even the most simple-minded pleasure, and another when I went to stand beneath the Cheffe's windows to watch for any sign I might interpret as meant for me or favourable to me, and that's how I lived, forever feeling my own unworthiness, which I got used to, which in time I stopped distinguishing from the gloomy thoughts that were the daily fare of my existence, that's how I lived, and in that grey feeling of worthlessness I married one of my co-workers, Sophie Pujol, I got married almost without knowing it, limply, smirkingly, to a woman as blasé and smirking as I was, who asked me, once the ceremony was over, "What have we done?"

Neither of us knew, but whereas I never saw an omen in anything – blinded to any presage or promise by a sense of my fall – Sophie Pujol would always believe that our serene, fraternal decision to divorce eight or nine months later had something to do with the news I'd heard in Le Select's kitchen, the news that La Bonne Heure had lost its star, Sophie Pujol was sure I'd seen it coming and when it did I felt we had to divorce, she wouldn't give up on that idea, she didn't hold it against me, anything but: she was as tired of that sarcastic marriage as I was, she was relieved to have it behind her, and while she was at it she gave up her place at Le Select, she opened her own restaurant, Le Pujol, facing the river on the right bank, she was soon a success, and still is.

It was Le Select's chef who told me with visible, vindictive delight that La Bonne Heure had lost its star.

I didn't believe it at first, I thought it had to be a jealous rumour. The Cheffe's daughter had only been in charge of the restaurant for twenty months.

Then came the confirmation, immediately followed by the announcement that La Bonne Heure was closing for good, or rather wouldn't reopen, it was on its winter break at the time.

Horrified, I bolted out of the kitchen and ran to see what was happening. I hadn't seen the Cheffe since I left, hadn't caught so much as a glimpse of her.

Even though I thought I'd made every possible effort not to mention her name or existence in front of Sophie Pujol, even though I'd succeeded and said absolutely nothing, Sophie Pujol would confess, a little after the divorce, that our marriage had been hard for her, however unserious, sardonic and casually friendly the climate of our shared existence, that she'd constantly felt the supernatural, sorrowful presence of another woman there with us, she'd tell me she always saw a shadow at my side, which I sometimes turned to without realising it, looking deep into eyes that weren't Sophie Pujol's but the eyes of that ghost who lived in the very heart of our marriage, who, even if we'd loved each other more seriously, would have prevented any communion between us, any full, sincere intimacy, and it was as if, Sophie Pujol would tell me, I'd never got over the death of someone I would always love more than any other, that's why our marriage was so hard for Sophie Pujol.

As always, no light shone at the kitchen windows or the Cheffe's apartment above La Bonne Heure.

I cupped my hands around my mouth as a megaphone, I shouted her name at the dark windows, I think I even shouted the daughter's name, and I shouted out "Sainte-Bazeille" too, desperately, aggressively trying to force the Cheffe to come out and stop my assault on the delicacy of that sacred name, "Sainte-Bazeille" I howled, filling my voice with all the misery, frustration and fear that were choking me.

Nothing moved.

I spent the next few days enlisting the help of the Cheffe's circle, or more precisely the very few people who might conceivably have some idea what had become of her, but no-one – not my former co-workers, not the two regulars who I thought privately called on the Cheffe now and then, not her sister Ingrid, whom those last two helped me to locate (she'd bought a bistro on the coast) – could tell me a thing, they hadn't heard from her either, they hadn't even seen much of the Cheffe since the daughter's return, they laconically told me, "It wasn't the same anymore."

No, certainly, it wasn't the same at all, and I knew a little about that myself, but didn't it mean something, I wondered, that the Cheffe had forged such fragile bonds, and with so few people, that she could disappear without their even knowing it, and particularly, once they did know, without their feeling any particular concern?

Because they'd heard about the loss of the star, and they more or less knew La Bonne Heure was closing, but none of them had raced to the Cheffe's side to pledge their friendship and support, no-one leapt up in alarm from their armchair when I told them the Cheffe, if she was home at all, seemed to be living in the dark and not opening her door to anyone, no-one found it unthinkable that the Cheffe could leave town and not tell them, I realised the Cheffe had no real friends, no-one who worried about her but me, and in my vanity and my cowardice, I'd left her.

And I thought that was a terrible mistake on the Cheffe's part, not valuing friendship, not cultivating it, but was it, since solitude was exactly the life she wanted?

Ten times, twenty times I went to the Cheffe's, I called out and waited, I paced up and down the pavement, but I never once glimpsed her, never saw the curtains shift or the faintest light filter out, so I finally convinced myself she'd gone away, and perhaps she'd told no-one, and never wondered if I might be devastated, worried and hurt, maybe she thought I'd lost all interest in her since I'd never once come to see her after I left La Bonne Heure, and since, as she might have heard, I'd married Sophie Pujol, or maybe by worrying me she was trying to punish and hurt me.

I liked that idea better than her thinking I'd stopped caring about her, thinking I was leading a life broken free from her own, thinking I'd loved her only for a time.

"My thoughts were never free of you, I haven't felt like my own man for as long as I've known you," I would later tell her, in the kitchen where her steady, tranquil voice would keep me up for much of the night.

And then, with the boldness bestowed by exhaustion, I would go on, "My ex-wife Sophie Pujol always thought you were what put an end to our marriage, I don't know, but she's sure of it."

"They have good food at Le Pujol," the Cheffe would answer, with enthusiastic conviction, "isn't that what matters most? Next to that, a marriage is nothing."

"Very true," I would answer, relieved, and we'd laugh together, I've never laughed with anyone as heartily, and with so pure a heart, as I did with the Cheffe.

Hopeless, deeply depressed, I gave my notice at Le Select.

I used my savings, which were fairly substantial since I had no real life outside work, to finance the kind of travels I once looked at with the same dubious incomprehension as the Cheffe generally gave outings and amusements, I flew to Vietnam, to India and Italy, to Japan, I signed up for organised tours, each time hoping against hope I might spot, among my travel companions or suddenly appearing across the lobby of an international hotel, the Cheffe's face.

I didn't admit it to myself, but I always chose countries known for their cuisine, I vaguely thought that if the Cheffe had made the very unlikely decision to travel it could only be to lands where she'd find ideas to further embolden her inventiveness, unknown ingredients to bring back, rare spices, plants that don't grow on our shores, never for a moment did I consider the possibility that she might give up cooking, no matter what happened to the restaurant.

Back home in Bordeaux after my last trip, I agreed to seek treatment for severe depression.

My money was gone, I had to work, I was finding it all hard to face.

I went to see Sophie Pujol, she consented to give me a job,

and we got along as well as could be expected. I was taking all sorts of pills at the time, I moved slowly, my work lacked precision, but Sophie Pujol was kind enough never to take me to task, and besides her restaurant was unfailingly packed.

Then, in a bar, I ran into the Cheffe's daughter.

Seeing my expressionless eyes, my grey, drooping face, she asked how I was and told me she was going through a hard time herself, though I saw no sign of it, she was rosy and plump, not cheery but more alive and more animated than in the days of La Bonne Heure.

She answered my urgent, avid, pointed questions about her mother by telling me she didn't know anything, the Cheffe had disappeared, leaving her a good deal of money that she, the daughter, had almost completely run through, living within her means wasn't her style, she confessed with a certain roguish charm, it was her mother's fault, she didn't know how to raise a child.

She bought me a drink, I paid for the next two, and, staggering and stammering from the alcohol and the pills, I heard myself offer to put her up, since, she'd just assured me, she had nowhere to go, she'd been thrown out of some sort of communal apartment where she'd found refuge, the story was confused and completely uninteresting.

I understood only that the Cheffe had taken the keys to her apartment, which gave me a short jolt of pleasure, and maybe it was in penance for that, and also because I felt vaguely sorry for the daughter, lost, indecisive, less disagreeable than before, that I offered to put her up until she could get back on her feet.

I must also have been hoping she'd tell me of her last months with her mother, and thinking some minor detail of that story might give me a clue to what the Cheffe could be doing now, and where and why, and apart from all that being with the daughter brought me closer to the Cheffe, in however warped, pitiable and degraded a way.

In my drugged stupor, and in the deep indifference the daughter inspired in me, I didn't suspect at the time that she accepted the invitation less because she truly had no roof for the night (she had other ways out, she still had more than a little money) than because she wanted to see, with a twisted, hard, unwholesome delight, how I would use her, as she later put it, and how the memory of the Cheffe tormented me, and on that latter point she was right but why did that narcissistic girl need to put herself in precisely the situation that would confirm her suspicion that I didn't care about her, that I only cared about the Cheffe, her soul and her cooking, the soul of her cooking?

Numb though I was, we soon grew thoroughly sick of each other.

Everything she did, said or suggested filled me with resentment or shame, just as a veritable loathing for me soon took shape in her narrow, self-obsessed heart.

The story of our relationship is the pitifully banal story of two people who come together for a while because they're broke and alone and don't know what else to do, and once the few good times of the early days are over they find themselves standing, stunned, bitter and vindictive, before someone they can't possibly love or admire, I'll take my share of the blame, I was close-mouthed and distant, roughly indiscreet when I wanted to learn more about the Cheffe, very rarely pleasant in a general sense, and utterly devoid of ambition, plans or good cheer, not to mention genuine warmth.

As for the daughter, she was listless and bored, she spent her time staring at the television she'd bought herself, talking of going back to Canada but never doing anything about it, sourly happy to be forcing her company on me.

The only question she would agree to answer was my question about the loss of the star: had that devastated the Cheffe? "Not at all," the daughter said with a disdainful sniff, "I got the feeling she wasn't sorry at all."

"Maybe not," I shot back, "but still, having to close La Bonne Heure, what a defeat, it's devastating! And it's all your fault."

The daughter gave me a glance of genuine astonishment. "I never forced her to listen to me, and I wasn't making her keep me around," she said, with her flat-footed logic. "And she didn't have to close the restaurant if she didn't want to."

"That was the only way she could find to get rid of you," I said quietly, the daughter let out a mean little laugh, and then, as usual, we sat for hours in silence, exasperated by each other for no precise reason, the daughter turned up the television to annoy me even more as, simply to irritate her, I walked back and forth in front of the set on the pretence of tidying the apartment.

Once I'd wormed out of her what little she could tell me of the Cheffe, not a day went by that I didn't bring up the subject of her going away, offensively insistent about it, never seeking a tactful phrase to hide the fact that I wanted her gone without further delay.

But before long evicting her was out of the question.

Cora tells me she wants to open a French restaurant in Lloret de Mar, she's learned to cook, and that's what she's wanted to do all her life, that's why she's come to Lloret de Mar. She's counting on me to help find a place and give her all the most useful advice. Smiling, staring at me with a faintly challenging gaze, she tells me a man who worked as long as I did with the Cheffe has to have lots of good ideas. I'm speechless, uncomfortable, the heat is appalling, what will my Lloret de Mar friends think, I want to run away and have nothing more to do with Cora, nothing more to do with Martine or Jean-Marc or Thierry, why can't I be left alone in Lloret de Mar, so I go out for a vigorous walk on the beach, and little by little my thoughts grow more peaceful and the idea no longer seems so unimaginable. I remember the pleasure I felt picking up Cora's knives, the little jolt it gave my heart.

We were living in a state of hostility so intense that she didn't send for me at Le Pujol when her time came to go to the hospital, she gave birth to our child with no friendly or familiar presence beside her, she alone chose the baby's first name, and she gave her her own surname, the same as the Cheffe's.

And when I finally heard and ran to the maternity ward, when I took little Cora in my arms, her mother turned her face to the wall, refusing to come together with me in any sort of happiness, however briefly, so I felt precious little to be happy about and in fact realised I was ashamed, I put the child down in her cradle, I felt unworthy of that sacred moment.

Even when the daughter came home to our apartment, I rarely had a chance to look after Cora or hold her in my arms, her mother didn't want me having anything to do with the girl, which in a strange way I could understand, since she hated me.

And then she took steps to finally do what she'd idly talked about long before, she flew off to Canada two or three months after Cora's birth, taking the child with her, leaving me more alone than I'd ever been.

She'd vaguely promised to send me an address where she could be reached, and having guessed from her tone that she never would I wasn't surprised not to hear from her, and yet I waited, hoping she'd call to ask me for money, but her greed was no match for her towering hatred, and I lost them both – forever, I thought at the time.

I opened a bank account in Cora's name, set aside some money for her.

So I too had my young elephant in a faraway land, I wanted her draped one day in the gold I'd worked to give her, even if I never saw her again.

That was the saddest time of my life, without question.

But I have to say I'd grown so dependent on my pills that I came to the end of each day with no particular awareness that I'd lived it, and in the evening I couldn't clearly remember what I'd done just that morning, or in what order I'd performed the various tasks whose undeniable result my uncaring eyes sometimes landed on, until finally Sophie Pujol urged me to take medical leave and, since she had little time and no doubt little desire to come calling (the slightest conversation bored me to exhaustion), I found myself with absolutely nothing to do, alone, and in a sense almost happy with so much emptiness.

One springtime evening, it was in that state of mental and emotional blankness that I walked with tiny, shambling steps to La Bonne Heure, my senses registering only the cold basement-like smell drifting from the hallways of apartment buildings whose doors had been left open onto the street, I loved that smell when I was a child, I inhaled it deep until my head spun, that cold saltpetre breeze.

I spotted a light behind the kitchen's grimy windows.

Derelict and befogged, I looked at that light and told myself there was no light there at all, only a projection of my grieving, regretful memory, and walked on.

Then I turned back, not under the impetus of some second, more rational thought but mechanically, like the zombie I'd become, I put my face as close as I could to the barred window, and after many long minutes, little by little, I convinced myself that the lights were indeed on in La Bonne Heure's kitchen.

Suddenly trembling all over, my forehead knocking the bars, I rapped at the glass, several times, harder and harder.

I stood up straight, I hurried to the restaurant door, I was afraid those truths would become dreams if I wasn't quick enough, the lights would go out, I had to catch reality off guard to keep it from mutating, such was my frantic, desperate reasoning – hurry, get to the door of La Bonne Heure before the Cheffe, if that really was her, could disappear.

And the door opened, the Cheffe pulling it towards her as she backed into the dimly lit dining room.

"It's you," she said quietly, sweetly, in the grave, clear voice I hadn't heard for more than two years, and it hit me just where I'd long since stopped feeling anything alive, simple, spontaneous, and I felt my shrunken lungs opening up, a searing pain ripped my chest as a feeble, forced smile deformed my mouth, and I walked in without a word, powerless to speak, my hands clenched over my left breast – how cold and constrained I must have seemed, how wooden and emotionless, I told myself, overcome, unable to speak a word, only aware of the dull stiffness, so contrary to what I was feeling, that was paralysing my features just when I longed for the Cheffe to recognise me as the love of her life, nothing less, because I'd so often imagined this scene that the most unlikely scenarios had taken on the texture of possibilities, and then likelihoods, so when I imagined what would happen if someday I saw the Cheffe again my daydream began at the moment when she laid her eyes on me and realised at last that I was the one man she could love, since I alone loved her blindly.

And now I was standing before her and my face was frozen, desperate, my eyes veiled, my silence imbecilic, oh I almost cursed myself for knocking at that window, I would have run away if my legs had had the strength.

"You don't look well," said the Cheffe, very gently.

To my deep embarrassment I began to weep, uncontrollably, as I hadn't since childhood, and even though I'd never so urgently wanted the Cheffe to see me as a man in the full desirable bloom of his maturity.

And I waved my arms every which way, trying to tell her:

"Please, don't pay attention, let my arms wipe these ridiculous minutes from your memory!"

Standing on tiptoe, the Cheffe gave me a hug, and for the first, for the only time in my life I was in her arms, my face pressed to her hair, which she still wore pulled back in that strict chignon, as if to forget and make others forget she had hair at all.

I bent forward, at one corner of my mouth I felt the faint graze of a kiss.

I turned my head a little to let the Cheffe find my lips if she wanted to kiss me again, but she gently pulled away, wiped my cheeks with the back of her hand.

Now she was studying me with concern in her eyes, a concern not without tenderness, I thought, which immediately brought me to life again, gave me the courage to look straight back at her, trying to make my mouth and eyes express everything I was feeling – an exhausted delight, a shivering joy, uncertain but so huge that it bordered on despair.

In the dimness of the dining room, the Cheffe's pale, shining, alert, polished face seemed to float above the dark patch of her apron, a darkness glistening here and there with damp spots, and I felt a violent longing to follow her into the kitchen and watch her imagine as I used to do, watch her try out procedures and combinations, watch her create, in that liberating nocturnal solitude, before my discreet, devoted eyes, recipes whose number and absolute originality were, she said, the only reason a person could have to go on with their humdrum life.

But though she went on looking at me with the greatest

affection, the Cheffe didn't invite me to keep her company in the kitchen.

She looked exactly the same as two years before, I noticed, and I felt all the more aware of my own dilapidation.

I tried to quell the hunger in my gaze as I looked her up and down, compact and self-assured, her beautiful, solid hands on either side of her apron, her smooth, shining forehead, her dark, calm, appraising eyes, the perfect, androgynous oval of her face, unframed by any lush mane of hair, she was the same, yes, you would never have thought she'd suffered a failure, never have thought she'd run away and hidden, whereas my own face clearly expressed the scale of my many disasters – professional, moral, emotional.

How shameful, how shameful to have her see me this way, I said to myself over and over, wishing I could hide my burning face.

The Cheffe saw my distress, my humiliation and misery, so she took my hand, pressed it between her cool, soft hands, and said to me with a smile, "You're going to have to snap out of this, my boy. You do know I'm planning to reopen next month?"

I stammered out something or other, she was barely paying attention. With one arm she gestured broadly around the dusty dining room and in a gaily eager voice asked me to name a date when I thought I'd be able to come back to work with her.

Yes, it was the Cheffe who by her long, unexplained absence had cast me into the depths of hopelessness and grief, but it was also the Cheffe who pulled me out, who literally saved my life.

She later told me she was deeply shaken by my wretched appearance when she first saw me in the doorway, she'd done her best to hide her pity and her shock, all she could think of was the urgent need to come to my aid, through the only remedy she had any faith in: work.

"Does that mean," I asked, horrified in advance by the implications of what she might answer, "that you wouldn't have called me back to you if I had been doing fine?"

"Oh, I don't know, don't fret, my boy," she said, evading the question, easy-going and reassuring, but also determined not to lie to me with assurances that she would have asked me back had the circumstances been different.

And then I realised: the Cheffe hadn't thought of me for the team she was putting together, I realised that, crushed.

I wondered if that rejection had something to do with Cora, if the Cheffe had heard I was the father and so wanted nothing more to do with me, wanted no part of anything or anyone connected with her daughter – or was it simply that like me she was still thinking I'd betrayed her when I left La Bonne Heure?

I couldn't possibly ask her that. But when, one day, as if in passing, she told me her daughter was living with a Canadian in Montreal and they had a little girl named Cora, I realised she didn't know the truth, and I was relieved and at the same time stung by a cruel jealousy of that stranger treating as his own the child stolen away from me, my little elephant, as all the while I diligently amassed her future finery, the mountain of gold I was hoping to heap on her.

I was relieved, but I would have liked to set the Cheffe

straight, to proudly tell her, "I'm your granddaughter's father" – thereby making official another bond between us, indestructible, innocent and irrefutable, how long the lack of any such unquestionable link had tormented me, how I'd envied her brothers and sisters for being united with her by blood!

But I didn't, and I vowed I never would.

If the Cheffe ever did find out it wouldn't be from me, and I didn't know if with that decision I was protecting or immolating myself, if I was protecting the Cheffe or heartlessly immolating something that was rightfully hers.

The Cheffe ordered me to come and work with her every day in preparation for the reopening. Sophie Pujol let me go without regret, and what she hadn't managed to bring about with all her patient friendship the Cheffe accomplished in three weeks of vigilance and affectionate severity: I stopped taking the pills.

Every morning, opening the door to let me in, she studied me with a cold, penetrating stare.

I set about refreshing the dining room, I painted the walls, waxed the woodwork, scrubbed the floor tiles with black soap, first finding in those tasks, unlike any I'd ever engaged in, a sort of furious sensual pleasure, and then a peaceful satisfaction, which, focused on the smallest detail, on the "job well and thoroughly done", opportunely reminded me that I was now clean.

Meanwhile, the Cheffe worked in the kitchen, and I hoped that as a reward for my efforts, in recognition of my new mastery over my unhealthy habits, she would invite me to join her there before the rest of the employees came along, but it wasn't to be, and when it came time for her to introduce her new dishes I found myself looking on with four co-workers, and inside myself I consented to that, I inwardly bowed down, I accepted that I'd still shown too little zeal and modesty to hope I might recapture so soon – if I ever would – the profound intimacy we'd built up in our work, that almost silent communion, stamped with a trust she'd never felt for anyone else, of that I was sure.

And so the Cheffe showed us the new menu she'd come up with. I liked it, yes, I liked it.

So I can't say how it was that a small foreboding came to me, a feeling that something wasn't right, or rather that there was too much of something I couldn't name in what the Cheffe was doing.

I couldn't put my finger on it, so I shooed that premonition away and admired the Cheffe's inventions as they deserved to be admired, no longer telling myself I was witnessing the beginning of her downfall.

The most recent dishes pushed her rigorism to the limit.

Young people who, like my new co-workers, didn't know the Cheffe might have described her style as very spare.

I myself saw an asceticism I'd never glimpsed in her work, and for a moment I thought it wasn't far from hatred, although that was so foreign to the Cheffe's nature that it left me at a loss.

But in her, I must make this clear, nothing showed, so it was with an unmixed, serene enthusiasm she introduced, described and explained her capon slow-cooked in borage broth, zander lightly browned in a chestnut leaf, yellow-beetroot compote, roasted porcini stuffed with walnuts confit, carpaccio of hare with peppery mint cream, all of them dishes that, along with the few others she went on to describe for us, quickly attracted a curious clientele when Gabrielle opened, inspiring reviews and comments that with one voice all said the Cheffe could still astonish and delight as she always had, and two years later those dishes earned her back her star, and this time the Cheffe showed neither shame nor unease nor, I think, any emotion at all, she was unmoored and uninterested, consumed by a cold, personal, pugnacious hostility to cuisine.

She would never have been able to work bored, or disillusioned, or weary, she would have closed the restaurant forever if she ever felt such feelings taking hold.

But she had no objection to doing battle.

She never told me anything of the sort when she kept me up all night in the freshly cleaned kitchen, I always found her serene and straightforward, intense and calm, she spoke to me as she would to the only friend she had, to be sure, but also neutrally, with no interest in me specifically, seeing me as the one person who, with his love and his loyalty, might know what to pass on and what might best be kept quiet, if anything had to be.

She didn't tell me about her new hatred of cuisine, or the way she was imperceptibly cutting ingredient after ingredient from her dishes, keeping within the boundaries of an exquisite simplicity but just on the brink, I anxiously told myself, of tumbling into fruitlessness, so she said nothing of what was troubling her, tormenting her, of what had abandoned her.

I only saw it because I loved her as I'd never loved and never would love anyone else.

And yet she thought she could keep that from me.

As one of those nights was coming to an end, I asked where she'd gone when she disappeared, I jokingly told her I'd looked for her all over the world, or at least all over Bordeaux.

She raised one eyebrow, first in surprise, then in amusement. "I wasn't far away, you know," she answered. Then she was silent. Finally she added, "I've also searched desperately for something I lost."

The years went by, each like the last, Gabrielle flourished and was praised to the heavens, but nothing reminded me of the joy, the goodness and the accomplishment of the old days, even if nothing seemed to have changed in the Cheffe's face or her ways.

I was certain she was lost, I was certain she'd lost everything.

I have a memory from those years, just one, of a moment when I saw the Cheffe's face as if sculpted from the pure gold of an untainted happiness, it was an evening in winter, during the few weeks, from January to February, when the restaurant was closed.

I stopped by to say hello to the Cheffe as I'd been doing two or three times a week, oh I would have gone to visit her every day if I hadn't been afraid I might be a nuisance.

She opened the door to her apartment, I immediately noticed her beaming, muted air and her bright blue blouse, its halo encircling her with a lunar glow. "I have company for a few days," she told me.

A little girl appeared behind her, tall and sturdy, with long brown hair and sharp, interested eyes that stared into mine but saw no sign of anything, I immediately thought, suddenly defenceless and powerless.

The Cheffe told her my first name and the child held out her hand. I kept it in mine for a moment. "Hello, Cora, pleased to meet you," I said quietly. She gave me a little nod of her pretty, thoughtful head.

Claiming I didn't want to intrude, I hurried out, my legs rubbery, hating and pitying myself at the same time, feeble and faint of heart, unable to bear with the same cheerful endurance what had been forced on me and what I'd chosen of my own free will.

A few days before her death, for some people so unexpected that they felt the need to invent a brain tumour she supposedly kept secret or decided not to have taken out (but what good does it do to ask why?), the Cheffe called to invite me to Sainte-Bazeille the next Sunday, at lunchtime.

She would close Gabrielle for the day, she told me in an exaggeratedly mysterious tone that wasn't like her, and we'd be joined by a number of her friends who, she was sure, would also enjoy an impromptu day in the country.

She explained how to get to the auberge she'd reserved for the occasion, just at the edge of Sainte-Bazeille on the Marmande side, and her artificially exuberant voice gave me an uneasy feeling, like the fact that she'd called instead of talking to me face to face in the restaurant.

When I got to the auberge, just off the main road, they told me the Cheffe was waiting in the garden.

I walked through the empty dining room, with its hard beige tiles, its polished wood furniture, and I found myself in an enchanted garden, oh, those are exactly the words that came to my mind.

The Cheffe was sitting at a little table on the grass, with black and white chickens wandering freely among the fruit-covered cherry trees. Between those trees, as if by chance, grew carrots, rocket, peas and beans, which those round, tidy chickens pecked at here and there, strangely perfunctory, as if they had everything they wanted and were doing all this purely for show, for the sake of the tableau.

The Cheffe heard me, stood up, luminous, pure and crisp in a white cotton dress I'd never seen on her before, with her open, unadorned face that in its perfection was nothing other than what it was, I couldn't help taking that face in my hands for a moment, and the Cheffe didn't pull back or protest, my heart was gripped by a sharp, limpid sadness that caused me no real pain.

The Cheffe invited me to sit down, then she called towards the auberge, and almost immediately we were brought two glasses and a bottle of Graves in an ice bucket.

I asked the Cheffe where her friends were. "What friends? There's only you," she answered with a smile.

She poured the wine, tilted her head back to feel the sun on her skin.

Then I decided to chase away the unease and anxiety that were stupidly keeping me from enjoying the moment, and I offered my face to the sun along with her.

When I quietly, happily told her how hungry I was, the Cheffe sat up, stretched out her arm, and pointed towards the chickens, the young vegetables, the ripe cherries.

She told me the meal was there, spare, magnificent and perfect.

We could imagine the taste of each element, and the taste of them put together. She would never invent anything simpler or more beautiful, and so our wine, that excellent Graves, was all we would need for our lunch, the culmination, she said with a painful seriousness, of the long ceremony that was her career.

Three days later, on Wednesday, the Cheffe died in her bed, with no sign of a fight.

I ask Cora if she's found a name for the restaurant she wants to open in Lloret de Mar. She tells me it will be just a first name, maybe preceded by "chez". She then tells me her grandmother's name, Gabrielle. "What a fine idea," I murmur, doing my best, for discretion's sake, to conceal at least some of my joy.

The MacLehose Press Editions:
A New Library from MacLehose Press

This book is part of a new international library of literature in translation. Join us on our journey to READ THE WORLD.

1. *The President's Gardens* by Muhsin Al-Ramli
TRANSLATED FROM THE ARABIC BY LUKE LEAFGREN

2. *Belladonna* by Daša Drndić
TRANSLATED FROM THE CROATIAN BY
CELIA HAWKESWORTH

3. *The Awkward Squad* by Sophie Hénaff
TRANSLATED FROM THE FRENCH BY SAM GORDON

4. *Vernon Subutex 1* by Virginie Despentes
TRANSLATED FROM THE FRENCH BY FRANK WYNNE

5. *Nevada Days* by Bernardo Atxaga
TRANSLATED FROM THE SPANISH BY
MARGARET JULL COSTA

6. *After the War* by Hervé Le Corre
TRANSLATED FROM THE FRENCH BY SAM TAYLOR

7. *The House with the Stained-Glass Window* by Żanna Słoniowska
TRANSLATED FROM THE POLISH BY ANTONIA LLOYD-JONES

8. *Winds of the Night* by Joan Sales
TRANSLATED FROM THE CATALAN BY PETER BUSH

9. *The Impostor* by Javier Cercas
TRANSLATED FROM THE SPANISH BY FRANK WYNNE

10. *After the Winter* by Guadalupe Nettel
TRANSLATED FROM THE SPANISH BY ROSALIND HARVEY

11. *One Clear, Ice-Cold January Morning at the Beginning of the Twenty-First Century* by Roland Schimmelpfennig
TRANSLATED FROM THE GERMAN BY JAMIE BULLOCH

12. *The Shape of the Ruins* by Juan Gabriel Vásquez
TRANSLATED FROM THE SPANISH BY ANNE MCLEAN

13. *Vernon Subutex 2* by Virginie Despentes
TRANSLATED FROM THE FRENCH BY FRANK WYNNE

14. *Stick Together* by Sophie Hénaff
TRANSLATED FROM THE FRENCH BY SAM GORDON

15. *The Tree of the Toraja* by Philippe Claudel
TRANSLATED FROM THE FRENCH BY EUAN CAMERON

16. *The Oblique Place* by Caterina Pascual Söderbaum
TRANSLATED FROM THE SWEDISH BY FRANK PERRY

17. *Tropic of Violence* by Nathacha Appanah
TRANSLATED FROM THE FRENCH BY GEOFFREY STRACHAN

18. *My Name is Adam* by Elias Khoury
TRANSLATED FROM THE ARABIC BY HUMPHREY DAVIES

19. *E.E.G.* by Daša Drndić
TRANSLATED FROM THE CROATIAN BY
CELIA HAWKESWORTH

20. *Katalin Street* by Magda Szabó
TRANSLATED FROM THE HUNGARIAN BY LEN RIX

21. *Balco Atlantico* by Jérôme Ferrari
TRANSLATED FROM THE FRENCH BY DAVID HOMEL

22. *The Lord of All the Dead* by Javier Cercas
TRANSLATED FROM THE SPANISH BY ANNE MCLEAN

23. *The Faculty of Dreams* by Sara Stridsberg
TRANSLATED FROM THE SWEDISH BY
DEBORAH BRAGAN-TURNER

24. *The Archipelago of Another Life* by Andreï Makine
TRANSLATED FROM THE FRENCH BY GEOFFREY STRACHAN

25. *The Last Days of El Comandante* by Alberto Barrera Tyszka
TRANSLATED FROM THE SPANISH BY
ROSALIND HARVEY AND JESSIE MENDEZ SAYER

26. *The Snares of Memory* by Juan Marsé
TRANSLATED FROM THE SPANISH BY NICK CAISTOR

27. *Echoes of the City* by Lars Saabye Christensen
TRANSLATED FROM THE NOWEGIAN BY DON BARTLETT

28. *Daughter of the Tigris* by Musin Al-Ramli
TRANSLATED FROM THE ARABIC BY LUKE LEAFGREN

www.maclehosepress.com